SLOW TREK TO TRIUMPH

A MATURE-AGE CHRISTIAN ROMANCE

JULIETTE DUNCAN

A SUNBURNED LAND - BOOK 5

PRAISE FOR "SLOW TREK TO TRIUMPH"

" TOTALLY ENJOYED THIS BOOK and I am sure you will too!!!" *~Bonny*

"This novel draws the reader into the story of a family so real that I couldn't help but be drawn into their tragedies and triumphs. These characters are not stereotypes. Rather they live true life with their faith and love for each other.They are dynamically as vibrant as the setting described throughout the telling of their story. *~UtGrandma*

"There is nothing to dislike, your books are uplifting and informative. You capture me from the moment I first started reading your books, I am emotionally moved by them." *~Julia B*

"These books are uplifting. Ms Duncan writes in a way that allows you to see not only the surroundings but feel real life feelings of the people. The love, hope, fears we all face in our lives are found in the words. But more importantly we hear and see how much better our lives are with the love of God at the center."

FORWARD

HELLO! Thank you for choosing to read this book - I hope you enjoy it and are blessed by it. Please note that as this story is set in Australia, Australian spelling and terminology have been used throughout.

Happy reading!
Juliette

BOOKS IN THIS SERIES

Slow Road to Love

Slow Path to Peace

Slow Ride Home

Slow Dance at Dusk

Slow Trek to Triumph

Christmas at Goddard Downs

Beneath the Southern Cross: Dawn of a Sunburned Land Series

Love's Unwavering Hope

Love's Rebellious Spirit

Love's Distant Dream

Love's Precious Moments

Love's Faithful Journey

CHAPTER 1

Frank could hardly keep track of the changes occurring in his life and that of his family, but this latest change brought a smile to his lips every time he thought of it. His youngest son, Joshua, had married Stella and they were now living at Indigo Downs, the cattle station Stella's family had owned and lost, and which Joshua had purchased back for her as a wedding gift.

The couple had left for their honeymoon right after the wedding, and since then, Frank had resumed the role of managing Goddard Downs, a role he was more than familiar with. He was, however, finding it difficult to rouse himself each morning, something he'd never had a problem with before. Perhaps it was the lingering heartburn that had been troubling him in recent times, but more likely, it was simply that he didn't want to leave Maggie. Whenever his gaze settled on his beautiful wife's sleeping form, he was tempted to stay with her and not go to work. He was getting soft in his old age.

In the short time Joshua had been running things, Frank and Maggie had settled into a routine of long breakfasts on their deck, followed by a Bible reading and a prayer time. Returning to the helm had all but ended that. Maggie had been more than understanding and never grumbled or complained, but he knew she was missing their time together as much as he was.

But that morning, as he sat down for a quick breakfast, he made a decision. He took her hand across the table and rubbed it gently with his thumb.

She lifted her gaze and gave a bemused smile.

"My love," he said, "I think we should take that trip."

Her eyes shot open. "Now?"

"Yes." He looked deep into her eyes that flickered with confusion.

"What about the station? All the work that has to be done? We still haven't found a vet to replace Stella, nor an extra hand to help with the drives."

He lifted a finger to her lips and hushed her. "Shhh, my love. All those things can be figured out. We need to take time for each other while we can. The station will survive without me for a while." He squeezed her hand and lifted it to his lips, kissing it gently. "I want us to spend time together, Maggie. Just you and me, before we get too old. What do you say?"

She stared at him for a long moment, their gazes locked, before she replied, "I'd love to, Frank, so long as you truly think you can afford the time."

"I'll make sure I can." He smiled, the delight in her expression warming his heart. "Broome it is, then?"

She nodded eagerly. "Why don't we make a road trip of it?

I'd love to be able to take our time and enjoy all the sights along the way."

"Funny you should say that. I just happen to have been working on the perfect rig."

"Oh?" she said, her brows furrowing.

He chuckled. "Come down to the workshop later and I'll show you."

"Okay." She leaned forward and searched his eyes as her own danced with merriment. "How long have you been planning this, Frank?"

He grinned. "Since the day we met."

"Oh, go on with you, Frank Goddard. Seriously. How long?"

He leaned back in his chair and sipped his chamomile tea. He'd gone off coffee recently after finding that Maggie's herbal teas soothed him better. He'd even started enjoying the flavour. He stared out across the lagoon where a family of ducks was enjoying an early morning paddle.

When had he started planning this? Good question. Julian's sudden death had made him realise once again that no one, other than God, knew how many days they had left on this earth. That day as they lowered his eldest son's body into the ground, he'd made a decision to cherish every day, to take pleasure in life, and to spend as much time with Maggie and his family as he possibly could. He didn't want to live his life with regret.

He faced her and drew a slow breath. "Since Julian's funeral."

Her expression sobered and an understanding passed between them. Words weren't needed. She knew how much

Julian's death had affected him, but God was gracious, and although he'd never fully get over his son's death, he, along with the rest of the family, was learning to live without him.

"I'll make some more tea," she said.

He smiled. "Thank you, my love. That would be great, and then maybe we can do a bit of planning before I head off. I told Liv I'd be in late this morning."

"Okay. I'll grab my notebook and laptop." Maggie returned a few seconds later with both items and sat beside him. He could hardly get a word in as she began to explore the possible routes, expounding on the pros and cons of each. She was so meticulous, and she had the best photo spots and attractions brought up within minutes, suggesting the places they could stop on their way to and from Broome, the seaside town where they'd honeymooned three years before.

"But when we get there, we'll have to stay in the same hotel we did for our honeymoon." She lifted her gaze from her screen and met his. Unspoken words passed between them.

Recalling those magical days and nights, their first as husband and wife, brought a smile to his lips. With its long sandy beaches and laidback lifestyle, Broome was the absolute best place for a honeymoon. But it was also a great place to camp. He made circles on her hand with his thumb. "Oh, I thought we'd camp."

Her eyes widened and disappointment flashed across her face until he chuckled. "I'm only kidding, my love. The hotel it is."

Her face broke into a relieved smile as she swatted him gently on the arm. "Frank. You do like to tease, don't you?"

He reached out and curled a loose tendril of hair around his finger before slipping his hand behind her head and drawing her face close to brush his lips across hers. "But I like this more."

Laughing, she returned his kiss before pushing to her feet. "You'll be fired if you don't get to work soon."

He grinned. "Bring it on!"

"You don't mean that, Frank."

"No, but I'm looking forward to taking some time off."

"So am I. It'll be wonderful." She wrapped her arms around his neck from behind and kissed his cheek. "Now, off you go."

He squeezed her hands and angled his head to smile at her. "Come down later and we'll tell the family."

"But we haven't decided anything definite yet."

"We've decided we're going. That's enough. And they'll need time to prepare for when we're gone."

She nodded. "You're right. I'll pop down a little later and you can show me the rig as well."

"You're going to love it." A grin grew on his face as he imagined her reaction when she saw the camper he'd been secretly working on for weeks.

She chuckled and ruffled his hair. "I'm sure I will."

AFTER FRANK LEFT, Maggie tidied away the dishes and made another cup of tea. Her mind was awhirl. She needed a few quiet moments to process what had just happened. With Julian's passing and Joshua moving to Indigo Downs, she'd assumed the trip she and Frank had been talking about since their wedding would be put off indefinitely. While she was okay with that, because Goddard Downs was his life after all, it had also saddened her. Spending time together, just the two of them, exploring new places, was something she'd looked forward to, but she was wise enough to know that best made plans often didn't happen. So Frank's announcement that he wanted to go anyway filled her with excitement and gratitude.

She carried her tea to the deck, and after easing into her chair, she opened her Bible to do her morning reading. Although she was studying the book of Hebrews, she opened it at her favourite Psalm, Psalm 100, and read it aloud, softly.

> *Shout for joy to the Lord, all the earth.*
> *Worship the Lord with gladness;*
> *come before Him with joyful songs.*
> *Know that the Lord is God.*
> *It is He who made us, and we are His;*
> *we are His people, the sheep of His pasture.*
> *Enter His gates with thanksgiving*
> *and His courts with praise;*
> *give thanks to Him and praise His name.*
> *For the Lord is good and His love endures forever;*
> *His faithfulness continues through all generations.*

Like the psalmist, Maggie's heart overflowed with gratitude for the many blessings God had bestowed on her. She took a deep breath and closed her eyes. *Lord, I give You thanks for Your goodness. For bringing me to this place where I know beyond a shadow of a doubt You want me to be, but I also give You praise that Frank and I can spend quality time together while experiencing Your amazing creation. Go before us and prepare the way for Goddard*

Downs to run without Frank. Bless the family and raise them up to be the people You want them to be. I pray these things in Your Son's precious name. Amen.

An hour later, she wandered down to the workshop. It was that time of year when the ground was beginning to cry out for rain, and she had to be careful where she walked as deep ruts had started to appear in the track. Once the rains came and the dirt became soft and pliable, the boys would grade the tracks, levelling them out and making them easier to traverse, although she wasn't sure which she preferred. Dirt or mud. She chuckled. How her thoughts had changed in the three years she'd lived here. She'd loved city life, but there was something special about living on the land. God seemed closer somehow. She knew that wasn't the case since God was everywhere, so she guessed the change was in her. She had more time to appreciate His goodness, to see His hand at work, and choosing to walk instead of driving the short distance gave her that extra time.

Her heart was light by the time she reached the large workshop where all the vehicle maintenance was carried out. By necessity, Frank had learned to change an engine, fix a gearbox, and he could troubleshoot almost any mechanical fault a vehicle might have. Julian had never learned those skills. He'd preferred someone else look after that messy part of the business. Joshua had taken an interest, but preferred looking after the horses. Nate, Olivia's husband, being city born and bred, was not mechanically inclined at all, and Sean, Frank's nephew, wasn't reliable enough. But David, Serena's husband, was a firefighter who didn't mind getting his hands dirty and was still trying to find his place at Goddard Downs. Frank had told

7

Maggie that he hoped he might pass his knowledge onto David over time, but it was looking more and more likely they'd have to employ a mechanic from outside the family. And sooner than later, if she and Frank were to take this trip. Another thing to hand over to God.

She poked her head into the workshop and frowned. Frank didn't seem to be there. In fact, it was so quiet she could hear the ticking of the clock on the far wall. She took a breath and a swig of water and was turning to walk up to the main house when her gaze caught sight of the rig. Her eyes widened, and then she laughed. She'd assumed Frank had fixed the old caravan they'd bought not long after they married, but this wasn't the caravan. It was a camper that fitted onto the back of a small truck, much like a tortoise carrying its home with it wherever it went. She'd seen them on the road, of course. Tourists travelled through the Kimberley in the dry season sporting all sorts of rigs, and she'd always thought a camper like this would be fun. And now, as she stepped closer and studied it, she thought it was the perfect setup for her and Frank. It wasn't large by any means, but it would give them the best of both worlds. Indoor sleeping and outdoor living, and they wouldn't have to drag a van over those corrugated dirt roads. She was investigating the slide out stove when footsteps sounded from behind. Turning, she came face to face with Frank.

His eyes danced as he searched hers. "What do you think, my love?"

"I think it's perfect." Smiling, she walked into his embrace and leaned against his strong chest.

He kissed the top of her head. "I think so, too. Let me show you inside."

"Frank." She chuckled at the suggestive tone of his voice. "I've already looked, and it's very cosy. I might even pass on the hotel, but right now, don't we have a family meeting to get to?"

He released a heavy sigh. "Yes, we do." He slipped an arm around her shoulders. "So, you like it?"

She looked into his eyes. "I love it. And I love that you want to do this trip. I can't wait to be travelling the open road with you."

He rubbed her arm. "We'd better go and break the news."

"Yes, we should."

They strolled the half kilometre to the homestead, chatting about where they would head to first, and what they'd need to take to last several weeks on the road before reaching any shops where they could restock. While joy bubbled through her, Maggie's mind whirled. There was so much to think about. How could they carry enough food to last three weeks? What about cooking utensils? And what clothes should they take?

"It's all in hand, my love. I asked Janella to order extra supplies this month. We're ready to go as soon as we tell the family."

"Oh Frank. I can't believe you kept this from me."

He chuckled. "I wanted it to be a surprise."

She laughed as she leaned into him. "You definitely succeeded."

∾

THE FAMILY WAS GATHERED in the main house. Everyone, including Joshua and Stella, was present, and it was a welcome sight to Frank's eyes. Although the couple now lived four hours' drive away, they'd agreed to attend the monthly family business meetings, and this was the first since their wedding.

"Good morning," Frank said brightly, looking at each face around the table. Maggie sat to his right, Serena and David were beside her, Olivia and Nate sat opposite, Joshua and Stella were at the other end, Sean sat beside Joshua, and Janella was to Frank's left. Sasha was minding the younger children who were playing quietly in the adjoining room. His granddaughter possessed a natural maternal instinct that her cousins responded to. They were always happy to have her look after them.

"First, I'd like to thank you all for being here, and a big welcome back to Joshua and Stella." As he gave the newlyweds a nod, a wave of pride swept through him. The change in Joshua since Julian's death was nothing less than remarkable, and although they all missed Julian greatly, God had used his death to work in Joshua's life, changing him from a troubled young man who had little idea of what he wanted, to a responsible, mature husband and leader.

"We have a lot of business to cover this morning, but before we begin, let's start with a word of prayer."

They joined hands and bowed their heads as Frank committed their time to the Lord. "Dear Lord and Heavenly Father, Thank You for Joshua's and Stella's safe return. We ask that You bless our time together and guide us as we make decisions that will affect us all. In Your precious Son's name. Amen."

After taking a sip of tea, Frank turned to Joshua. "How are things at Indigo? Settling in okay?"

Joshua crossed his arms. "Yes, but we need to find some hands before we get the new herd. We've put the word out but haven't advertised yet. We'd rather try for hands we've at least heard of before looking for new ones."

Frank nodded approvingly. "Good idea."

"Less time training, too," Stella chimed in. "We want to get the new herd settled well before the next rainy season."

"Indeed," Frank agreed. "Speaking of which," he squeezed Maggie's hand, "we have an announcement."

As expected, all eyes turned to him.

"What is it, Dad?" Olivia folded her arms and studied him with narrowed eyes, her gaze darting between him and Maggie. He'd known that his daughter would have the most issue with them disappearing for a few weeks, so he replied to her.

"Maggie and I have decided to take a trip."

Olivia frowned. "Now? With everything that needs to be done?"

He nodded. "Yes. I've thought and prayed long and hard about this. Maggie and I need some time alone, and I'm sure you'll survive without us for a while." Breaking his gaze with Olivia, he looked around the table, his gaze taking in each of the other family members in turn. "We'd love you all to work together to ensure everything runs smoothly while we're gone."

"How long are you going for?" Olivia barked.

"We haven't fully decided, but perhaps a month. Once we

have a better idea, we'll let you know. We just wanted to give you a heads-up so we can start getting things ready to leave."

"But we still have to find a vet to replace Stella, and some new hands…" she continued.

"You're more than capable of handling all of that, Olivia." He raised a brow and gave a pointed look.

She huffed out a breath and shook her head but remained silent.

Usually, he would never have contemplated taking an extended trip with so many tasks outstanding, but things had changed. He cast his gaze around the table. "This will be a time for you all to step up. To learn some new skills. To work together. I have confidence in you all, and I know you'll be fine." He placed his hands on the table. "That's all I have to share on my end other than saying I expect to have an update from Mr. Tamala sometime soon, but Joshua and Stella will be handling that arrangement going forward since the new herd will be under their supervision."

He didn't miss how his statement caused the corners of Joshua's lips to rise in a half-grin, half-smile. His son needed his space, an opportunity to shine, not only as a man, but as a husband and as head of his own house. Frank was glad they'd finally come to a place where they could each be the men they were meant to be. It was long in coming. Julian would have been proud to see how his younger brother had stepped up already. That thought caused Frank's heart to feel heavy. It wasn't that long ago Julian was chairing these family meetings, eager to show himself as responsible. He never had anything to prove in Frank's eyes, but he didn't seem to understand that.

Frank handed the floor to Joshua who proceeded to explain

the process they were undertaking to select the new herd. Stella added her points on the selection process and stated that she would be personally choosing the new cattle, especially the studs, whose breeding prowess would improve the herd's quality for years to come.

Finally, once those matters were settled and everyone's questions answered, Frank opened the floor to any other business. "Does anyone else have anything to say?"

"I do," David said quickly, sitting straighter and clearing his throat.

Silence fell on the room before Frank nodded. "Good. The floor's yours. Over to you."

"Thanks." David smiled as his gaze swept around the table. "Good morning to everyone. As newcomers, Serena and I don't have much to contribute normally, but there's a matter which I believe affects us all and is about to directly impact Serena."

Leaning forward, Frank crossed his arms on the table and pinned David with his gaze. "Newcomers or not, you're family, and that gives you a right to speak."

David gave an appreciative, and a relieved, smile. "Thank you."

"So, what seems to be the trouble?" Frank asked.

David released a heavy sigh. "It's the rains. We've only had one Christmas here, but in that time, we got to see how isolated Goddard Downs becomes during the wet season, and how dangerous it can be. Serena's programme with the children is doing well, and this place is a sanctuary for them, but if they can't come during the rainy season because it's not safe to travel, everything she's been trying to do with them could be derailed. Months without being able to come could do more harm than good."

"What do you have in mind?" Frank asked.

"A bridge."

Everyone's eyes widened and an audible gasp rounded the table.

David continued quickly. "I'm suggesting we build a bridge to provide safe passage to and from Goddard Downs, eliminating its isolation during the wet season. Having a bridge will also help in an emergency."

"And it would mean the children can come here safely all year round," Serena added. "They already experience so many disappointments, I don't want to add to them."

Frank took a slow breath. He'd raised the idea of a bridge years before when his father still held the reins, but the idea had been vetoed because of the cost. Now, however, the station was in a much better financial position. He glanced at Maggie. She'd been silently listening and met his gaze, hope filling her eyes. The project with the children had helped Serena overcome her own issues, and Maggie would welcome the idea of a bridge if it would help both her daughter and the children.

He faced David and gave a nod. "I like the idea."

"A bridge, Dad? Really?" Olivia protested, leaning forward. "Don't get me wrong, I'm all for anything that would make the station safer and enable Serena to carry on her programme, but we're talking about building something that none of us have any idea how to do, nor of the costs involved. It could cost more than it's worth." She folded her arms and sat back in her chair with a stony expression on her face.

Of course, Olivia would be negative. "We won't know that

until we investigate," Frank replied, trying not to be too conde-scending. "How do the rest of you feel?"

Janella spoke first. "I think it's a great suggestion. I've always thought something needed to be done. I think we all have at one point or another, but no one ever said anything."

"It's because we're used to it," Frank said. "We've grown up with the rains and the flooding, and we've just accepted that's the way it is. David and Serena haven't." He nodded at the pair. "Sometimes new eyes are all that's needed to find a solution. Sean, what do you think?"

Blinking, his nephew straightened and ran his hand across his shaggy hair. "Ah… I…I think it's about time. I could help."

"How are you going to help with that broken arm?" Olivia asked almost derisively before turning her gaze to Frank. "I think we should stick a pin in the entire thing until we have more information to base a decision on."

"We aren't deciding now, Liv," Frank said, holding her gaze. "But yes, we need information. David, can I entrust you to undertake some research?"

"Certainly. I'll make a few calls and see what the process would be."

Olivia drew a long breath and blew it out. She sat forward in her chair. "Okay. I'll get some quotes and see just how much this idea will cost, although I think it's going to be more than we can afford. We'd have to engage engineers and get the land surveyed, and then we'd have to find a construction company who could build it, plus pay for all the materials, and it wouldn't be a small bridge."

Frank smiled. His daughter would do a thorough job of gathering details, even if she didn't support the idea. "Perhaps you and David can work together and report back at the next meeting. I'm thinking we should call an interim one before Maggie and I leave. Five days to put everything together?"

Olivia's eyes shot open. "Five days? That's not long enough."

"We need things to move quickly. I want to have this matter tabled or actioned before Maggie and I leave. A week from today should be enough time."

"At least that's better than five days," Olivia said, rolling her eyes. "Are we done?"

"I think so, unless anyone else has something they want to raise?" Frank waited a moment, and when no one responded, he called the meeting to an end.

MAGGIE RETURNED to the cottage to start planning their trip while Frank settled into his office for the day. He was pleased with how things had gone at the meeting, although there'd been little to debate other than the bridge. David's idea was a good one and worth investigating. If it proceeded, it would be another change, but one that Frank would welcome. He was more than used to the access issues the station experienced during the wet season, but having vehicular access all year round had to be beneficial.

CHAPTER 2

rank's one-week edict to Olivia had sent her into overdrive. She'd taken over his office by mid-morning, the need to make calls in private the excuse, which meant he was forced out of the office for the rest of the day. Not that he minded, since he had plenty to do elsewhere. With no vet around, he was the one tending to the needs of the cattle.

By mid-afternoon, with the sun beating down on him, he'd had enough. He leaned against his truck and took a slug of water.

"You alright there, Frank?" David called out from where he was unwinding a reel of barbed wire.

"I'm fine," Frank said, straightening. Though he didn't feel fine, he didn't want a newcomer like David knowing. Nor outdoing him.

He pushed on, ignoring the tiredness and ache in his chest,

but by the end of the day, he was struggling to keep his eyes open. He couldn't remember being so tired.

He finished checking the mob of cattle in the high paddock and drove back to the homestead to grab some paperwork from the office before heading home, but the armchair on the verandah, with its soft cushions and footrest, called to him. Would it hurt to close his eyes for a few minutes?

Succumbing, he eased into the chair, put his feet up, slipped his hat over his face, and closed his eyes. But guilt nibbled at him. How had he become so lazy that he needed a nap at this time of day? Had his time taking a backseat caused him to lose his edge? No. He couldn't accept that. He'd worked hard his entire life. He was used to it. A few months of late mornings couldn't possibly have made him so sluggish. Was it age? He considered himself in the prime of his life, despite the silver hair and five grandchildren under his belt. He didn't feel old. He wasn't old. Then what was the reason for this tiredness? Why did he feel ten years older than he was?

"Are you alright, my love?" Maggie's soft voice called from somewhere beyond the darkness behind his eyes.

"Perfectly." He pulled the hat from his face and smiled. "I was just thinking."

"About anything in particular?" she asked as she walked over and slid onto his lap.

He wrapped his arms around her waist as she snuggled close. "Not really. How's the trip planning coming along? I'm guessing you've got the entire thing completely organised by now," he said, chuckling.

"You know me too well." She chuckled with him. "I've

drawn up a plan but it's at home. I thought we could go over it after dinner."

"Sounds good. So, what brings you here?"

"I came to give Serena a hand. Oliver was fussing and she had an online meeting with the school district."

Frank lifted his brow. "Everything alright there?"

"There were some questions about what she's planning to do when the rainy season comes. That's been one of their biggest concerns all along."

"This morning's meeting was right on cue, then. I'm very glad David made the suggestion."

"I was surprised you warmed to it. All the years you've spent here, and it never occurred to you to build a bridge, then David arrives and immediately sees the need and is bold enough to speak up about it. That had to be confronting."

"Yes and no. I raised the idea many years ago when I was his age, but my father dismissed it because of the cost."

Maggie straightened. "Really? I wasn't aware of that."

He shrugged. "Not many do."

"Well, I think this must be God's timing."

"I wouldn't doubt it. A bridge could mean big changes for us. Positive changes."

"There've been so many already, even in the three years I've been here."

"And here's another. I think I need to start exercising. I eat okay, but I think I may need to work out. Julian used to suggest it from time to time, but I never considered it seriously."

"Don't you get enough exercise working on the station?"

"That's different. I'm not as young as I think I am. If I want to keep up around here after we come back from our trip, then

I need to get fitter. I can't go running around mending fences and driving cattle if my body feels older than it is. I need to keep my strength up if I want to keep up with the boys."

Maggie chuckled. "That's it. Having David here, young and strong, has you thinking about your strength all of a sudden."

"Can't a man think of these things?" he said with a laugh.

Maggie leaned closer, brushing her hand gently over his hair and gazing into his eyes. "There's nothing wrong with your strength. There's no need for competition, but if you feel you need to exercise, then, by all means, do so. I'll join you."

"Would you?" He'd expected Maggie to approve, but hadn't considered she'd want to join him.

"Why not? If you want to be healthier, then I should as well. We're in this together, after all."

Frank's smile widened. "That we are." He planted a kiss on her cheek. "Let's head home so we can make a start, and we can also look over the plans for the trip."

"Music to my ears," Maggie replied, smiling. "Let me say goodbye to Serena and then I'll meet you by the Jeep." She slipped off his lap and headed inside while he started towards the office to gather his things.

Olivia was still in his chair but was so engrossed in her telephone conversation that she barely rose her hand in acknowledgment. She was so dedicated. Her entire life, she'd been the child he had to worry about the least. She was resolute and always in control, but she was also thoughtful and discerning. She'd made few mistakes in her life, but it meant she lacked the wisdom that experience and mistakes often brought. On the flip side, she'd been spared the pain of those lessons.

He mouthed for her to enjoy the rest of her day before

turning and heading to the door. The sooner he got home, the better he'd feel. A nice cup of tea and Maggie's company would soon dissipate all the aches and pains of the day.

When he went outside, she was putting her bag into the back of the Jeep. "That was quick," he said.

"Yes. Serena and Oliver were taking a nap, so I didn't bother them."

He nodded and got into the driver's seat while Maggie climbed in the other side. Slipping his hand across the console, he took hers and looked into her eyes. The soft, tender expression he found there made him even happier he'd decided to take time out to spend with her. He kissed her knuckles gently. "Let's go home."

He put the key in the ignition, but before he could turn it, Janella appeared at the top of the verandah, waving her arm frantically in their direction before rushing down the steps. She was breathing heavily when she reached them.

"What is it, Janella?" Maggie asked, leaning across the console.

"I...I got accepted to culinary school," she said between gasps.

"That's wonderful! Congratulations," Frank said. Following Julian's death, his daughter-in-law had buried herself in the kitchen and the children, emerging only because of Serena's youth programme, and the young man, Jonah, she'd met and helped. Frank was glad she'd finally found a pursuit outside of the station and the children, although this was another change that would affect everyone. *Who would take over the cooking?*

Maggie beamed as she leaned across him. "I knew you could do it, Janella. That's wonderful news."

"Thanks, but...I...I don't know what to do. I only applied because Jonah asked me to. I wanted to support him, and he refused to go ahead unless I did. I never imagined I'd be accepted." Her gaze lowered and she stared at her hands. "I don't have time to go to school now."

Frank frowned. "Why not?"

She lifted her gaze, her dark eyes troubled. "I'd have to leave the station. I can't do that. Especially now. There's so much to get settled with everything that's happened in the past months. I can't take two years to go to Darwin just to follow some pipe dream I never had in the first place."

"What about Jonah? Was he accepted?" Maggie asked.

"I have to call him and see if he's heard. I do hope so. He's so talented. He'll make a great chef someday."

Maggie reached for Janella's hand. "And so will you. Where do you think he got the inspiration? Who helped him improve his skills and put everything together for him to apply? That was all you, Janella. Don't discount yourself."

"You're more than capable, Janella," Frank added. "You've been preparing gourmet meals for us for years. That's no easy feat."

"That's different, Frank. Everyone here is happy to eat whatever I cook. This is a school. People are going to criticise; it's their job. They'll soon realise I'm not that good."

"Rubbish," Maggie interrupted. "You're a wonderful cook. Stop saying otherwise."

"I have to agree with Maggie, Janella. You'd make a wonderful chef. Plus, being in Darwin would mean that you'd be close to Caleb. That has to be a positive."

She smiled. "Of course. I miss him so much. But there's a lot to consider. I can't just run off. It isn't only about me."

Frank nodded. "You have a point, but I'm sure the rest of the family would agree with us and tell you to grasp this opportunity with both hands."

"Please, don't tell them," she said abruptly. "I'd rather we kept this between us."

"If that's what you want," Frank replied, although he wasn't sure why she'd want to keep it quiet.

"How long before you have to respond?" Maggie asked.

"A week."

"Well, I for one hope you go, but it's your choice."

"We'll support you whatever you decide," Frank said, "but I think we should pray about it."

"I will. I am," Janella said.

"That's great, but I'd like to pray for you now, if that's okay."

"Oh. Yes, of course." Janella nodded, a grateful smile on her round face.

Frank climbed out of the Jeep and Maggie followed suit, quickly running around to the driver's side where they both placed their hands on Janella.

They bowed their heads and Frank began. "Father, You are the Author and Finisher of our faith. You knew us before You formed us in our mother's womb, and to each of us, You have appointed a purpose on this earth. We may not know what Your plans are, but You said in Your Word that if we seek, we shall find; if we knock, it shall be opened to us, and if we ask, we shall receive.

"Father, we come seeking Your will for Janella. She's been a faithful servant, Lord. She's raised her children in the love and fear of You. She stood by Julian's side and supported him, and today, she's seeking guidance for her future. We ask that You bless her and give her peace. May Your hand be upon her. She never means ill for anyone, Lord. She always wants the best for those around her, but now, let her see that You may have a new purpose for her life and let her be open to that. We ask these things in Jesus' precious name. Amen."

"Amen," Maggie and Janella both echoed softly.

"Thank you, Frank," Janella said, the smile on her face even broader and more genuine than before.

"Don't thank me. I was just doing what I felt we should. It's always best to bring God into the middle of such decisions."

Janella nodded. "Very true. I'll let you two go now. I realise you were heading home."

"It was no trouble," Frank replied. "We're always here for you, Janella. You know that."

"I know. Thank you." Smiling, she stepped up and gave him a kiss on the cheek.

"I look forward to hearing what you decide," Maggie said, giving her a hug.

"I'll be sure to tell you once I know."

"Great." Maggie smiled and walked around to the other side of the Jeep.

Janella stepped back and waited while Frank climbed in.

He turned the key and raised a hand before pulling away. As she waved back, he couldn't help but think this was another pivotal moment in their lives.

"I'm so glad she got accepted," Maggie said as they drove down the track towards the cottage. "It'll be good for her."

Frank nodded. "I agree. I only hope she takes it up."

"You don't think she will?"

"I don't know." He shrugged. "Life in the city would be very different for her. But it's in God's hands, and we have to trust that she'll listen."

"Agreed. He knows best." She placed her hand on his thigh as the Jeep bumped along the rutted track beneath the setting sun.

The long day was behind them, and he looked forward to a relaxing evening with his wife. Getting fit could wait another day.

CHAPTER 3

*J*anella's news was the perfect end to Maggie's day. Frank's suggestion that their trip should be sooner rather than later, followed by the afternoon spent with little Oliver, and now, learning that Janella had been accepted into culinary school had been the icing on the cake. The day couldn't have been more wonderful.

Once they reached the cottage, she set about preparing dinner. Frank would be hungry, and although family dinners at the main house had resumed, they still liked their private dinners at least three times a week. Today was one of those days.

While he went to shower, she pulled the lasagna she'd made the previous day from the fridge and cut two large squares, placing them side by side on a baking sheet before popping them into the oven. The pieces only had to be warmed, and their new oven only needed a few minutes to get to the right temperature.

By the time he joined her, the table was laid with sparkling water, a tossed green salad, lasagna and some crusty bread. "Bon appetite," she chuckled as she presented her table.

"Lovely." He stepped towards her, kissing her on the forehead before pulling a chair out for her. She loved his gentlemanly ways. It was so refreshing.

They talked a great deal as they ate, about the small things, their day, the beautiful sunset they witnessed on the way home, and plans to spend some time on the deck watching the water after dinner. Finally, the topic turned to their trip.

"So, show me what you've come up with," Frank said as he wiped his mouth with a napkin. He'd refused the leftover apple cobbler she'd offered, but she indulged herself with a slice, along with some whipped cream. He was already taking his new fitness plan seriously. She'd start tomorrow.

She rose from the table and collected her notebook and laptop from the kitchen counter where she'd left them. She'd spent several hours after the meeting ended researching where to go and where to stay. The camper had solar panels and Frank had told her they'd also take a generator, so they didn't need to stick to a tight schedule and could basically go wherever they fancied, but that went against her grain. She liked to plan and know where she was going, although when she was younger and still married to Cliff, she'd entertained the idea of caravanning across the country and going wherever the wind took them, but it never happened. Her ex-husband didn't want to miss any important political opportunities, and the idea of sleeping in a caravan instead of a hotel didn't appeal to him. Now he was living in a small room, unable to go out, and receiving medication to treat his psychotic disorder.

She couldn't help but feel a moment of sadness for him. After all he'd done, and everything he'd strived for, he now had nothing. Mandy, his second wife, had remarried and he never saw their daughter. Serena and Jeremy visited on occasion, but not often, since he'd made it clear he didn't want them to come to the secure hospital to see him. She could understand that. It would be humiliating for him. Maybe one day he'd get better and be released, and regain some semblance of a normal life, but in the meantime, all they could do was pray for him.

"Maggie?"

She blinked. "Sorry, my mind wandered a little," she confessed with a chuckle. "Let me show you the route I thought might work."

Frank leaned closer to look at the laptop screen.

"From here to Broome is about a seven-hour drive, but there are lots of places to stop along the way, as you know. I'm thinking we should go up to Mitchell Falls, for one. It would take three days to get there and back, but we should only go if you think the truck would make it. The track's rough and it's not recommended for trailers."

"The truck will be fine. I've always wanted to see the falls, so that's a great idea. After that?"

"Derby, and then Broome. But I'd also love to see Cape Leveque. But then, do you think we could head south and see the wildflowers? And I'd love to go to the Karijini National Park and Monkey Mia to swim with the dolphins. And then there's the Pinnacles, and Perth, and Albany…"

"Whoa." Frank chuckled. "How long are you thinking we'll be gone?"

She shrugged. "I don't know. How long *can* we travel?"

"To do all of that would take at least a month, but we'd be driving non-stop. To take it slowly and enjoy the sights, I think we'd need three months."

"Can we be away that long?"

"I don't see why not." His eyes twinkled as a grin grew on his face. "I think it might do the family good to survive that long without us."

She smiled broadly. "I love the sound of that. Three months with you, camping out, sounds wonderful."

"I totally agree, but will Serena be able to cope without you?"

A small breath escaped Maggie. That was her major concern. But Serena was resourceful, and Oliver was a good baby. "They'll be fine."

"Good. So, three months it is. And if we leave in ten days' time, Olivia and David should have the information on the bridge before then."

"I'll start packing, but first I'd better do the dishes." She stood and started clearing the table.

"No, I'll do that," Frank said, taking the plates from her hands. "You cooked. I'll do the dishes."

"Okay. Thank you. I'll make some tea to have on the deck."

"Sounds wonderful. I'd like some of that chamomile," he said while collecting the salad bowl and placing it on top of the plates before walking to the sink.

Maggie filled the kettle, turned it on, and while waiting for it to boil, grabbed the mugs and the teabags. Frank made quick work of the dishes, which she ended up wiping, and once they were done, he carried the tray containing their tea out to the deck. He set the tray on the small table between their chairs, and as she sat, she gazed up at the sky. It was filled with a sea of stars, all twinkling like diamonds. She sighed. "I'll never get tired of looking up."

"I agree. It's amazing." He reached over and took her hand and gently stroked her skin with his thumb.

She exhaled a long sigh of contentment. She was so blessed. Frank was rougher than Cliff in many ways, and yet he was far more tender and loving. He was the kind of man movies were made about—the rancher on his horse, spending his days herding livestock, living life with passion. Dependable. Strong. Trustworthy. If ever there was a depiction of a perfect husband, it was Frank. At least, in her mind.

She turned and faced him. "I feel so blessed to be married to you, Frank."

His forehead creased and a bemused grin filled his face. "How'd you get to that from gazing at stars?"

She chuckled. Shrugged. "I don't know."

Their gazes held for a long moment before he said, "Come here." He rose to his feet and gently pulled her up to meet him. She stepped into his arms as he wrapped them around her, holding her close but tenderly. His lips pressed against her forehead as they swayed to imaginary music. Not only was he a great horseman, father, and rancher, he was also a terrific dancer.

She breathed deeply, clearing her mind as she nestled against his chest, searching for the sound of his beating heart. After some time, her thoughts turned to the bridge. "Do you think the bridge will get built before the rains come if the price is right?"

He chuckled. "How can the bridge be on your mind? I

thought you'd only have thoughts of me." He pulled back and grinned.

She chuckled with him. "I'm sorry. I just thought of it."

"It's okay." They resumed dancing. "With David and Olivia on it, I don't doubt it could get done. They're both very capable people, and from what I've seen, David's not afraid of hard work and challenge."

"He certainly faced many challenges as a fireman, and even more winning Serena's heart. I'm so glad they're here with us now. I feel that the family, and the station, are becoming stronger."

"You're right, my love. This family has faced many trials in the past few years, but God has brought us through every one of them and made us stronger because of them. I'm sure He gave David the idea for the bridge. I'm sensing it's come at the right time."

Maggie nodded. "From the very beginning, when I look back and see the tapestry the Lord has woven to get me from one stage of my life to another, I can't help but smile. I can see it all in hindsight, how each step I took and each mistake I made brought me closer and closer to you and the life we now have. I never thought I'd get divorced, and once I had, I never imagined remarrying, but God saw it all. He led me here." She lifted her chin and gazed into her husband's eyes. "To you."

Frank's smile was brilliant, even in the dim light. He lowered his lips to hers and kissed her deeply. She breathed in the scent of the oatmeal soap on his skin. She loved him so much. She loved their life together. She couldn't imagine it without him now. In all the years she had with Cliff, she could never have imagined loving like this, feeling this way, or having such a life. She felt freer now than she ever had. Her eyes stung as the kiss deepened.

"Maggie, what is it?" Frank asked as they parted.

"Nothing," she replied, wiping her eyes.

"You're crying," he said gently. He rubbed her back soothingly as he hugged her. "You can tell me."

She laughed and sniffled simultaneously. "I'm being silly, that's all."

"No. You're never silly."

"I'm just so happy," she confessed. "I'm so very happy."

He hugged her tighter. "I'm glad. I'd hate to be the only one feeling that way."

They both laughed and continued their music-less dance. This trip couldn't come soon enough.

CHAPTER 4

*J*anella sat quietly on the edge of her bed in the semi-dark as the laugh of a kookaburra ushered in the dawn. Sasha lay asleep on the other side. It'd been a long time since her daughter had crawled in bed with her. Julian had never encouraged the children to join them as he always felt their marital bed was a special place just for them. It was only on the odd occasion when one of the children was sick that he allowed them to snuggle down between them. However, it wasn't illness that brought Sasha to her bed sometime during the night, but comfort. More than ever, they needed each other.

There was so much change going on at Goddard Downs. Janella sometimes wondered what Julian would say if he were there to see it. Would he be proud? Hopeful? Sceptical? Joshua's new marriage, Caleb's departure for school, the acquisition of Indigo Downs, and now the talk of a bridge. *And her acceptance to culinary school.* It all seemed too much, but it was all happening. But one question remained. *Was she ready?*

Slipping to her knees, she closed her eyes and clasped her hands.

> *Our Father in heaven,*
> *Hallowed be Your name.*
> *Your kingdom come,*
> *Your will be done,*
> *On earth as it is in heaven.*
> *Give us today our daily bread.*
> *And forgive us our debts,*
> *As we also have forgiven our debtors.*
> *And lead us not into temptation,*
> *But deliver us from the evil one.*
> *In Jesus' name. Amen.*

Taking a deep breath, she rose to her feet, stretching her arms above her head before leaning to one side and then the other. The day wouldn't wait for her to answer that question—there was a lot to do, and she was the one to do it. If breakfast for the family and station hands was to be ready on time, she needed to get moving. Her lingering doubts could wait or join her as she carried out her tasks. Either way, she had no time to waste.

She showered quickly, the cold water jolting all traces of sleep, before dressing in jeans and a navy-blue button-down blouse with a tank top underneath. She paused to look at her reflection in the mirror. Her youthful hourglass was gone, and she looked more like the vase on her dressing table, with more bulge in the middle than anywhere else. She hadn't noticed the pounds piling on since Julian's passing. She'd never been a small woman, but before, her curves were more appealing. She took a deep breath and released it slowly. At least her clothes still fit. Just. She turned and left the room. Sasha would find her way to the kitchen when she woke, so there was no need to rouse her.

The kitchen was quiet as Janella began her usual prep. The stillness allowed her mind to wander. She envisioned herself walking the streets of Darwin amidst the hustle and bustle of crowds and traffic. The thought made her shake her head. It was ridiculous. She wasn't a city-dweller. There was no way she could be happy there. Mornings filled with honking horns instead of the sound of kookaburras and willy wagtails. No, it wasn't for her. How could she live in a crowded apartment complex after living here, where their nearest neighbour was three hours away?

But she couldn't help thinking of Caleb and Julian at the same time. She missed her son so much, and she was sure that Julian would encourage her to go if he could. He'd always wanted her to stretch her wings, and she'd always resisted. Julian would say she'd never know if she liked it until she did. But he wasn't here to tell her that.

She clenched her jaw at the cruel reality. Julian wasn't going to return. She wouldn't see him again until the day she joined him in heaven. All she had left of him were memories, photos in frames, and their children. Tears built behind her eyes. But no. She wouldn't cry. This once, she'd stay strong.

It still hadn't sunk in fully that he was gone, even though it had been almost a year. It still hurt. Sometimes she forgot and woke up expecting to find him in the office or getting coffee in the kitchen to start his day. He'd be so proud of how well Caleb was doing, and Sasha, too. Their daughter was maturing before her eyes. Janella couldn't get her out of the kitchen, or her own wardrobe, though Sasha only ever borrowed clothes that were old and didn't fit Janella anymore. She sighed. *What am I to do about all of this, God? I don't know what to do.* Sniffing, she steeled herself and continued to crack eggs into a bowl for the French toast she was making.

Half an hour later, Sasha joined her in the kitchen. Janella smiled. "Good morning, sweetheart."

"Good morning, Mum," Sasha replied, wrapping an apron around her waist and stepping to the counter. "What do you need me to do?"

"You can get the sausages and start on those," Janella replied, flipping the toast over in the pan, the scent of cinnamon wafting up to meet her.

"Okay," Sasha replied cheerfully.

Janella glanced over her shoulder. Sasha wore a smile as she retrieved the sausages from the fridge and grabbed a frying pan to cook them in. She was so happy working in the kitchen, and Janella was so pleased to have her there. Since Caleb left for school, Sasha made more time for her. It was as if she knew Janella needed her close. But one day her daughter, like Caleb, would leave for boarding school and she'd be left alone. Her heart sank. One day, she *would* be alone.

"Sash, are you looking forward to going off to school and joining Caleb one day?" she asked off-handedly. She truly didn't know how her daughter felt about it. It was a couple of years away, but still.

"You know I love it here, Mum, but I miss Caleb. Plus, his school looks so cool. I can't wait to go."

Janella blinked rapidly to push back the sudden stinging in her eyes. The words came out of her mouth without thought. "If I went with you, would you like that?"

"Are you thinking of moving to Darwin when I go to school?" Sasha asked, her eyes widening.

Janella paused, mouth open but words absent. The news of her acceptance was on the tip of her tongue, but try as she might, she couldn't utter them. It was as if her tongue was tied.

"Mum?" Sasha repeated when she didn't answer immediately.

Janella forced a smile. "No. Of course not. I was just asking."

Sasha looked at her thoughtfully. "Maybe you should think about it. I'd like to have you there, then you, Caleb, and I can be together."

Janella stopped to look at her daughter. "But don't you think I'd be out of place in the city?"

Sasha continued to unwrap the sausages as the pan heated up. "Why would you be out of place?"

"Look at me," Janella said. "I'm not exactly a city woman. I'm not fashionable at all."

"You don't do too badly, Mum. Yes, your clothes are a little old, but they're nice enough."

"But other than those couple of short visits with Caleb, I've never spent any time in Darwin. I wouldn't know where to start if I lived there."

Sasha dropped the sausages into the pan. They sizzled immediately. "Neither did Dad or Caleb when they first went, but they did just fine. And don't you always tell me that I'll be fine when it's my time to go? If you think I'll do well, then why wouldn't you?"

Janella didn't have a response. She always encouraged her children, but when it came to herself, it wasn't so easy.

She returned to the French toast and kept her news to herself.

LATER THAT EVENING, Janella found a quiet seat on the verandah and called Jonah. She'd tried to reach him the day before but he hadn't answered. Surely, if he'd been accepted, he would have been eager to let her know. That made her wonder if he hadn't been, and that seemed unfair. If she could give him her place, she gladly would.

She was about to hang up when he answered. "Hello?"

"Jonah... It's Janella."

"Janella? Hi! How are you?"

"I'm good."

"Me too," he said excitedly. "I got accepted! My letter came this afternoon. Can you believe it? I'm going to culinary school."

Her chest swelled with pride. Jonah had made it. "I knew you could do it," she said. "I never had a doubt."

"I did," he admitted. "If it wasn't for you, I would never have thought of applying. My dad wants to thank you. He's doing well these days. No drinking or any of that anymore. We're spending time together. Again, that's all because of you."

Janella shook her head. "It wasn't me. I just did what was right. If it was anyone, it was God."

"If it was God, then I thank Him. I never thought I'd see Dad get up each morning to go to work. I thought I'd be looking after him forever. Then I met you, and everything changed."

Tears of joy welled in her eyes. She'd never made such an impression on anyone's life before, not even her children's, at least not in her mind. She'd always taken the back seat since Julian had been such a powerful figure. "I just helped you see what was in you all along."

"What about you?" Jonah asked. "Did you get accepted?"

She paused. If she told him, would there be any going back? Would that be her decision made? But how could she not tell him? She couldn't lie. She hesitated, then answered in an almost subdued voice, "Yes. I got accepted."

"That's great! We'll be at school together. You can help me, and you'll get to be near your son," he said excitedly. "This is going to be so cool."

She gulped. How could she tell him that she hadn't decided whether she'd be going or not? How could she destroy his enthusiasm? She couldn't. "I'm sure it will be," she said.

"I have to formally accept the offer, but my dad thinks I should go there first to see if I like it. Would you come with me?" he asked. "You've been to Darwin before. I've never been there. Neither has my dad."

Her lips parted. If she went to Darwin with Jonah, might it help her decide as well? See if she could fit in? But could she leave the station to find out? Maggie and Frank were leaving on their trip soon, but the school needed an answer in a week, the amount of time Frank had given to investigate the bridge construction. Could they spare her for a few days?

"Janella?"

"Yes, sorry Jonah. Of course, I can go with you."

"Great! I'll tell Dad. I'm so excited. I never thought I could do anything like this. I didn't think I was smart enough, or good enough."

Janella shared his sentiments. "You need to have more faith in yourself and allow God to lead you."

The words struck her as she uttered them. She should be taking her own advice. "Is your dad there now?" she asked.

"No. He had a late shift at work today."

"Okay. I'll call him in the morning and make arrangements for the trip."

"Thanks. I don't know what I'd do without you."

Janella smiled. "I'm sure you'd survive. Have a great night, Jonah."

"You too."

Ending the call, she stared out into the darkness, her heart pounding. Darwin. She was going to Darwin. With Jonah. It didn't mean she would accept the offer, but it was a step closer. She had to tell Frank and Maggie. She went to call Maggie's number, but then hesitated, only to press it before she changed her mind.

Maggie answered almost immediately.

Janella swallowed hard and cleared her throat. "Jonah got accepted to culinary school, but his dad wants him to go to Darwin to check it out before he accepts the offer. His dad can't go with him, so he asked me if I'd go. I told him I would, but I want to make sure I can be spared for a few days." She was talking fast, but she had to get it out before she lost courage.

"That's wonderful, Janella. And if you go, I'm sure it'll help you decide whether to accept, too." Maggie's voice was filled with joy. "Let me get Frank."

Janella held the line for only a few moments before Frank joined Maggie on the other end. "Of course, you should go, Janella," he said. "How long do you think you'll be away?"

"A few days at least. I have to let them know in six days' time, but I should know in less than that."

"I think it's wonderful you're going," Maggie chimed in. "I'm sure you'll see that this is what God wants for you."

Maggie sounded so sure, but Janella still had doubts. "I guess we'll see. I don't want to keep you much longer. You must be trying to relax and enjoy some time together. I'll go now."

"We can talk in the morning," Maggie said. "If you want any help making arrangements, just let me know. I'd be happy to help."

Janella smiled. "Thanks, Maggie, you're a wonderful friend."

"We want the best for you, Janella," Frank said, "no matter what that is. If going to Darwin will help make the choice clearer for you, I think that's great."

"You need to be open to this being the path God has for you," Maggie added.

"I know." Janella drew a deep breath. That God might have something like this planned for her was beyond amazing. But still, her heart beat like a drum just thinking about it.

"Good night," Maggie and Frank said together.

"Good night," she replied. The tiniest of smiles crept onto her face. Could this truly be what God wanted for her?

CHAPTER 5

*F*rank sipped his tea as the family gathered around the table for their meeting. A week had flown by quickly, and in that time, he'd gotten a lot done. The camper was almost ready for their trip. He'd gone over the truck's mechanicals to ensure it was in tip-top condition. The last thing he wanted was to break down in the middle of nowhere. He wanted everything perfect for their trip of a lifetime.

He leaned to his right and whispered into Maggie's ear. "Where are David and Serena?"

"I'm not sure. They knew the meeting was this morning. I reminded her yesterday."

Frank drummed his fingers on his leg. David's attendance was essential to the meeting. He was to report his investigations into the bridge construction. There'd be little point in having it if he failed to show. "Maybe you should check on them."

Maggie nodded but had only gotten to her feet when both

David and Serena, with little Oliver in her arms, rushed into the room. "Sorry we're late," David apologised. "The little guy gave us a difficult time last night."

Frank chuckled, relief flowing through him. "We've all been there, son. Take a seat. I think we can start now." He set his cup of tea aside and bowed his head to pray. "Father, we thank You that You've allowed us to gather together once more in Your name to discuss the matters of this station. Lord, we know that we can make plans, but it is only by Your grace and mercy that we accomplish them. We commit our endeavours to You. In Jesus' name. Amen."

He cleared his throat. "Before we go into the matter of the bridge, I want to address Janella's absence. As you know, Janella left for Darwin to visit Caleb for a few days. She's also accompanying Jonah, the youth from Serena's programme who got accepted into culinary school."

He shifted his gaze to Serena, who was sitting at the end of the table rocking Oliver in her arms. "I want to offer my congratulations, Serena. I'm sure this is only the first of many successes your programme will have in the lives of children in this area, and I daresay further afield. You're doing a great job with them."

A small round of applause erupted, and Serena smiled. "Thanks, Frank, not only for your kind words, but for allowing us to host this aspect of the programme here. I couldn't have enjoyed this success without your support. *Everyone's* support." Her gaze swept around the table but settled on Maggie.

The smile on his wife's face reflected her immense pride in Serena's progress since her unfortunate accident. It didn't seem that long ago she was afraid to step out and be seen in public because of her scarring after being involved in a bomb attack in Paris when she was a journalist, but now, she stood in front of rooms filled with teenagers and young adults, speaking to them about self-esteem, achieving their goals, and perseverance in the face of challenge. The change was remarkable, wrought by God's gentle hand on her life.

Frank shared Maggie's joy in Serena's success and hoped she would have many more. He wished he could have shared Janella's good news as well, but his daughter-in-law had made it clear before she left that she still didn't want anyone to know about her acceptance into the culinary school until she'd made a decision. Still, her absence had to be explained.

"Now, Olivia and David, what information did you get concerning the building costs?"

His daughter straightened and opened the manila folder sitting on the table in front of her. "You didn't give us a lot of time, Dad, but I was able to get some gross estimates for what the construction would cost. I had to keep my list of options small, so I only got ten to compare."

Frank chuckled under his breath. "Only ten?"

Olivia looked up at him, oblivious to his amusement. "Yes. I would have gotten more to be completely thorough, but I figured ten would have to do."

"Of course," Frank agreed, bemused.

"You don't leave anything to chance, do you Liv?" Joshua added with a laugh.

Olivia looked at him pointedly. "I don't. Especially as substantial a project as this one. The wrong move could cost the station millions."

Her statement was a sobering remark that ended the

laughter immediately. There was a reason she was the one responsible for the management of the station's finances.

Frank thanked God silently. *And there couldn't be a better person.*

Olivia continued explaining the quotes she'd gotten, weighing in on the pros and cons of each. Finally, she summarised the project. "I believe it's too expensive. The construction companies require far too much to build the structure, and that doesn't include the costs for land surveying, the design, and building materials. Nor if we run into any problems. However, I did ask that the companies give me their best prices based on the simplest design and the shortest amount of building time." She passed copies of the documents around for everyone to look at.

Frank took a copy and scrutinised it. Olivia had left nothing out. There were estimates for everything.

"If I may?"

Frank looked up to find David with his hand raised. "Yes, David?"

"Olivia has done an amazing job gathering this information, but I also got some figures from a few friends in Darwin. I think you'll find that the job can be done a lot cheaper, especially if we all pitch in to cut down the cost of labour."

Olivia narrowed her eyes. "How could your numbers be lower than mine?"

"I called in some favours. There were some guys I met a few years ago. Their construction company was nearly lost during a fire, but we were able to save it. They said if I ever needed help, they'd be happy to assist. I contacted the main guy, and he sent these figures to me. You can all have a look. I didn't copy enough for everyone, so you'll have to pass the sheet around."

Olivia's hand shot out first. She wouldn't believe anyone could outdo her unless she saw it for herself. Everyone was silent as she studied the numbers. Slowly, her expression softened. "He agreed to this price?"

"He did," David confirmed. "He also called in favours from some of his associates and got us reduced prices for design and surveying. And all within the timeframe we're looking at. Also, I asked some former fireman buddies of mine who have construction experience to pitch in. It'll save us even more on labour."

"We can help," Sean and Nate said simultaneously. They chuckled at their synchronicity.

"You go first," Nate offered, leaning back to wrap an arm around his wife's shoulders.

"I said before that I could help," Sean said. "I've always thought a bridge would make sense, so I'd like to be a part of the project."

"Your arm isn't even healed yet," Olivia challenged. "And what about the drives? We can't allow them to slip because you've all divided your time between them and building a bridge."

"We'll manage," Nate assured. "Sean's arm will be right as rain soon, and then he can do anything that needs to be done."

Frank stifled a laugh as Olivia shot her husband a pointed look. Nate would pay for supporting Sean later, he was sure. "I don't see dividing their time as a problem," Frank said. "I think Nate, Sean, and David know what they can handle. Am I right?"

"Yes," they each replied in turn.

Frank held out his hand, and Olivia passed the paper. He glanced over the numbers, which were far less jarring than those she'd presented. "This is good, David. Very good." He looked up. "Did they give any idea when they could start if we decide to proceed?"

David nodded. "They're just waiting for my call. The surveyors can be here within a couple of days, and then we'll have to meet with the designer after that."

"Dad and Maggie are leaving in a couple of days, and I'm sure Dad will want to have some input. Am I right, Dad?" Olivia asked.

"Yes," Frank confirmed, nodding.

David was unfazed. "I figured as much, which is why I arranged for a virtual meeting. Frank can sit in from wherever he is as long as he has an internet connection."

"You thought of everything," Olivia commented, turning in David's direction. Despite her initial reservations, she sounded impressed.

"I was raised by a very organised aunt who made sure that whatever we did, we did it well," he said with a grin.

"A very wise woman," Olivia noted.

Frank thanked God that Olivia seemed to be on board, and it warmed his heart to witness the exchange between the younger generation. They'd need to work together while he and Maggie were gone for three months. They all would. Speaking of which, he had to inform them of the final plan for their trip, but not until after the vote on the bridge. He passed the paper David provided to Maggie to review. Soon the paper made its way around the entire table and back to David.

"If everyone's had a chance to look over the numbers, why don't we take a vote?" he said. "All in favour of the bridge, raise your hand."

One by one, everyone raised their hand, although Olivia was still a little hesitant. Frank was sure that she was still concerned about the costs, but the figures David presented made it possible, and no one could argue the fact that it would be an invaluable feature for the station to have.

"It's unanimous. We're building a bridge," Frank declared. "David, call your friend and let him know that we want to get started as soon as possible. Have him send official estimates to Liv so she can make arrangements to meet with the bank about a loan." He turned to his daughter. "Let me know if you need anything from me before we leave."

"How long are you going to be gone?" Olivia asked, leaning forward.

Frank exchanged a smile with Maggie as he reached under the table and squeezed her hand. "We've decided that we want to take our time and enjoy this trip, so we'll be gone at least three months."

Olivia's voice was piercing when she responded. "Three months, Dad! Are you sure?"

"Of course, he is, Liv," Joshua piped up. "Stop worrying so much. We can handle everything here." His son had remained quiet for the entire meeting, whispering to Stella from time to time, but now he spoke up. "Dad knows we can handle it, otherwise he wouldn't be going. Isn't that right, Dad?"

"Absolutely," Frank confirmed. "I trust you all to work together to see this project to completion and to ensure that everything runs smoothly on the station while we're gone.

Joshua, you need to stay on top of the Tamala situation. I won't be completely out of touch during this trip, but I won't be checking in that frequently, either."

"You don't have to worry, Dad. I've got it under control." The confidence in Joshua's voice made Frank smile. Indeed, his son had come into his own.

"Thank you, everyone, for your input today. I think we've covered everything we need to. Maggie will provide you with a map of our planned route so that you'll know where we are. The camper's ready, and all we need to do now is some last-minute packing."

"I'm sure you'll have an amazing time." Stella leaned forward, smiling. "Perhaps Joshua and I will get to do something like that in the future." She turned and grinned at her husband. "Camping out under the stars sounds wonderful."

Joshua chuckled. "I do enough sleeping under the stars on the cattle drives. I don't think I need that on a holiday, too."

Stella pouted and Joshua leaned in to kiss her cheek. "But for you, I'd do it."

Frank smiled. "Wise man, Joshua. A happy wife makes for a happy life."

"You got that right," Nate agreed, and everyone laughed.

"I think we can call this meeting adjourned," Frank said, pushing away from the table.

"What I wouldn't give for some of Janella's treats about now," Sean commented.

"I know what you mean. She makes the most amazing food," Nate said.

The urge to tell them the news was on the tip of his tongue, but Frank held it in. He respected Janella and would honour her wish to keep her news quiet for the time being. He wondered how she was doing in Darwin. He'd call her before they left, but in the meantime, he had a trip to finish getting ready for.

He kissed Maggie on the cheek and told her he had to tidy a few things in the office, but he'd be right back. She was chatting with Serena, but she looked up and they shared a smile that spoke volumes. They couldn't wait to leave. Only one more night.

Frank excused himself and headed to the office. As he sat at the desk, he took a moment to study the photos filling the walls. A lifetime of memories, but he was sure many more would be added to the collection. A graduation photo of Janella, perhaps.

He bowed his head and prayed. *Lord, whatever Janella decides, let Your will prevail.*

CHAPTER 6

*W*hy did it have to itch right up to the elbow? Sean shoved the ruler as far up the space between his arm and the cast as he could and moved it around vigorously. He closed his eyes and groaned with satisfaction as it finally found the spot. He was tired of the cast. Each day when he woke, he longed to see it gone, but the doctors said he still needed another couple of weeks. It had been a bad break he'd gotten from coming off a bull at a rodeo, and it was taking longer than expected to heal.

"You look busy," Joshua commented as he strolled into the kitchen and poured himself an orange juice. He didn't live there anymore, but he still had free rein to come and go as he pleased, and today, they'd all gathered to see Uncle Frank and Maggie off on their three-month holiday.

"You may not think it, but this is work. Do you know how difficult it is to get to the right spot?" Sean asked, biting his bottom lip as he scratched harder. It was utterly satisfying.

Joshua gulped down his juice. "I know what you mean. I broke my arm when we were kids, remember?"

Sean nodded as he recalled that summer when Joshua wound up in a cast for eight weeks. They'd been climbing giant boabs when he fell and landed on a rock. With their enormous trunks, the giant boabs were difficult to climb, but that one had a split up the middle causing the tree to branch off in two directions. They thought they could shimmy up the middle and reach the boughs. They were wrong, and Joshua paid the price. "How could I forget? Olivia scolded me for days, saying it was me who encouraged you to climb that tree."

Joshua chuckled. "She refused to listen to explanations. She was so sure she knew what had happened."

"But I wasn't the ring-leader that time. You were," Sean replied.

"Yeah, but who'd believe that?" Joshua laughed as he finished his juice.

"True. When there was mischief to be had, I was usually the one leading the charge," Sean admitted. "We had some good times."

Joshua met his gaze and nodded. Did his cousin feel the same sense of loss that he did? It made him sad to recall their abandoned past. The closeness they'd shared when they were younger was gone, but Sean no longer saw that as a bad thing. He'd always gotten Joshua into scrapes, and though his cousin had been a willing participant, he'd come to realise that the real reason Joshua followed him into one half-cocked idea after another was to ensure that Sean came out alright. Joshua had his back.

But now, with Stella in the picture, Joshua had left all that behind. He'd grown up and was finally gaining respect from the family. Even Uncle Frank appeared to treat him with more consideration than ever before.

"At least we have our memories," Sean added before the mood took a nosedive.

"We do," Joshua said with a smile. He walked to the sink and rinsed out the glass. "I have to stop by the office to check on some things with Liv before Dad and Maggie ship out. Meet you out front?"

"Sure," Sean replied, placing the ruler on the table in front of him. The itch was all scratched out, at least for now. Joshua left, but he remained at the table. His cousin was happy, and he was happy for him, but it didn't change the fact that he missed him. What would it be like at Goddard Downs with both him and Uncle Frank gone?

Sean lived under no pretences. If it hadn't been for his uncle spearheading his return, he doubted very much that he would have been welcomed back again after the way he'd behaved. Not that he would have blamed everyone. He'd made a fool of himself, acting like a petulant child because Joshua wanted to grow up. It had taken him a long time to realise that, and he was trying daily to make up for it, but as far as he could tell, he wasn't making much headway. His arm made him feel useless for the most part. Every day when the others headed to work, he felt like a giant toadstool just sitting there, eating and drinking and doing nothing to earn his keep. No one said anything, but it was the way he felt. He got up from the table and took the ruler with him. He never knew when another itch would hit, and it was best to be prepared.

The rest of the family was gathered in a small group around

Uncle Frank and Maggie's rig, inspecting it. Gadding about in a rig like this was the sort of thing his uncle would like, but Sean was surprised that Maggie seemed enthusiastic about their trip and their plans to rough it. She didn't seem that kind of person. Sean didn't know why, but he had her pegged as a woman who'd prefer hotel rooms and bubble baths to a basic camper on the back of a truck, but that showed how little he knew her. He hadn't tried to get to know her, and it was one of many things he had to correct.

"The rig looks great, Uncle Frank," Sean said. His uncle and Maggie had just finished chatting with one of the hands who'd walked off after tipping his hat.

Uncle Frank turned in his direction and smiled, his face brightening. "Thanks, Sean. She's a beauty, isn't she?"

"Better than that," Maggie agreed, stepping closer to Uncle Frank. "She's perfect."

He slipped his arm around her waist and kissed the top of her head.

Sean smiled awkwardly and averted his gaze. Witnessing the affection between the pair made him feel strange, as if he were intruding on something private.

"I'm sure you'll have many adventures out there on the road," he continued, forcing himself to look at his uncle.

"I'm sure we will. We've not done anything like this before, and we're looking forward to it, aren't we, love?" He squeezed Maggie closer.

"Absolutely," she replied, smiling up at him with such a look of love it made him squeamish.

The others joined them. Nate's arm was draped around Olivia, Joshua stood with Stella, his arm also around his wife.

David and Serena stood together, a little family with their baby, while William and Isobel hovered around Sasha. Sean was the only person on his own.

Years of chasing skirts and the next good thing, and what had it gotten him? Back at Goddard Downs, feeling like the odd man out, that's what. A pang of longing rose inside him as he looked at the couples. Everyone had someone. Everyone knew their place. He had no one, and he didn't know his place.

He was grateful that Uncle Frank had welcomed him back after he broke his arm, but now he was leaving. How would the others treat him with Uncle Frank gone? Olivia certainly wasn't his greatest fan and he guessed she'd give him an even harder time when Uncle Frank wasn't there to temper her. He sighed. He had no option but to hang around and put up with whatever came.

Uncle Frank glanced at his watch. "It's time we hit the road."

One by one, each person stepped forward to hug him and Maggie and wish them safe travels. Standing back to let the others go before him, Sean watched the loving exchanges and promises to check in.

"We'll take care of everything, Dad. You don't have to worry about a thing," Olivia assured her father.

Uncle Frank kissed her forehead and hugged her. "I know, Liv."

Finally, it was Sean's turn.

His uncle looked him in the eye. "Help take care of this place until we get back, Sean."

A lump formed in Sean's throat. He swallowed hard. At

least his uncle believed in him. "Of course, Uncle. You can count on me."

Uncle Frank clapped a hand on his shoulder and smiled. "I know I can, son."

That was the greatest affirmation Sean had ever been given. But could he live up to it?

"Dad, before you go, can we pray for you?" Joshua interrupted, effectively ending the moment.

Sean stepped back. He didn't want to be involved in this praying thing. It was all a load of hogwash as far as he was concerned.

Uncle Frank nodded. "That'd be great. Thanks."

The family gathered in a circle. Uncle Frank waved him over. He had no choice but to join them. They all bowed their heads. He did the same, although it felt stupid standing outside, holding hands, talking to someone he couldn't see.

Joshua began praying, and that in itself felt weird. Wrong. His cousin, with whom he shared so many adventures, praying? He shook his head as Joshua began.

"Heavenly Father, watch over Dad and Maggie as they begin their trip. Keep them safe and let them have the most amazing time. May they be aware of Your presence as they travel through this incredible land. Refresh them, Lord, and may they return richer and fuller in every way. Bless them, Lord. In Jesus' precious name we pray. Amen."

Uncle Frank thanked Joshua for the prayer, as amen after amen followed and the last of the hugs and well wishes were given. Finally, he and Maggie climbed into the cab. The engine roared to life, and moments later, they pulled out of the station with all the family waving and calling out their last goodbyes.

The group lingered for as long as the truck and its turtle-back camper were in sight, but once it was gone and all that was left was a cloud of red dust, they began going their separate ways.

Joshua headed in Sean's direction and walked in step with him. Not that Sean had anywhere in particular to be going, unlike the others who all had jobs to do. "Hey Seano," Joshua said. "Stella and I are about to head off but come for a visit when you can."

Sean looked up and smiled. "Thanks, mate. I'll take you up on it as soon as I can. I'm looking forward to checking out your new digs."

"Great." Joshua smiled and gave him a pat on the shoulder "Take it easy, Seano."

"You too," he replied.

Joshua headed to his truck where Stella stood waiting. They both climbed in and were gone a few moments later.

Sean released a heavy sigh and lifted his hat, wiping the sweat off his brow with the back of his hand. Although Joshua might welcome him at Indigo, he doubted Stella would, even though she'd told him she'd forgiven him. *God forgave us, why can't we forgive you?* Her words echoed in his head. It was a conversation they'd had when she and Joshua had first returned from their honeymoon.

But that kind of forgiveness and acceptance was foreign to him, and he would expect her to turn him away if he showed his face on their doorstep. So nope, he doubted he'd be paying Indigo Downs a visit anytime soon.

CHAPTER 7

*E*xcitement and anticipation filled Maggie the moment she and Frank headed down the track, leaving Goddard Downs and the family behind. She'd leaned out the window and waved until all she could see was dust. Despite the days of planning and preparation, she still found it hard to believe they were actually taking this trip, and it hadn't felt real until that last moment when they pulled away from the homestead and headed towards the open road.

She reached across the console and squeezed Frank's hand. "We're off!"

He turned and grinned like a Cheshire cat. "Finally."

Although she knew this part of the track like the back of her hand, travelling with the camper attached to the back of the truck meant Frank had to drive more slowly than usual to avoid the ruts, allowing her to take in the scenery with fresh eyes.

She remembered the first time she'd driven along this road

and how the vibrant colours had captivated her. The rich, red earth, the burnt ochre of the rock formations that were as old as time, and the deep blue of the sky.

The Kimberley had such stark contrasts from one season to the other. Balmy days with clear skies gave way to torrential rains that turned the firm earth to muck within seconds and turned rivers into raging torrents.

"The bridge will help a lot when the rains come," she said.

"It will," Frank agreed. "Let's pray that everything goes to plan while we're away. It'll be something to see when we return."

"It sure will. No more helicopter flights just to go shopping. That will be a change." She chuckled lightly as she settled back in her seat to enjoy the scenery.

Before long, the majestic Cockburn Ranges rose up ahead of them, framing the scenery like a work of art. A group of wallabies lifted their heads as they passed, and every now and then, another vehicle came towards them, whipping up dust for them to drive through. Soon, they came to the Pentecost River crossing. At this time of year, the river was shallow and easy to navigate, but during the rainy season, it would become treacherous and only the brave or stupid would try crossing it. Much like their river. Saltwater crocodiles were often sighted, so swimming was out of the question.

As they approached the crossing, Maggie peered ahead, leaning forward in her seat while snapping photos.

Frank slowed the vehicle to not much more than a walking pace as another vehicle, a large 4WD towing a camper trailer, trundled across the river towards them. Frank lifted his hand as they passed each other. The gravel crunched under the tyres as he manoeuvred the rig into the water and across the riverbed. Every now and then, they rolled from side to side as the truck drove over larger boulders that were hidden under the water. Maggie held onto the grabrail. Before long, they came up the other side. Frank pulled over so she could take some more photos. With the ochre range in the distance, the river reflecting the deep blue of the sky, and the red road carving a path through the sparse vegetation on either side, it was a gorgeous picture, worthy of hanging in their living room.

"It's so beautiful," she commented.

"And there's plenty more like this to see along the way."

Their first destination was Mitchell Falls, a nine-hour drive from the station, but they'd been told that the last section of the track was challenging and would be very slow going, so they'd decided to camp along the way and continue the following morning.

The terrain grew drier and dustier as they continued along the Gibb River Road. Termite mounds in all shapes and sizes dotted the sparse land. Maggie had read that some mounds reached seven metres high and could weigh ten or more tonnes.

She spotted a group of wild donkeys grazing on some tall grass. "Can we stop a minute, Frank?" she asked.

"Sure." He pulled the rig onto the verge and turned off the engine.

Maggie climbed out and tiptoed towards the donkeys. "Come on, Frank. I want you in the shot," she called softly, not wanting to disturb the animals.

He gave a nod and followed her. "Where do you want me?" he whispered.

"Over there." She pointed to a large termite mound. "Stand beside it and hold your hand out as if you're presenting. The donkeys will be right behind you. It'll make a great cover shot for our photo book."

He chuckled indulgently. "Whatever you wish, my love."

She grabbed his hand as he passed her. "Thank you."

Lifting her hand to his lips, he kissed it gently. "Anything for you, Maggie."

She exhaled a long sigh of contentment. This trip was already the best thing that had happened to them, and it was only day one.

He took his place right where she'd instructed. Five donkeys stood together behind him, their coats varying in colour from pale tan to a dark grey that looked almost black. Maggie laughed as they raised their heads to look in their direction as if posing for the camera. She took several shots.

"Shouldn't you be in the photos as well?" Frank questioned.

"Yes, but someone has to take them."

"What about the tripod? I'm sure we packed it."

Maggie glanced at the camper. "Yes, but I don't know where it is. I should have left it out."

"We should get it. I don't want to be the only one in all the shots."

"Okay. But you'll have to find it. I put it somewhere in the back, and I'm sure that you, Mr. Packing Expert, put it away so neatly I wouldn't have any chance of finding it."

He grinned coyly. "That, I most likely did. There's only so much space in there."

She stepped towards him. "I know, but that's why *you* should go find it while I stay here and see what else there is to photograph."

He chuckled. "You win."

While he searched for the tripod, Maggie walked slowly through the tall grass. It rustled in the wind and tickled her legs. She'd worn stretchy denim shorts that came to just above her knees, and she was wearing her sturdy boots. It was unlikely she'd come across a snake, but it was better to be safe than sorry.

A couple of wallabies raised their heads and twitched their noses while sniffing the air. Janella had told her during one of their lunchtime conversations that over nine different species of wallabies inhabited this area, but which kind these were, Maggie wasn't sure. Still, she focused her camera and took several snaps as they nibbled on the grass.

"Found it!" Frank called.

Within seconds, the wallabies hopped away.

Frank made a face. "Sorry."

"It's okay," Maggie replied. "I got some good shots."

After he set up the tripod, she placed the camera on top and set the timer. "To the mound," she said. They hurried to get in place before the timer went off. Frank wrapped his arm around her shoulders as she nestled under his arm and hugged him tightly. She grinned as the camera timer chirped rapidly followed by the sound of several images being taken. It was a lovely beginning to their trip.

∾

THEY TRAVELLED ON, but with Maggie wanting to stop every few minutes to take photographs, the day quickly slipped by and before they knew it, the sun was dropping towards the horizon. Frank suggested they find a place to set up camp for the night before darkness settled over the land. Maggie agreed. It was much easier to get things organised while they still had daylight to see by, especially on their first night.

They found a spot beside a dry creek bed, a short distance off the road. Although it was listed in their guidebook as a camping spot, no one else was there. However, the fireplace looked like it had been used recently.

Frank carefully parked the truck beside the dry creek, ensuring it was level. While he erected the awning on the side of the camper, she took several photos of the amazing sunset. Frank had assured her that erecting the awning was a one-man job and that he was okay doing it on his own.

Several boab trees stood in the distance, sentinels of the arid land. Their sparse boughs rose into the air like arms to the heavens. Behind them, the sky was deep crimson and orange as the sun slipped slowly below the horizon. It was spectacular.

"Are you seeing this, Frank?" she asked, her gaze focused on the horizon.

"You should see it from where I'm standing," he called out.

Turning around, she burst into laughter. He was staring at her. She immediately understood his meaning.

"It looks good from this angle too," she said, grinning.

She continued to take photos until the vibrant colours faded and darkness chased away the last remnants of light. Frank had gathered a bundle of loose timber from the surrounding area and was lighting a fire by the time she returned to the camper.

She put her gear away and started dinner. They'd packed everything they needed to make their favourite meals, but Maggie had also packed some pre-prepared ones for when they wanted something quick and tasty. Like tonight. She pulled the chicken and pasta salad she'd made the day before out of the small fridge, grabbed some crusty bread, and placed both on the folding table Frank had set up outside the camper.

"I'll grab the plates," he said.

"Great. Thank you."

Returning moments later, plates in hand, he sat opposite her at the small table and smiled. "Thanks, my love. It looks delicious. Shall we say grace?" He held out his hand, which she took.

"Heavenly Father," he began, "we pause to give You thanks for Your many blessings. For this beautiful place, this wonderful country, for giving us each other, and for the chance to take this special trip, and for this food. In Jesus' precious name. Amen."

He squeezed her hand and then let go. The night was slightly chilly, but the fire made it cosy and warm.

Maggie gazed around as she nibbled on some bread. "It's wonderful out here."

Frank nodded. "It sure is. There's nothing better than camping out like this, away from the crowds."

"Do you ever wonder what it looked like as God was creating the world?" Maggie asked, the darkness around her reminding her of the story of creation.

"I've never thought of it, to be honest, but I suppose it might have looked something like this."

She looked up at the sky. Stars twinkled overhead; an errant cloud floated by. "If I could, I'd love to see what God sees. I'd want to know what He thought and saw as He was making everything. What He thinks of it now."

Frank chuckled. "This is a very deep conversation for a first day. But I like where you're going."

"I'm glad," Maggie said, smiling.

"There's so much we don't understand, and I don't think we can in this life," he said. "The limitless wonder of God is simply too great for us to comprehend. But, I believe, He gives us glimpses and shares His heart with us when we give Him the room to do so. We're so often consumed with living that we forget He's there." He looked at her. "Who knows? Maybe He wants to share something with you about His creation, and that's why it's on your mind now."

She considered the statement. "Perhaps," she finally replied. "If He is, I'm ready to listen."

"So am I," Frank said. "This trip is going to change a lot of things for us. I can feel it."

She smiled broadly. She hadn't told him the feelings she'd had the past couple of days, the expectancy. Something was awaiting them on this trip. She didn't know what it might be, but whatever it was, it would change everything. She trusted God to see them through whatever lay ahead.

They enjoyed the rest of their meal in silence, taking in the peace and solitude. Once the meal was over, they cuddled together in front of the fire.

"Can we sleep out here tonight?" Maggie asked, snuggling closer.

Frank brushed her hair gently with his hand. "We could. I did throw our swags in."

"Great. I want to sleep under the stars tonight. I want the sky to be the last thing I see before I fall asleep, and the first thing I see when I wake up."

He chuckled. "Then it's settled. Tonight, we sleep under the stars. But first, let me kiss you." He lowered his face and his lips found hers. He kissed her gently while the fire crackled beside them and the stars twinkled overhead.

CHAPTER 8

*D*arwin wasn't quite as bad as Janella had expected. It wasn't as daunting as she thought it might be, though there was plenty about it that was. The bus system, for one. Although she'd driven her Jeep the whole distance from Goddard Downs, she wasn't prepared to drive in the city.

"Come on, Janella, or we'll miss the bus," Jonah called as he raced ahead of her. The boy's long strides took two of her shorter steps to keep up with, and when he was in a rush or excited, there was no slowing him.

"We'll make it just fine," she replied, walking at her usual pace. "You said we'd miss it last night, and we didn't. We won't miss it today, either."

"But today isn't yesterday. We could've just lucked out," he protested, walking back to her side as if his presence would spur her along. He was mistaken.

"Jonah, I'm not making myself hot, sweaty, and miserable,

or worse, falling over, just to please you. I'm sorry, but no. I'll keep my own pace, and I promise you, we won't miss the bus."

He groaned but stayed beside her. She smiled as she glanced at him. He was a good boy, much like Caleb, and she wanted to see him succeed. He hadn't had the same opportunities as Caleb, who'd had a loving and supportive family around him, but that meant Jonah's success was all the more special because he'd overcome those circumstances and was determined to make a life for himself.

"I can't wait to get to the school. It's going to be great," he said for the tenth time that morning. He was so overjoyed with being accepted that it never occurred to him he might not like the place once they got there. Janella doubted she'd like it. She so easily got lost in buildings and corridors. If she arrived at an entrance other than the one she was used to when she visited Caleb, she often took the wrong path and had to ask for directions to find reception. Today, however, they weren't visiting Caleb. They were going to the Webber School of Arts and Sciences to inspect the campus and take a tour.

They reached the bus stop in plenty of time, as she'd predicted. While they waited for the bus, she listened as Jonah continued to talk about the school and his excitement at going.

The bus arrived and they took a seat near the front. She preferred being near the door, especially if there was a chance that the bus could become crowded. She hated the feeling of being bunched up with other people, especially ones she didn't know.

"Keep still, Jonah," she whispered. He was leaning forward, hands clasping the rail in front of them as he peered past her out the window. He was almost like a kid in a lolly shop for the first time.

"I'm just trying to see. It's so different to Kununurra."

She looked out the window and had to agree. The streets were lined with fancy hotels and expensive looking shops, nothing like those in Kununurra. The people even dressed differently. Smarter, more fashionable. Some women even wore high heels.

"Would you like to change seats?" she asked.

His eyes widened. "Could we?"

"Sure."

The remainder of the ride was quiet as Jonah's eyes were glued to the window. They arrived at the campus ten minutes later. She hadn't been sure what to expect, although she pictured in her mind an ugly, concrete building, so when the bus pulled up in front of a large expanse of grass with a duck pond in the middle, she thought they were at the wrong stop.

She leaned forward and asked the driver. "Are you sure this is the Webber School of Arts and Sciences?"

"Yes, ma'am. This is it."

As they disembarked, she thanked the driver for the safe ride. The man smiled and raised a hand as the doors closed.

Standing on the grass, surveying the campus buildings in the distance, her stomach fluttered as if a whole family of butterflies had been set loose. If Jonah hadn't been with her, she would have jumped straight back onto the bus.

He seemed nervous, too. He stood there, jiggling his arms and legs. What they were embarking on was truly starting to sink in. Had she made a mistake thinking either one of them could fit in? Maybe they should just go home and forget all about the school.

She glanced at him and slipped her arm around his shoulders. No, for his sake, she had to be the adult. "Come on, Jonah. Let's do this."

They walked down a path towards the collection of one-story buildings. The signage was clear and they found the Vocational office easily.

"Welcome to Webber," an attractive redhead greeted from behind a low counter. "How can I help?"

Janella stepped closer. "I'm Janella Goddard, and this is Jonah Barambah. We were both accepted into the culinary programme."

The woman pulled a large book from under the counter and flipped it open. She moved a long, painted fingernail down the page before looking up with a smile. "Yes, Mrs. Goddard. We're expecting you. Please, have a seat over there. Someone will be with you shortly."

Janella and Jonah sat together on two of the plastic seats lining the wall. A group of people were already seated. Some appeared to be of mature age, while others were obviously younger. Much younger. She assumed they were all there for the tour.

"I feel nervous," Jonah whispered.

She patted his arm gently. "You'll be fine." If only she could convince herself of the same thing.

Their guide joined them a few minutes later, and as she suspected, the others seated nearby were also part of their group. By the time they started down the path, there were fifteen in total taking the tour. Jonah stayed close to her at first but quickly ended up with a group of boys and girls who appeared to be of similar age.

"You look as nervous as I feel," a short blonde woman said. She was slender with a bright smile and youthful voice, but the strands of grey in her hair suggested she wasn't as young as she initially appeared.

"Is it that obvious?" Janella replied with a tentative smile.

"No, I just recognise it," the woman said, extending her hand. "I'm Kathy. Kathy Tate."

"Janella Goddard."

"Nice to meet you. Are you here for the Commercial Cookery course or something else?"

"The Commercial Cookery course," Janella replied.

"Me too! Looks like we'll be classmates."

"Wonderful. I thought I'd be the only one my age here," Janella divulged.

"I thought the same," Kathy replied. "I'm glad I was wrong. Bill..." she called to a tall, slender man with glasses. He was balding, and what remained of his hair was more salt than pepper. "Bill...this is Janella. She's taking the Commercial Cookery course as well."

He turned and smiled. "Great. The more, the merrier," he said cheerfully, extending his hand. "I'm William Winter, but you can call me Bill."

"Nice to meet you, Bill. I'm Janella Goddard."

"Where are you from?" he asked.

"I live in the Kimberley on a cattle station," she replied.

"A cattle station? That's a rough life. When I was a boy, I wanted to run away and become a cowboy," he said, laughing. "My mother quickly got that out of my head."

"Where are you from?" Janella asked.

"Originally from Sydney, but my family and I moved to Darwin five years ago. My wife, Alice, has family here."

"Do you have children?" Janella asked, shifting her gaze between the two.

"Four," he answered.

"One for me," Kathy said.

Janella smiled. "I have two. A son and a daughter."

"Lovely," Kathy said, smiling. "It looks like we have even more in common. I'm happy I decided to come. I was so nervous that I was thinking about refusing the offer."

Bill's eyes widened. "You did? I felt the same, but my son told me I should go for it. I've always been the cook in the family, and I wanted to try it professionally, but I was never brave enough. Now that most of the children are out of the house, I figured I could give it a shot."

Kathy and Bill's confessions gave Janella hope. She wasn't the only one who'd considered quitting before they'd even begun. What a coincidence that they should be there together on that day. It was uncanny. *'For I know the plans I have for you,'* declares the Lord, *'plans to prosper you and not to harm you, plans to give you hope and a future.'*

She slowed as the words settled on her mind and her heart. *Was this truly God's plan for her?*

Kathy stopped and turned around. "Janella, are you alright?"

Janella drew a deep breath and smiled. "Yes, everything's just fine."

∼

LATER THAT EVENING, as she and Jonah relaxed in their hotel room with takeout and movies, that verse stayed with Janella. *Was culinary school truly the Lord's will for her?* And if it was, what was His purpose for her going? *What might follow once she finished?*

"What did you think of the school, Janella?" Jonah asked as he took another slice of pizza from the box and took a large bite. For someone so slender, he ate a great deal.

"I think it was wonderful," she admitted. "I didn't expect the people to be so friendly or the campus to be so peaceful or beautiful."

"What were you expecting?"

"I don't know," she answered. She hadn't given it much thought; she simply felt that it wouldn't be for her. She'd never imagined that she'd like it.

"Have you decided? I have. I'm definitely going. The place is neat, and I made some friends already."

"So did I," Janella said, smiling.

"Does that mean you're going to accept the offer and we'll be studying together?" The hopefulness in his voice was unmistakable. He wanted her there, wanted her support, and she wanted to give it. There were plenty of reasons to accept. The campus wasn't as overwhelming as she thought it would be. She'd be closer to Caleb, and the course was only two years. Caleb would still be at school by the time she finished. But then, he'd be going to university. The thought was jarring. Her son at university. She couldn't think that far ahead. And by that time, it would be Sasha's turn to attend boarding school like her brother, father, and grandfather before her. And finally, Frank and Maggie were encouraging her to do it. Everything was pointing to her accepting the offer.

But if she did, she'd have to find somewhere to stay. Having lived at Goddard Downs most of her life, she'd never had to look for accommodation. Where did one start? She had no idea.

'For I know the plans I have for you,' declares the Lord, *'plans to prosper you and not to harm you, plans to give you hope and a future.'*

Really, Lord? If You want me to do this, You'll have to lead the way.

She let out a big sigh. "If I accept, we'd be able to share accommodation. I'm sure your father would feel better about that, plus it would cost him less."

Jonah grinned. "So that means you're going to do it? You're going to accept?"

She wanted to tell him yes, but she couldn't. She still wasn't sure. "I was just thinking out loud," she replied. "Weighing the options."

"I'm part of your decision?"

"Of course you are, Jonah. You're like one of my children. How could I not consider you in all of this?"

He smiled and leaned closer, resting his head on her shoulder. "Thanks, Janella."

She smiled and patted the side of his head. "You're welcome. I promise you that no matter what, I'll be there for you. I won't let you down, even if you're here and I'm back at Goddard Downs. I know you'll make it here. You're going to be so successful."

He lifted his head and looked at her. He was still so young

in so many ways, though he was beginning to look a lot like the man he would become. "So will you, Janella. I know it." He took an audible breath. "I...I love you, Janella. You're...you're like a mum to me."

Tears pricked her eyes. Jonah didn't know it, but God had used him to pull her out of the miry pit after Julian's death. Helping him had helped her heal and prepare to move forward. Now, she stood on the cusp of another life altering event. She leaned forward and kissed his forehead. "I love you too, Jonah. Like a son."

CHAPTER 9

*T*he next day, which was a Saturday, Janella and Jonah were on the bus again, but this time, they were on their way to see Caleb. With her future weighing heavily on her mind, she'd tossed and turned all night and had barely slept. If only she knew the right path to take. It was time to discuss it with her children, starting with Caleb. She'd told him she'd come to Darwin to check out the culinary school with Jonah but hadn't told him she was considering going herself.

The entire bus ride she was silent as she prayed for clarity and direction. Jonah seemed happy looking out the window.

The bus dropped them off at the entrance she was familiar with, and within a few minutes, they came to the main reception area.

"I can't believe your son goes to school here," Jonah said, his eyes large with wonder. The buildings and grounds were huge and impressive, with staircases and manicured gardens, sports ovals, and grandstands. So different to the pre-fabricated classrooms and dirt playgrounds in Kununurra.

"Believe me, you aren't the only one," Janella replied. She recalled the awe she'd felt during her first visit to the school. It was as far removed from their life on Goddard Downs as she could imagine, and she feared Caleb would be seduced by its grandeur and never want to come home, despite him being adamant he would return to Goddard Downs one day and take over the running of the station. She smiled at that thought. Julian would have been so proud to hear him talk like that.

The same man who'd been on duty when she last visited sat behind the reception desk. He looked up as she and Jonah approached. "Good morning. How can I help you?" His smile was practiced but warm, but then a glint of recognition flashed across his face. "Caleb's mother, right?" he asked as his smile grew brighter.

Janella was taken aback. "Ah, yes. That's right."

"I remember you from your last visit," he said. "I guess you're here to see your son?"

"Yes. He knows I'm coming."

"I'll call him down. Just a moment, please."

She nodded and took a step back as he picked up the phone and called someone, she presumed the dorm master. Moments passed as he nodded and mm-hmmed. He ended the call and looked up at Janella. "Caleb will be down shortly."

"Thank you," she replied.

"You're welcome to take a seat." He waved to the row of chairs behind her.

"Great. Thank you." She gave a nod and began ushering Jonah to the chairs, when the man cleared his throat. "I'm sorry," he said, "I didn't get your name the last time you were here."

Janella paused. Surely he had access to Caleb's records. *And why did he want to know her name, anyway?* But he'd asked, and it would be rude not to respond. She turned around and said, "Janella. Janella Goddard."

"I'm Wade Johnson. Caleb tells me you live on a cattle station."

"Yes," Janella replied tentatively. *What was Caleb doing, divulging personal information to a stranger?*

"His face lights up when he talks about it," Wade said.

"Really?"

"Yes. I can tell that's where his heart is."

She nodded. "It's the only home he's known."

"He also told me that his father passed recently. I'm so sorry." Wade spoke with compassion and empathy, and all of a sudden, a lump formed in her throat.

She swallowed hard. "Thank you."

"It must be hard for you." He looked at her with such understanding that she wondered if he, too, had lost someone recently.

"It hasn't been easy," she admitted, "but we're getting along." Something about him put her at ease, and she was even tempted to tell him her reason for visiting Darwin, other than to see Caleb, but footsteps rushing down the stairs drew her attention. Seconds later, her son stood before her.

"Caleb!"

"Mum," he said, wrapping his arms tightly around her.

"Let me look at you," she said, turning him around in a circle. He'd grown taller since the last time she'd seen him, but he also looked thinner. "What are they feeding you?"

He laughed. "No one cooks like you do, Mum, but the food here's not bad."

"Hmmm, I think I'll treat you to a big lunch. Try to fill up those long legs." She ruffled his hair and placed a hand on his shoulder, smiled at Wade, and then ushered him towards the door.

"See you, Mr. Johnson!" Caleb called back, waving.

"Have a good day, Caleb. I'll be off duty by the time you get back."

Caleb nodded. "Have a good one. See you tomorrow."

"Good afternoon, Mrs. Goddard. Hope to see you again soon." Lifting a hand in a wave, Wade gave a smile that not only revealed his white teeth but made her heart jolt. Her mouth went dry as their gazes briefly connected, and he gave a nod.

"Ah...yes. You, too." She quickly turned away and made a beeline for the door. What had just happened? *Was he flirting with her?*

WHEN JANELLA INTRODUCED Caleb and Jonah after exiting the reception building, they immediately hit it off and agreed they wanted pizza for lunch. Caleb said he knew a great pizza joint down at the jetty. Janella groaned. *Pizza again?* But she sighed and gave in.

They strolled the short distance to the waterfront and found the place Caleb had mentioned. The smell of Italian herbs, garlic bread and pepperoni wafted from the restaurant and made her mouth water. Perhaps she could grow used to eating pizzas more than once a year.

They placed their order and sat outside at a table with a large umbrella. The harbour looked glorious, and since it was a Saturday, boats of all shapes and sizes were coming and going. She could sit there and people and boat watch all day, but that wasn't what she was there for.

During the meal, she tried to bring up the subject of school, but she couldn't. They were having such a wonderful time, and she didn't want to ruin it with her doubts and misgivings. After the pizzas had been devoured, they strolled further along the jetty and came across an ice cream parlour. The boys pleaded with her to get one.

"Okay, but I don't know that I can fit one in."

"Come on, Mum. How often do you buy an ice cream for yourself?" Caleb asked.

She shrugged. The answer was never.

"These ice creams are the best. You won't regret it."

She let out a sigh and chuckled. "Oh, okay. What flavour do you suggest?"

They stepped closer to the display cabinet. "My favourite's cookie dough, but you might prefer salted caramel."

"Salted caramel?"

"Yeah. I think you'd like it."

She wasn't so sure. It seemed a strange combination. She'd heard of it but had never tried it, although she did like caramel. And she liked salt. She'd just never put the two together.

"Okay. You've convinced me. I'll have salted caramel. Now, Jonah, what would you like?"

His eyes were like saucers and her heart melted. He was having so many new experiences, and she was simply glad that she was there to witness them. "I'm not sure," he finally said. "There are so many to choose from."

"Have the cookie dough with me," Caleb said.

"Okay." Jonah smiled and looked relieved.

Janella placed the order with the young girl behind the counter, and soon they each had an ice cream in their hands. The scoops were much larger than she'd expected, but the moment she took her first lick of the salted caramel she knew she'd finish it. It was the most scrumptious thing she'd ever tasted.

"Like it?" Caleb asked.

She nodded as she caught a random dribble with her tongue. "It's delicious."

"I thought you would think so."

They continued walking, but finally, she couldn't take it any longer. She had to talk to Caleb about the offer. "Let's go sit in the park for a while," she said when they came to the end of the jetty walk.

They headed up a set of stairs and entered the park nearby. It overlooked the harbour and perhaps offered the best view she'd seen so far. She found a park bench and suggested they sit for a while. Jonah said he needed to go to the toilet. Janella wondered if he was just making an excuse to give her time with Caleb.

After he left, she turned to Caleb and simply looked at him for a few moments. Why was it so difficult to speak with him about her going to culinary school? She had no doubt he'd tell her to do it, but that's what worried her. As soon as she told him she'd been accepted, there'd be almost no way out. Not that she really wanted one, but it was the first major decision she was making on her own. *What if she made a mistake?*

'For I know the plans I have for you,' declares the Lord, *'plans to prosper you and not to harm you, plans to give you hope and a future.'*

She swallowed hard and said, "Caleb, I need to talk to you about something."

As she'd expected, he was ecstatic when she told him. "Mum! You have to take it. It'll be so cool having you and Sasha live in Darwin."

"It isn't that simple," she said, her gaze dropping to her hands.

"Why isn't it?"

How could she explain? *I'm afraid. I don't think I can do it. I'm not good enough.* She drew a deep breath. "It's complicated."

"I don't think it is, Mum. My entire life, you've done nothing but take care of other people. Dad. Sasha. Me. Everyone at home. Not once did I see you do anything for yourself."

"What's wrong with that?" she replied.

"Nothing. But maybe it's time you do." He paused, and then added, "Dad would have wanted you to do it."

Janella nodded slowly. "Yes, he would have."

"Plus, Mum, I want you here." Tears pooled in his eyes.

"Caleb."

"I miss you." He sniffed and glanced away. "My friends are great, and so's school, but it's not the same as having family

83

around." He took her hands. "But it's more than that. I really think you'll do well. You're an amazing cook, and I think this is what God wants you to do."

Tears of her own stung her eyes. Was this the confirmation she'd sought?

"Dad thought you could do more. I think you can, too. You can do anything you put your mind to, Mum. God will give you strength, just like He did me when I first came here."

She nodded. God *was* her strength, and if this truly was the path He was leading her on, He would help her through it. She had to stop listening to the lies that told her she couldn't do it. The little voice that said she wasn't good enough, that she wasn't cut out for life in the big city. She *could* do it. In God's strength, she could.

"You told me I had to come here when I wanted to stay home," Caleb continued. "You said that Dad believed in me. Well, he believed in you, too. Doesn't that mean something?"

"You truly think I can do it?" she asked softly.

Caleb nodded. "You're my mum. You can do anything."

Janella laughed and pulled him into a tight embrace. She needed to hear those words. It was the confirmation she needed. She squeezed him tighter and ruffled his hair. "Come on, we'd better go find Jonah."

"So, does that mean you're going?" Caleb asked.

She took a deep breath and nodded. "Yes, I'll do it."

He broke into a huge smile and threw his arms around her neck. "I love you, Mum."

"And I love you right back, Caleb."

When they separated, Jonah was standing there, looking at them quizzically.

"Come on, Jonah, you may as well join in." She waved him over. "I've decided. I'm accepting the offer."

His face lit up. "Really?"

She nodded. "Really."

THEY WALKED BACK to the school a short while later. Wade wasn't there, but another man, lanky and stern looking, waited for Caleb at the desk. She promised to see him again before she returned home.

After leaving Caleb, she and Jonah did a bit of sight-seeing, and when they returned to their hotel after dinner, he grabbed the remote to watch movies while she stepped out onto the balcony where it was quiet. She took her phone out and searched for Maggie's name amongst her contacts and composed a message.

Dear Maggie, having a great time here. The campus is much nicer than I imagined. I talked it over with Caleb and made up my mind. I'm going to accept the placement at Webber. I'm going to school! Love Nella

She hit send and watched until the small tick appeared in the corner. She'd done it. There was no going back. Once Maggie knew, Frank would know also, and they'd never allow her to back out. She was going to attend culinary school. She was going to chase a dream she never knew she had.

Before I formed you in the womb, I knew you. Before you were born, I set you apart.

She leaned against the rail and looked out across the city. The lights looked like stars bound to the earth, prevented from flying. She'd been that way her entire life, holding herself back because she didn't think she could fly. But the Lord said that He gave strength to the weak and that those who waited on Him would renew their strength. They'd run and not grow weary. They'd walk and not faint. If other people could soar like eagles, then why couldn't she? It was time she tried.

CHAPTER 10

*B*ack on the road, the early morning sun cast its brilliance across the landscape. It was glorious. In fact, everything around Maggie was. It was as if the day was waking up, full of expectancy and wonder.

"I'm glad you suggested we head out early. It's so gorgeous," she said, turning to face Frank.

"And we should reach Mitchell Falls by mid-morning," he replied, smiling as he held his grip tight on the wheel as they bounced over the corrugations in the road.

"Sounds good. I can't wait to see them."

"You do know it's a three-hour walk once we get there, and three hours back?" He cocked a brow.

"So you've told me several times." She chuckled as she studied his profile. He was grinning and it made her glad. Already he seemed so much more relaxed than he'd been in the days leading up to their departure.

"Have I?" he asked.

"Yes, you have. And I'm not worried. Are you?"

"Nope. I'm fit and raring to go."

Four hours later, after manoeuvring over and around numerous culverts in the track, and bouncing around as if they were on a ride at a fairground, they reached the final turnoff to the Mitchell Falls camping grounds. Maggie hoped the eggs she'd packed had survived.

The campground catered mainly for tent campers and off-road camper trailers. The road wasn't suitable for caravans, and now Maggie knew why. The truck had handled the road well, however, just as Frank said it would. She was glad their camper was on the back of the truck and they weren't towing. It made everything so much easier.

The sites were clearly designated, so after self-registering at the box, they chose one that was in part-shade, part-sun. They needed sun for their solar panels, but part-shade was also good, since it was already past thirty degrees and climbing.

Hopping out of the cab, Maggie took in her surroundings, shading her eyes with her hand. She liked it immediately. The campground was spread out, so even though other campers were there, it didn't seem crowded. She'd not been to Mitchell Falls before, although it had been on her bucket list of places to visit for many years. Cliff had suggested they take a cruise along the coast from Darwin and fly in on a helicopter. She'd thought that was a lazy way of seeing the falls and said she'd rather camp and hike. Consequently, they never went. But now, she was so glad that she and Frank were getting to do it together.

While he quickly set up the solar panels and checked that

everything was working correctly to charge their batteries, she made coffee and sandwiches to take on the hike.

She checked her laces and grabbed her backpack from the front seat of the truck. "Are you ready?" she asked as he did a final adjustment to the panels. He'd brought an extra-long cable so they could be further from the truck and catch as much sun as possible during the day.

"I think so. I'll grab my pack and I'll be good to go," he replied. Moments later, he stood beside her with his pack slung over his shoulders and buckled across his chest. It was pre-packed with everything they'd need for the hike other than food, which she was carrying. First-aid kit, spare clothes, and water. He slipped his arm around her shoulders and kissed her cheek. "Let's go, my love. I can't wait to see these falls."

They walked to the trail entrance and started along the dusty track that ran between sparse, low-lying vegetation. The path veered left, and they soon came across a rocky outcrop. The rocks had been worn smooth by persistent rains, and lush green vegetation had found a gap to spring up between them. There were places where walking was easy, and others where they had to hop from rock to rock. They stopped several times to take photos along the way, the untamed scenery the perfect backdrop. Despite the wildness of the land, markers along the way ensured they stayed on the trail. They stopped at Little Mertens for more photos. Little Mertens was a small curtain of water that cascaded over sandstone into a pool below. It was an hour from the campground, but it took them half an hour longer with the number of photo stops. They lingered near the top looking down into the dark water.

"These lands are spiritually significant to the Wunambal

people," Frank commented, gazing into the pools. "Don't go near the edge, Maggie."

Hearing the alarm in his voice, she edged back a little but continued to take shots. "That's their rock art?" she asked, focusing her camera on the drawings etched onto the rock face.

"Yes," he answered. "The Wunambal are Janella's people."

She stopped shooting. "Really? I didn't know that."

He nodded. "Ancestrally, at least. Her family stopped practicing their beliefs a generation or more ago, but she was raised to understand the significance of the land, as well as the love of God."

"Sounds like the perfect mix," Maggie replied, lowering her camera to her side. "Sometimes I think all of our modern ways have pushed us further and further from the life God intended."

"I think that way too, sometimes," Frank said. He uncapped his flask and took a sip of water. "We should press on if we want to get to the falls and back before dark."

She nodded her agreement and they set off again.

Three and a half hours later they arrived at the falls. Although the walk had been tiring, the sheer beauty of the falls and the cascading pools made her forget her aching muscles and sore feet. "This is amazing, Frank. I'm so glad we came."

When he didn't respond, she turned around. He was sitting on a rock with a bottle of water to his head. He looked a little pale and was breathing hard. She hurried to him and squatted down. "Are you okay, Frank?"

He nodded. "Just a little peachy."

She frowned as she cast her gaze over him and placed a hand on his forehead. He felt cool to touch, so it wasn't a fever.

"Maggie, I'm fine," he assured. "It was a bit more of a hike than I expected. It's been a long time since I walked that far."

She chuckled. "We should have started our exercise regime sooner."

"Seems that way. But you made it look like a walk in the park." Grinning, he took her hand and kissed it.

"I'm not so sure about that. I think I'll pay for it tonight."

"Come sit by me," he said, patting the rock next to him.

She removed her pack and lowered herself carefully onto the rock. It was such a gorgeous day. The sky was an azure blue with not a cloud in sight. Children were laughing and splashing in the clear water while their parents looked on. It was idyllic.

When Frank slipped his arm around her shoulders, she leaned against him, relishing the warmth of his embrace. "Let's stay for a while," she said. "It's so peaceful and beautiful."

"I'd like that," he said, rubbing her arm gently.

She couldn't think of a more magical place. As she gazed across the falls, Psalm 145 came to mind.

I will exalt You, my God the King;
I will praise Your name for ever and ever.
Every day I will praise you
and extol Your name for ever and ever.
Great is the Lord and most worthy of praise;
His greatness no one can fathom.

Yes, Lord. Thank You for this amazing place. Its beauty speaks of You, its Creator. No one is like You, oh Lord. My heart swells with praise and gratitude as I think of Your immense greatness, and I humble myself before You.

As Maggie rested against Frank's shoulder, the sounds of nature permeated her heart and soul while the sun warmed her body. When a rock wallaby appeared on an outcropping, she grabbed her camera, quickly focusing the lens before she took a shot.

Finally, it was time to start the trek back to the campsite. They didn't want to risk being out after dark. Frank took his time, and Maggie slowed her pace to match his. It surprised her that the hike was taking so much out of him but decided not to mention it. He was already feeling threatened by David's arrival at Goddard Downs and she didn't want to make him feel any worse, but the fact remained. They were both getting older, and at some stage Frank might need to modify his role on the station and hand some of the more physical jobs over to the younger ones. But would he? She somehow doubted it. He'd try to keep up with them for as long as he could, even if it killed him. That thought jolted her. *What if his breathlessness was something more than simply being a little out of condition?* She shook her head. No. There was nothing wrong with Frank. They just needed to slow down a little. Take it a bit easier.

They reached the campsite just after sunset. There was still enough light to see where they were going, but only just. Smoke from campfires filled the air while cockatoos squawked in the trees as they settled in for the night.

Holding hands, Frank and Maggie headed for their camper.

Another rig, similar to theirs, was parked in the next bay. The occupants were sitting in foldout chairs around a small fire. Maggie nodded and smiled as they passed by.

"Oh no," Frank muttered.

"What's wrong?" She looked at him, her brow crinkling.

He shrugged off his pack and set it on the ground. "I didn't pick up any firewood before we left. I'll go find some now."

She rubbed his arm. "Don't worry about it, Frank. It's fine. We can sit inside tonight." After a six-hour hike, the last thing she wanted him to do was forage for firewood in the dark.

Facing her, he smiled, his eyes twinkling. "I was looking forward to another night under the stars."

She grinned. "That would be nice, but I'm sure we'll have plenty of other nights to stargaze."

"Okay. So long as you're sure."

"I am," she said. "Now, perhaps you should go for a shower while I get dinner."

"Are you saying I smell?"

She chuckled. "Just a little."

"Well, I never..." Laughing, he shook his head.

"Excuse me," a female voice called out.

Maggie and Frank both turned. The couple they'd passed were walking towards them.

"Hello," Maggie said, smiling.

"Hi," the woman replied. She was plump, with silver hair and cheeks so rosy they stood out in the semi-dark.

"Hello," Frank said. "How can we help?"

"We wanted to help you," the woman said.

"Oh?" Frank replied.

"We heard you say that you don't have any firewood," the man said, his voice soft, but raspy. "We've got more than enough, so we brought you some." He held out an armful of thick branches and twigs.

"Thank you," Frank said. "That's very kind of you."

"It's no problem at all," the woman replied. "I'm Mable Henry, and this is my husband, Ned."

"I'm Frank, and this is my wife, Maggie." Each couple shook hands.

"Nice to meet you both," Mable replied. "We always make sure we have more than enough wood so we can share if someone's in need."

The cheerfulness in her voice made Maggie smile. "That's very thoughtful. Thanks again."

"You're welcome. And you're welcome to join us for dinner if you'd like," Mable continued. "We're having chicken soup, nothing fancy, but there's more than enough to go around. It'll save you having to cook."

Maggie turned to Frank and spoke in a quiet voice. "What do you think, Frank? Should we accept?"

"Sure. Why not?" he replied.

Maggie nodded and told Mable they'd love to join them. "Chicken soup sounds wonderful. We can bring some crusty bread."

"That would be lovely, dear. Ned's partial to crusty bread," Mable answered. "Come over when you're ready."

"Great. Thank you. We won't be long."

A short while later, after they'd both showered, they walked the short distance to Mable and Ned's.

Sitting at the table enjoying a bowl of warm, tasty soup and crusty bread, Maggie learned that the pair were doing the big loop and planned to travel around the country over the period of a year. They didn't have a tight schedule. In fact, they simply went wherever they wanted, whenever they wanted.

Maggie marvelled at their plan. "That's wonderful," she commented. "I can't imagine travelling for a whole year, not knowing where you'll be from one day to the next, but it sounds exciting."

"It is," Mable replied. "We're Christians, and although *we* don't know where we're going, God does." She chuckled.

"You're Christians? So are we!"

"Really? We had a feeling you might be. This trip isn't only a vacation for us. When we decided to do it, we asked God to use us in whatever way He saw fit. Whether that's supplying firewood and a meal, changing a flat tyre, or perhaps even sharing the gospel."

"That's amazing," Maggie said. "I'm so impressed. And inspired." She couldn't contain the excitement welling inside her. "Would you tell us your story?" she asked.

"Certainly," Ned replied, leaning closer to his wife of fifty years. He wrapped an arm around her, and Maggie could see that even after so many years of marriage, the love between the couple was still strong. Maggie shuffled her chair closer to Frank, resting her head on his shoulder as Ned told their story.

"We were living in Adelaide and attending church there. We'd both been feeling that something was coming into our lives, but we didn't have any idea what. Then Mable had a dream about us travelling. I thought it was crazy. But then, I had the same dream a few weeks later."

"That's when we decided to pray on it," Mable interjected, a big grin on her face.

Ned continued. "Yes, we prayed on it, and months later, we got an answer when one of our daughters surprised us with a gift of money and told us to use it for a vacation. She wasn't sure what prompted her to do that other than a prompting from the Lord." He squeezed Mable's hand. "We then knew it was what the Lord wanted and that it was time to move. We bought this rig and left home three months ago. Since then, we've been going wherever the Lord leads us, using our time to minister to those we meet."

Maggie looked up at Frank. His eyes were bright and fixed on Ned as he spoke, and there was a grin on his face. "You spend your days travelling and ministering to people?" he asked.

"Yes," Ned answered, nodding.

"We always wanted to be missionaries but going overseas never seemed to fit into our plan," Mable explained. "Now, we're doing it, but differently. We're ministering to those who need to hear the Word, or we give a helping hand, right here at home."

Ned squeezed her hand. "You'd be surprised by how many people here in our own country don't know, or don't want to know, about the Lord. We take the opportunity whenever we can to share the gospel."

"That's a noble task you've undertaken," Maggie commented. "I'm sure God's blessing you abundantly."

"Yes, we feel very blessed. But that's not why we do it."

"I'm sure." And Maggie was. This couple exuded genuine joy in their mission to share the gospel with strangers, to offer a helping hand where needed, and to minister whenever a need arose.

She squeezed Frank's arm gently. Perhaps the Lord had something similar in mind for them.

That night, as they settled down to sleep inside their camper, Maggie couldn't help but think about what God might have in store for them.

CHAPTER 11

*T*he ruler was at work again. The itch wasn't unbearable, but it was aggravating, and Sean couldn't wait for it to be over. Why healing had to involve such a ridiculous process he would never understand, but he was happy to have the itches since it meant his time in a cast was coming to an end. It couldn't come soon enough.

He growled as he tried to reach the exact spot. The family was seated around the dining table, same as they had for every meeting he'd ever been a part of. However, as frequent a participant in these meetings as he was, he'd never been to one where Frank wasn't there. It felt strange to see Olivia in his seat.

"Would you stop that?" she said sharply, looking at him with annoyance.

"Sorry. It's itching. I can't help it."

"It's distracting," she replied, pursing her lips.

"That's an understatement," he retorted, ruler still going.

She groaned and rolled her eyes while shuffling the papers on the table before her. "Can we start?"

"Sure," Nate said. It was obvious he was trying to appease his wife. She could be temperamental at times, at least in Sean's opinion. Highly strung. Everything had to be perfect. He couldn't imagine living like that. It seemed so time consuming, so stressful. He couldn't tell her that of course. She thought she was on top of everything, so saying that she was anything but would only offend her, and that was the last thing he wanted to do. Instead, once his itch was satisfied, he set the ruler aside.

"Okay, we have some things to go over if this project is to proceed," she began.

"If?" David asked. His question reflected Sean's feelings, but he wasn't bold enough to utter them.

"Yes, 'if,'" she repeated. "The bank's requesting certain adjustments before they'll approve the loan."

"What kind of adjustments?" Joshua asked, leaning forward. He glanced at Stella, who was also frowning.

"They can see the benefit of the bridge, but they're not sure they can justify the loan without further confirmation that we can service it, especially since we also carry the loan for Indigo. They also want to ensure that if they approve it, we'll be prudent with the management of the project since we're effectively overseeing it ourselves. They're going to require full access to the site for inspections, and they'll only agree to payments on a stage-by-stage basis."

"Like if we're building a house?" David inquired.

Olivia lifted her gaze and nodded, her expression passive before she returned her focus to the documents. "Yes, exactly like that. These are the things they're asking for." She passed Sean the document first since he was sitting beside her.

He took it and glanced over the requirements. The bank was doing its due diligence. They required confirmation that the respective parties they were employing were legitimate since they were from outside the area. They were also requesting a schedule for work so that payments could be made by transfer for each stage of the process. They were suggesting five site visits at various stages of the process to ensure the money was being spent as they said it would be. Nothing strange there.

"We'll also need to do a schedule if you all plan to help with the construction because we have to look after our paying guests and do the drives. We're booked right up to the rainy season," Olivia said, releasing a heavy sigh. Her gaze travelled around the table. "I honestly don't know how we can manage to build a bridge while catering to our guests at the same time, especially since we're shorthanded. I'd rather put the bridge on hold until next year when Dad will be back."

Silence filled the room as everyone's gazes settled on her.

She held her hands up. "I take that as a no, then," she said.

"We voted on this, Liv." Joshua leaned forward. "We agreed that if the bank was prepared to lend us the money and we could get the right people on board, we'd proceed. We haven't hit a roadblock yet, so yes, it's a no. If that makes sense."

"Okay. We'll keep going with it." She released a huge breath. "Providing some of the labour will save money, as long as we don't all burn out in the process."

"We'll be fine, sis. It's not forever," Joshua said.

"How are you going to run Indigo and still help out here?" she asked, narrowing her eyes. "That's a tall order."

"Stella tracked down Indigo's previous leading hand, Daku Henderson, and he's agreed to come back." Joshua folded his arms across his chest. "He's amazing and I have no issue leaving him in charge so I can help out here when the time comes."

Stella spoke up. "And a few of the men and women who worked on the station before want to come back now that they know we're up and running again. We didn't need to interview them because I've known them most of my life and know their work ethic. We still need more hands, though. We've got interviews lined up over the next few days."

Sean hid his disappointment. He didn't know why, but he thought Joshua might have wanted him to work with him at Indigo. After all, they'd always worked well together. But he hadn't. All he'd done was invite him for a visit. Perhaps it was Stella, or perhaps Joshua simply didn't want him around. He had a new wife and a station of his own to manage. He was starting over. Why would he want the past in front of him as a reminder of all his mistakes?

"Good. You're on track, then," Olivia said. "When do you think you'll be getting the new cattle?"

"I'm not sure yet," Stella confessed. She looked at Joshua, and Sean didn't miss the exchange between them.

"We'll get them when we get them," Joshua replied. "Dad left that in my hands, and I have it under control. I've already spoken to Tamala, and he's all squared away."

Sean couldn't help but grin as Joshua put Olivia in her place.

She seemed to get the essence of the response, since she quickly backpeddled and changed the subject. "So, I was thinking that only one guide will be needed for the smaller drives, which means that Joshua, David, and Nate should be able to alternate between the drives and working on the bridge, but when the larger groups come through, at least two of you will need to be available."

She looked at the other men but overlooked Sean. He clenched his jaw silently. This was how it usually was. Everyone talking, everyone doing something, and him stuck in the middle. He'd never been much on giving input before, but that didn't mean he couldn't, or didn't want to.

He narrowed his gaze. "Where do I fit in with all this? I'll be able to help as soon as this cast is off."

"You won't need rehab time?" she asked, angling her head, eyeing him with her cool gaze.

He shrugged. "Don't think so."

"Well, I'm sure if you can help, that will ease the load. Thank you, Sean." Olivia's gaze softened, and she almost smiled at him, but she still sounded condescending.

"You're welcome." He gave a nod and crossed his arms.

She drew a long breath and placed her hands on the table. "Okay, I'll put together the financials for the bank and make plans to meet with them again this week."

"When do you need my guys to come out?" David asked.

"And what about the survey?" Joshua asked. "Don't we need that done first to see if we can even build where we want to? Where *do* we want to build this thing, anyway?"

"That's what the surveyors will do," Olivia replied. "They're the best ones to determine the most suitable spot."

"Yes, but we should have some idea of where we think it should go," Joshua continued. "What do you think it'll cost to have them traipsing up and down the place looking? We should tell them where we think it should go and have them tell us whether it's feasible or not."

David nodded. "I agree. We don't want to waste a second on this. It'll just add to the completion time, and the longer it takes, the more likely we'll run into the rainy season. If that happens, we won't get anywhere, and we'll be forced to wait months before we can resume construction."

"And there's no telling what damage could happen if the river floods. We could end up spending even more money on repairs or replacement than the initial construction," Joshua added.

"Which we don't want," David said.

"Okay. Okay." Olivia held up her hands. "David, since the bridge was your idea, you have to have some idea of where you think it should go. Why don't you meet with the survey team and take them there?" she suggested.

Little Oliver began to fuss before he could reply. Serena stood and tried shooshing him, bouncing him up and down in her arms. Adoration was evident in David's eyes as he looked at his wife and son. Sean felt an acute sense of sadness. He couldn't remember his father looking at him like that. He wasn't close to his father. Never had been. It was a strange thing, since he was an only child. His parents loved each other, but there was a separation between him and them. He'd started getting into trouble when his mother got diagnosed with MS and his dad seemed more interested in helping her than him, or at least that's how he saw it. The last conversation he'd had with his father hadn't gone well. They hadn't spoken since, and that was over a year ago. Maybe he should call. Find out how Mum was doing, if nothing else. Last time he'd seen her she was in a wheelchair.

But no, his father wouldn't want to hear from him, even though his mum might. He pushed the thought aside and refocused on the conversation going on around him.

"So, it's agreed. You and Joshua will go out and identify a place today," Olivia stated, her gaze on David. Sean felt as if he'd missed an entire conversation. When had they decided that?

"We'll head out there right after the meeting," Joshua replied. He turned to Stella. "Do you mind going back on your own? I can get a ride home later."

She frowned. "Did you forget that we have interviews today?"

"No, darling, but I'm sure that you and Henderson can handle them." He placed a hand over hers and another look passed between them.

Her expression brightened, but Sean groaned. Since when had his cousin become so mushy? A shudder ran down his spine.

"Yes, I guess we can manage," she said.

"So, that's sorted." Olivia gathered her papers and pushed her chair back, making to stand.

But Sean had a question and he put his hand up. "Have we decided on a design for the bridge?"

Everyone looked at him.

He gave his input. "I think a truss bridge would be best. People have been using that design for years, because it's strong and relatively inexpensive in comparison to suspension type bridges."

"Sean, what are you talking about?" Olivia laughed. "What do you know about bridge designs? The last time I checked, you didn't have a degree in engineering. In anything, actually."

Her words stung. It may have been a joke to her, but it wasn't to him. Yes, he wasn't as educated as the rest of them, but that didn't mean he was stupid. "I did some reading," he replied curtly. "It's the easiest way to learn about things."

Her lips pursed.

"Why don't you join us, Sean?"

David's request took him by surprise. "Join you? Where?"

"To find a location for the bridge. I think you could be useful. You've lived on this station for a long time, and I'm sure you could think of some good places." David smiled. "Plus, I think you'd like to get back out there. You can ride a horse with that arm, I'm sure."

The chance to be useful? Sean didn't hesitate. "Definitely. Where were you thinking of heading to first?" The prospect of getting away from the homestead and out in the field again was intoxicating.

"I'm not sure," David replied. He looked to Joshua. "Did you have a place in mind to start?"

Joshua nodded his head towards Sean. "I think Sean can help you with that. I should get back home to help Stella with the interviews."

"That's okay," Stella countered. "I can handle it if you want to help out here."

Joshua took her hand. "I'll be better off at home with you.

Sean and David can handle this. Can't you?" He turned and looked at both him and David.

Sean nodded. "Yep. It's all under control." He knew exactly where to go, although he wouldn't mention it yet. The place held painful memories, but it was the ideal place for a bridge.

"Do you have any idea where we should start?" David asked, leaning forward, finding his gaze. He looked eager to get going and Sean could see that he wasn't the kind of man who dawdled on things.

"Yeah, I have a good place in mind," he replied softly. It didn't matter how many years had passed, speaking of the place where his aunt lost her life was always difficult. His gaze held David's. There were questions there, but he didn't ask immediately, and Sean didn't offer any further explanation. He'd tell David where they'd be going after they left, but until then, he'd stay quiet.

Olivia cleared her throat. "Do what you need to do and let us know when you've decided on a good spot. You should probably have a couple of places in mind in case the first one's not feasible."

David nodded. "Roger that."

The meeting was virtually over after that. Olivia continued to talk but Sean's mind was elsewhere. He was thinking of the river, the overflowing banks, and the spot where he thought the bridge should be built. It would be difficult for the family to cross there, at least to begin with, but he truly believed it was one of the best, if not *the* best, place to build it.

Once the meeting was ended, David proceeded out the door and Sean followed. "You ready for this?"

David chuckled. "For what?"

"This isn't going to be an easy task, you know that, right?" Sean wasn't sure how much David knew about the individual members of the family, but he was about to find out.

"I'll see you later, honey," Serena said as they stood at the top of the verandah stairs. She was still bouncing Oliver.

"I'll be back soon," David replied, kissing her lightly on the cheek before turning to Sean. "Now, what were you saying?"

"Olivia."

"Ah, Olivia," David said, smiling. "What about her?"

"You know she's going to want to oversee every aspect of this, don't you? My cousin isn't the kind of woman who can simply let you do things. She has to be involved."

"I got that."

"She means well," Sean stated, wanting to be sure David understood. Olivia never meant ill; she simply didn't come across in the right way at times. "She's a bit controlling," he continued. "But it's only because she likes things done properly."

"I can understand that," David said as they walked towards his Jeep.

"I hope so, or else it's going to be a very long couple of months for you."

"What about you?" David questioned. He raised an eyebrow. "Won't it affect you, too?"

"Not really," Sean replied nonchalantly. "I came to understand my cousin a long time ago. At least I think I did. Take the good and try to ignore the annoying," he said with a laugh.

David chuckled. "Duly noted."

CHAPTER 12

*D*avid worked surprisingly fast. Sean couldn't believe how quickly he was able to get his construction friend into action; the engineer was ready to start work on the design and building of the bridge. Nor could he believe how quicky Olivia had secured the loan approval from the bank, although, once determined to accomplish something, there was little his cousin let stand in her way. At the end of the week, when she announced she'd secured the loan, everyone was speechless.

That morning, Carter Johansson, the engineer, was due to arrive with David's friend Patrick Carpenter. Sean woke early but didn't eat. He felt anxious about the proceedings. They were entrusting him to present the places that he and David had identified as potential locations for the bridge. It was his time to shine. He didn't know why the task made him so nervous, but it did. Perhaps it was the look his uncle had given him, and those last words: *Help take care of this place until we get back, Sean.* He wanted to make his uncle proud. He wanted to thank him in some way for allowing him to return to Goddard Downs.

Sean raked nervous fingers through his shaggy hair as he waited for the men to arrive. He paced the yard, the urge for a cigarette burning the tip of his tongue. He'd given up the habit after he'd broken his arm, but when times of anxiety arose, the urge to take a drag reared its ugly head. He stopped pacing, closed his eyes, and took a deep breath. There was nothing to be nervous about. He had it covered. It was just another trip around the station, no big deal. He opened his eyes as a large truck with a covered tray pulled into the station. *Here we go.*

He stepped towards the approaching vehicle as David appeared through the front door with Nate hot on his heels. There was a huge grin on David's face as he jogged towards the first truck. Nate picked up the pace behind him, and the pair reached the truck as it stopped several feet from the house. Sean hurried to catch up and reached them just as David greeted one of the men in the cab. "Patrick! Good to see you."

"David, how're you doin' mate?" A well-toned blond-haired man in a polo shirt and khaki shorts jumped from the truck's cab and came around the front. The two men hugged briefly, slapping each other on the back in camaraderie before stepping back.

"Glad you could make it out so quickly," David said.

"I gave you my word, and I always keep my word," Patrick replied. He turned to the passenger door as another man, just as well built but shorter and stockier, with dark hair and a short-sleeve, button-down shirt, stepped out. "David, this is Carter Johansson. Carter, this is David."

David shook Carter's hand. "Nice to meet you. This is Nate and Sean."

Sean and Nate stepped beside them and extended their hands.

"Nice to meet you all," he said, shaking each of their hands. Patrick had a firm grip, and Sean noted that he met his eye when he took his hand. It reminded him of something his uncle had told him as a boy. *An honest man will shake your hand firmly and look you in the eye.* He wasn't in the habit of holding peoples' gazes, but he wasn't always an honest person, either. He wondered if his uncle's words held any merit. He'd see soon, he supposed.

Patrick chuckled once the introductions were over. "I was telling Carter about that bar we went to in Melbourne a while back. Umm...what was the name of it?"

"The Pequod," David answered with a chuckle.

"That's it! I told you they named it after some fictional something or other," Patrick continued, looking at Carter.

"It's from Moby Dick. It's the name of the boat they sailed on," Nate added.

Sean looked at him in surprise. How could any of them remember such a silly name? As the men continued discussing the bar and the book, he wished he'd at least visited the joint so he could join in the conversation. He'd visited plenty of other bars in his time, but not that one.

"It was quite a place. You should check it out when you're next in Melbourne," David said to Carter.

Patrick and Carter walked with David and Nate as they headed towards the house to meet Olivia before they headed out. Sean lingered behind. His confidence was waning, and it unsettled him. He'd never experienced feelings like this before, and it was alarming. It was as if every inadequacy he'd ever suppressed was leaking through the cracks and beginning to surface. He couldn't let them. There was no telling what might happen if he did, and he wasn't about to find out.

After Olivia met Carter and Patrick and quizzed them not so subtly about their qualifications, David told the others to follow him in his Jeep. Soon, they were heading across the station to the furthest spot that he and David had identified as a potential suitable location for the bridge. Sean sat in the back seat of the Jeep while David drove. Nate sat in the passenger seat beside him. "They seem like nice guys," he commented, turning to David.

"Yeah, Patrick's a good guy. He's very grounded, and he's been a great help with me and my walk."

Nate nodded. "Ah, I see. How is that going?"

"I'd say pretty well. I'm not where I'd like to be, but I take each day as it comes, knowing that I'm in the process."

"It's always hardest in the beginning, trying to shake off the old and become new, but it's worth it. You have to give yourself a little grace. You'll get there." Nate smiled.

Sean frowned. *Walk? What walk? What were they talking about?* He peered at them from his seat, feeling like a child, and they the parents, involved in a conversation that was beyond him. He took a deep breath and looked out the window. A wallaby was nibbling on some sprouting vegetation and looked up as they passed. A few birds were flying overhead, and the sky was a pale blue instead of the richer blue he was used to at that time of year. He tried to find anything to distract him, but despite his best efforts, Sean couldn't help but listen as Nate spoke again.

"I remember when I first became a part of this family. I'd never been around people who talked about God or prayed as much as they did. I was raised in a semi-religious family, but the only time we went to church or spoke of God was Easter and Christmas."

"Sounds familiar." David chuckled.

Nate nodded knowingly. "How about Serena?"

David smiled at the mention of his wife's name. "She's amazing. She's such a different person now. Ever since she decided to give things over to God, she's been a lot less stressed, way more peaceful, and less focused on her fears."

"I haven't had a chance to say it, but I think what she's doing is great. Encouraging children to believe in themselves and strive to reach their goals. It's making a huge difference in their lives, and did you see what it did for Janella?"

David nodded. "I did. She came alive again after she met that boy, Jonah."

Sean remained silent while listening. Everything was clear now. The walk they were talking about, the changes, was all about their belief in God. He huffed silently and leaned his head back, closing his eyes. Still, he listened.

David talked about himself and Serena, the way their relationship changed, and how they'd almost lost the chance to be together because of her fears over her injuries. How God changed that, changed her, and brought them together as He worked on them both. Now, they were going to church when they could, they prayed and read the Bible, and they trusted

God to keep the promises He'd made. Sean wondered what promises those could be.

It all sounded good, great even, but he had his doubts. He knew about God, of course, but God had never done anything for him. He very much doubted that God cared one way or another about him. All that faith stuff was good for them, but he'd rather stick to his way and figure life out for himself. It'd kept him so far, even if he had messed things up.

They arrived at the first location half an hour later. Again, Sean felt like the fifth wheel. The four other men seemed to fall into easy conversation, while all he could do was give information about the terrain, the drives, and what happened during the rainy season. Nate gave input here and there, but since he spent most of his time at the homestead and not in the fields, he wasn't much help, and David hadn't been there long enough to know much. Primarily it was Sean who had to advise Carter, but in between the conversation about dirt and rain, the four men talked about books, university, and God. Things Sean knew little about.

At location after location, Carter's team repeated their routine of measuring and taking samples. Sean wasn't entirely sure what they were doing, but it was gruelling work under the blazing sun. It was easier handling the heat on a drive. The continuous movement created a breeze and made the heat more tolerable, but standing around watching others work made it almost unbearable. Plus, he was bored. He'd rather be doing anything than standing around doing nothing.

Finally, they arrived at the area of the river where his aunt lost her life.

"Tell me about this spot," Carter said as he began pacing the ground. He dug his boot into the dirt near the bank and made some notes on his pad.

"This place can be dangerous," Sean started. "The water rises fast, and when it does, the whole area floods. People have lost their lives here."

Carter's brows lifted. "I'm sorry to hear that. Family of yours?"

"My aunt," Sean said solemnly.

"My condolences," Carter said.

"She was a hero," Nate added. "She saved her two grand-children from drowning before losing her own life." His gaze locked onto the place where Aunt Esther had gone into the water. They all knew the spot. How many times had Sean come there with Joshua over the years? How many times had they lamented his aunt's loss?

"She *was* a hero," Sean agreed softly.

Nate met his gaze, but neither said any more.

David was silent, but Sean sensed that he felt what they did. Loss was something everyone could understand.

The longer Sean watched them working, the more he thought this was the right place for the bridge. He didn't know why. But he knew this would be the place. Carter and the others could do their tests and whatever reports they needed to do, but something inside him said this was it.

"Alright, I think I've got everything I need," Carter stated after more than half an hour of surveying and talking to his team.

"So, what's the verdict?" Sean asked.

"I've got to get back home and do my analysis. I should

have a report and a bridge design ready for you within a week. Maybe less. Does that work for you?"

The question was directed to David, who looked at Sean and then Nate as if wanting confirmation. Finally, he spoke. "That'll work fine, but can you email it? We only get regular mail once a week out here, and we'd like it as soon as possible so we can start construction. We need to have this finished before the rains come."

"I understand," Carter said, closing his book, his arms settling at his sides.

"We should get back to town now. We don't want to be on the road after dark," Patrick stated.

David nodded. "We'll head back now. I'm sure you want to get home to Jean and the children."

"Yes, she's planning something special tonight. I have no idea what, but I'll be in trouble if I get home late," Patrick replied with a laugh.

Everyone was married. Sean groaned. It seemed that the world was conspiring to point out how alone he was. Not waiting for the others to join him, he trudged to the Jeep and climbed in the back. Leaning his head against the seat, he closed his eyes and they remained closed until they reached the homestead.

Though they were closed, he didn't fall asleep. He listened as Nate and David continued talking like old friends. Their camaraderie reminded him of how he used to be with Josh. How he missed that. He missed his cousin. Not the scrapes they got into so much, but hanging around together the way they used to. He understood why things couldn't be that way, but it didn't make it any easier. He'd fooled himself into thinking they'd always be together. Partners in crime. He'd never considered life without Joshua by his side. Even when Josh wasn't always interested in what he was planning, he was always there to keep him out of trouble. Now, he had to keep himself out of trouble, and so far, he'd done a pretty good job of it. At least, he thought he had.

When they arrived at the homestead, Sean jumped out of the Jeep before David and Nate climbed out. Carter and Patrick stopped their truck but didn't get out. Patrick leaned across the passenger side and spoke out the window to David. "Take care, mate. We'll be in touch soon."

"Thanks again for coming," David replied. "We look forward to hearing from you."

"We'll get the final survey to you in the next day or so, and the plans will follow," Carter added. "We'll try not to keep you waiting."

"Thanks. Do what you have to. No matter what, I'm sure we'll get this done," David assured.

The two men gave their final goodbyes before Carter put the truck into gear and they headed down the track, dust billowing behind them.

Turning to Sean, David placed his hand on his shoulder. "Good work today, mate. We wouldn't have achieved so much if you hadn't come along."

Sean shrugged offhandedly, although David's praise was a pleasant surprise. They would have eventually gotten through without him. "It was no big deal. It didn't take much to point out a few spots."

"Yeah, well. Your input was invaluable."

Nate excused himself and headed inside, hunger his excuse.

David remained next to Sean. "I didn't know about your aunt," he said.

Sean shrugged. "You weren't here. How would you know? Besides, it's been a long time."

"Yes, but that doesn't mean it no longer hurts. I wouldn't have wanted to upset you or Nate," David continued.

"Don't worry, mate. Everything's fine. When we get the report back and can get started, everything will get better. We need this bridge. We should have had it a long time ago, but we're getting it now, and that's all that matters."

David agreed. "You hungry? I think Olivia was making lasagna today."

"Not really," Sean answered. "I'll eat later. I'm kind of tired."

"Alright. Catch you later."

"Later." Sean lifted his hand in a wave and watched as David disappeared into the house. How good it must be to be him or Nate, having someone waiting for you at the end of the day. Someone to share a meal with and ask about your day. Maybe one day he'd find someone. Then again, maybe he wouldn't. Who'd be interested in a jerk like him?

CHAPTER 13

*T*he next day, Sean woke with a headache. He often woke with a headache when he'd had a restless night, and last night he'd tossed and turned, although it was hard turning with his stupid cast on. The question of whether he'd made a good choice coming back to Goddard Downs still lingered in his mind. Now, laying on his bed and looking up at the ceiling, he wasn't sure. Goddard Downs had been home for so long, but now it felt odd, as if something was missing with Joshua gone. No one else seemed to feel it. Everyone was going on as if everything was normal, but it wasn't for him. Nothing was normal.

Swinging his legs onto the floor, he walked to the bathroom to take a shower. He'd mastered the art of bathing with one hand weeks ago, and now it came effortlessly. He didn't have to think of where to put his arm, it went there automatically. Once he was clean, he had to decide what to wear. His wardrobe consisted mainly of T-shirts and jeans, but today he felt like wearing something different. Perhaps an outfit change would improve his sombre mood. A button-down shirt, perhaps. Something a bit smarter. He chose a dark blue plaid shirt and light blue jeans, and once dressed, looked himself over in the mirror, raking his good hand through his hair. He needed to get it cut, but there was something about the long layers that appealed to him.

No one was around when he reached the kitchen. The remnant of breakfast sat in pots on the stove, and the aroma of Anzac biscuits wafted from a cooling rack. Sasha must have been up early baking before her lessons began. He fixed a plate of scrambled eggs, sausages, and toast and poured a large glass of orange juice and a small cup of coffee. After the night he'd had, he needed a pick me up.

He sat alone as he ate, staring out the window. An old bicycle leaned against the side of the shed that he hadn't noticed before. It looked too small to be man's bike, but it might be fit for Caleb. He wondered who it belonged to. He'd never seen anyone riding a bike. But then, up until recently, he'd always avoided the homestead, preferring to bunk in with the hands, or take a swag and a horse and sleep under the stars.

Finishing his breakfast, he washed the dishes and headed for the yard to inspect the bike and see what else he might have missed in his efforts to avoid the main house and the family.

"Cousin Sean," Sasha said as he poked his head in the living room to see if anyone was there on his way out.

"Hey, Sash. What are you doing in here?"

"Just working on some recipes. I want to surprise Mum when she gets back." She held up a notebook.

He stepped into the room to take a look. It seemed that his

little cousin was turning into her very own Sara Lee. He was proud of her. At such a young age, she'd already found her place on the station. He was still struggling to figure his out. "Looks good, Sash. I hope I get to be the taste tester."

She smiled brightly. "Of course! I was thinking of making this chocolate gateau tomorrow, along with a berry compote."

"The more you talk, the hungrier I'm getting," he said with a chuckle.

"I like baking. I get to spend more time with Mum when I do, and I like the way people look when they eat what I make."

Sean had heard something similar from Janella. Sasha was very much her daughter in all the best ways. "Don't quit. You can make whatever you want and we'll devour it, but I'm sure your mother has told you that before."

Sasha chuckled. "Yes, she has," she replied, before her expression grew sombre.

"You're missing her?" he asked.

She nodded. "I know it's silly since she'll be home in a few days, and she's only been gone a few more, but I do. I miss Mum when she's not here. She's my best friend."

Having a parent as a best friend? It was a strange concept, but not completely odd since on the station there were few people for Sasha to associate with, especially with Caleb gone. It was a strange time for her. She was nearly thirteen, and it was time she met new people. Spread her wings a little. Living on the station might be great in many ways, but it was isolating, and she had no friends that he knew of. Just her mum.

"You'll see her soon," he assured, smiling at her.

She continued to write in her notebook with a contented grin on her face. She was so happy to simply plan a recipe and execute it. He couldn't help but feel a tiny bit of envy. He was more than twice her age and had yet to find contentment in anything.

"What time is it?" she asked suddenly, a concerned frown on her face.

"Just after nine."

"Oh no! Class!" She jumped to her feet, book in hand, and ran for the door. The School of the Air, although it was online, was as punctual as any formal school. Tardiness didn't go down well. Often, when they were younger, his cousins would have to end their talks to attend class. At that time, it seemed like such a fun thing to do, when he was forced to sit in a classroom with teachers he hated and who seemed to hate him. Caleb, Sasha, and everyone else at Goddard Downs had a different upbringing. Sometimes, and it was only sometimes, he wondered what it would have been like if he'd been born his uncle's son. He shook the thought from his mind and headed outside, shielding his eyes with his hand against the brilliant sun.

It was another cloudless day, but the wet season was coming. Sooner than they wanted to believe, the rains would come, turning the parched earth into sludge, and their chance of making progress on the bridge would be almost impossible. They had to do everything they could now before running out of time.

Shoving his good hand deep into his pocket, he headed for the shed and the bicycle. As he reached it, Troy, one of the hands walked by. Sean stopped him. "Hey Troy, do you know who this bike belongs to?"

He shook his head. "It's been standing there for months. I

think it was something Frank found in the shed. He said he was going to fix it up, but I guess he didn't get around to it."

Sean looked at the rusted metal and peeling paint. The frame was larger than it seemed from the kitchen, and although worn, it appeared sound and almost rust free. The tyres were completely flat but still had plenty of tread. He pulled the bike off the wall to get a better look. "I can fix this."

His words were random, a thought spoken out loud, but the moment he uttered them, he knew he'd do it. He smiled to himself. It was the perfect gift to give his uncle when he returned. If Uncle Frank wanted it fixed, then he would do that for him. He might not be able to do more, but he could do this. He looked around the yard. Everyone was busy, so no one took notice of him. However, as he stood there, *he* noticed more. The paint on the buildings was faded and peeling in places. He kicked at the boards near the base of the shed and a few came loose.

"This place is falling apart," he muttered. He spotted another hand crossing the yard and called to him. "Mack!"

"Hey, Sean. How's your arm?"

Mack Johnston was a tall man, heavyset, with dark olive skin, light brown hair, and dark eyes. He'd worked as a foreman at another station, but after suffering some health issues, had joined the team at Goddard Downs and was responsible for maintenance.

"Mack, when was the last time these boards were repaired?"

He scratched his head as he considered the question. Finally, he answered. "About three years ago. Your uncle hasn't been concerned about certain maintenance issues in a while, not with all the trouble regarding the cattle ban. He wanted me to focus on more important things."

Sean nodded. He understood his uncle's concerns. Still, things were better now. The cattle drives had seen to that, and with the new deal with Tamala, there was more than enough money to arrange for a few repairs. He was sure Olivia would approve. Repairs now would cost less than repairs later, and, along with the bridge, they could be looked at as one large plan to improve the station.

Sean spent the rest of the day with Mack, noting the things that needed fixing and making schedules for things that could be done in the future. It felt good to be doing something constructive and helpful for a change.

"I'll get this all together and typed up to give to Olivia," Mack stated once they'd finished their walkthrough.

"Don't tell her it's from me," Sean said quickly.

Mack looked at him curiously.

"It's better if it comes from you. It'll show that you're ahead of things and make you look good."

"And what about you?"

Sean shrugged. "What about me? This isn't my usual responsibility. I just wanted to help. No one needs to know about it," he answered, somewhat defensively. He doubted very much that anyone would listen to him if he brought it up. They were more likely to take Mack seriously.

"Sean? What's going on?" Joshua's voice was unexpected. Sean hadn't expected his cousin to be back at the station until the next family meeting.

"Mack and I were just going over a few repairs. Can't have Indigo outshining Goddard Downs," he said jokingly.

He turned and looked at the truck. Stella was climbing out, her long legs easily reaching the ground. They usually travelled together, so that came as no surprise. What was surprising, however, was the person who emerged from the back seat.

Sean didn't realise his jaw had dropped until Joshua pointed it out. "Pick up your lip, Sean. It's just Elizabeth. She's staying at Indigo with us for a week or so to help Stella get the place more hospitable."

"What're you talking about? I wasn't staring," Sean grumbled.

"I didn't say you were. I said close your mouth," Joshua reiterated with a laugh. Mack laughed with him and Sean felt distinctly put on the spot. He felt it more as Stella's cousin, Elizabeth, walked towards them. Her dark curly hair was in a ponytail on top of her head, and she was wearing shorts and a sleeveless T-shirt that clung to her curvy body. He had a hard time tearing his gaze away.

"Hi, Sean," she said softly. It'd been over a month since he'd last spoken to her. They'd talked a little after Joshua and Stella's wedding, but she was always busy and it never seemed like a good time to catch up.

"Elizabeth," he replied, tipping his hat. "Nice to see you."

"You, too." She gave a friendly smile, and the corners of his mouth tugged upwards. Ever since the wedding, Elizabeth had regularly been in his thoughts.

She grabbed him by his good arm. "Come on, Sean. Let's catch up before you and Joshua hog each other's time." She led him away before he could respond. Not that he wanted to. He liked her. At first, he thought she was a bit forward, but the more he got to know her, the better his opinion of her became.

Once they were away from the others, she folded her arms and began talking. "So, how've you been?"

"Good," Sean answered hollowly.

She laughed. "Don't kid me. I know you haven't been, so why bother telling me otherwise?"

"I didn't."

"You just did. Are you going to lie and say that you weren't lying?" she challenged.

He liked her feistiness. She always spoke her mind and the truth, no matter what others thought. Yet, it was never in a way that was overbearing or intrusive, at least not to him. She just stated facts and exposed the obvious. He wished he wasn't so obvious.

"How are things around here?"

"As you might expect," he answered, expelling a deep breath.

"Still feeling out of sorts? I know you were concerned that things might be weird with Joshua gone."

"Yep. Things are exactly as I thought they'd be. Worse now that Uncle Frank's travelling."

"Yes, Stella told me that he and Maggie are on a three-month road trip. Sounds exciting," Elizabeth said with a grin. "I'm sure they're having an amazing time. There's so much to see out there. I hope one day I can take a trip like that."

Sean considered the statement *and* the speaker. "You'd do something like that?" He blinked. Somehow, he'd imagined she'd prefer five-star hotels and restaurant meals to camping out and one-pan meals cooked on an open fire.

"Yes. Why not? It'd be fun to spend so much time with the person you love. On the road, with no one else, just you and that special person spending all that time with each other. Seeing amazing sights. Having experiences of a lifetime. What's not to like?"

Shrugging, he groaned inwardly, feeling deflated. She must have met someone else. "Whatever. All this couple stuff isn't for me."

She glanced at him but said nothing.

"It's not that I don't approve," he added. "I'm just tired."

"Of what?"

"Of being *that guy.*" He expelled another long breath. He didn't know what it was about Elizabeth, but he felt as if he could talk to her. She was the only person, other than Joshua, he felt he could share stuff with who might understand.

"The guy who's on the outside looking in, envying everyone," she replied, snatching the words from his mind as if she were reading his thoughts.

"Yes," he said with some relief. It was good to admit his feelings instead of trying to hide them. "Also, no one listens to me here. I feel useless."

She thwacked him on his good arm.

"Ouch! What was that for?" he asked, holding his arm.

"That's to get you to stop being such a baby and grow up," she said dryly. "You're whining. Whining never solved anything. If you want things to change, then you need to do something about it."

"Like what, Miss Know it All?"

She laughed. "Ha! I don't know everything, but I come close," she teased, her eyes twinkling.

He couldn't disagree. "Well?"

"Well, if you want to be heard, then you have to open your mouth. I know you. You're not the kind of guy who'll say what needs to be said when your feelings are on the line. You have plenty to say when you don't care about the outcome, but when you do, it's not so easy."

How did she know this? He doubted many understood that about him, and yet she did. "Why do you say that?" he asked.

"You ran away so you wouldn't have to deal with Joshua and Stella getting married. You ran away from home to get away from your parents. When it comes to what you're truly feeling, being vulnerable, you aren't the kind who stands and fights. That's why you don't have what you want. You've gone after what comes easy, but the best things in life have a cost attached. Don't let anyone fool you. Even salvation isn't free."

He blinked rapidly. *How had they gotten there?* "Salvation?"

"Yes," she answered. "People like to say that salvation is free, but it's not. It cost big time. It cost Jesus His life."

Once again, she had a way of making him mute. He didn't share her feelings about God, but when she spoke, her passion almost made him want to. Almost. She believed so fervently, but she didn't bombard him with a barrage of words. She believed everything she said, and it was the way she lived her life, each and every day. He admired that kind of conviction. "So, what are you saying I should do?"

"I'm saying, it's time you got off your butt and did something about what you want. Whatever that is won't come to you simply because you think about it. You have to take action."

"But no one listens—"

A finger shot up to his lips to silence him. "Stop. There's your first problem. Unconscious use of language."

He looked at her beyond the finger at his lips. "What?"

"If you keep speaking ill, that's what you'll get. The power of life and death is in the tongue. What we speak can destroy or give life to what we want."

"They're only words," he challenged, raising a hand to gently remove her finger from his lips. Once her finger was gone, a tingle remained.

"No. Words have power. Tell a child terrible things about themselves, and they'll most likely become what you say. Encourage and love them, and they'll blossom and become the kind of people you'll be proud of."

He scoffed. "Well, that explains a lot." And it did. His dad had always told him he'd never amount to anything, and he hadn't.

She nodded, as if she understood. "Start changing what you say, and it'll change the way you think. A better attitude makes the process easier. Try it and see what happens. It works. Believe me."

He looked at her with scepticism.

"You need to give of yourself," she continued. "People can benefit from all of your experiences. You may not see it, but anyone who's lived the life you have has a lot to share. Our testimony isn't just for us. It's for others."

"A testimony?"

She smiled. "Yes, a testimony. You have one."

"No, I don't." He didn't have anything to give people. What he'd been through in life couldn't help anyone, except to show them what not to do. Who wanted to know that?

"Try something new, Sean. What do you have to lose?"

"Yes, Sean. What do you have to lose?" Joshua strode towards them, his brow creased.

"Nothing, cuz. Nothing at all."

"Good. Sorry to interrupt whatever you were talking about, but Stella needs you, Liz."

She nodded, but before she left, she reached out and squeezed Sean's hand. "Be bold, Sean. People care about you more than you think." She smiled and walked off.

As he watched her go, he wondered if there was any truth in her words. Something inside of him wanted to believe what she'd said, but a part of him still doubted. *Why would people care about him after all the messes he'd created?*

His gaze locked onto her swinging ponytail as she continued to the house. Man, she was something else.

CHAPTER 14

Frank enjoyed Fred and Mable's company. The couple had delighted him and Maggie with their stories, but it was their insight that grabbed his attention the most. They'd shared a lot during the few hours spent together around the fire, leaving an indelible impression on him.

He and Maggie had talked into the night, and as a result, their plans had changed. Maggie's rigid schedule went out the window for a more spontaneous and carefree experience. Whatever was supposed to happen, would. They wouldn't worry about getting to this place or that on time and seeing everything. Instead, they'd simply enjoy every second they had together and make each moment special.

"I'd rather photograph *you*," Maggie said, brushing her hair from her face as she stood in front of a large boab tree. The trunk was six times her size and twice her height, with branches reaching out in all directions as if trying to catch the very rays of sunlight shining down on her.

Frank smiled. "I know you would, but I refuse to let all of the pictures on this trip be of me. If you had your way, you wouldn't be in one of them." He checked her image on the camera screen. She was radiant. He could look at her all day and never be bored.

"Come over here with me," she said, beckoning to him with one hand. "The idea is for both of us to be in the photos, isn't it?"

"I will, my love, but first, I want to capture you."

She smiled. "You already did that."

A grin spread across his face. "And what a fortunate man I am."

"We are both blessed," she replied. The grin on her face matched his, and the warmth of her love shone through. He was glad they'd tossed aside their plans and were allowing God to direct their trip. It was a novel idea, but one that appealed to him. Maggie as well. It was funny, but the older they got, the more they wanted to rely on God. When he was young, he'd thought he could conquer the world on his own. It was only when he truly acknowledged his need of God that he achieved the success he craved. Now, more than ever, he was willing to hand the keys of his life over to the Lord. He set the timer on the camera for twenty seconds and then sprinted to where Maggie stood.

"Get on the other side," he said, rushing to the right of the tree and trying to wrap his arms around it. Understanding his intent, she quickly did the same. Laughing, they turned to face the camera as the alarm chimed moments before the camera snapped.

As they strolled back to the truck, Maggie's phone dinged

several times. The reception on their phones had been spasmodic, and whenever they were in a spot that picked up a signal, even for a few seconds, several messages often came through at once. They must have just walked into one of those spots.

His phone dinged as well. The message was from Olivia and had been sent two days earlier.

Dad, the loan has been approved. We're proceeding with the bridge unless you tell us otherwise. Hope you're having an amazing time. Love, Olivia xx.

Short and to the point. Typical Olivia. He chuckled to himself as he sent back an even briefer reply.

Happy to proceed. Having a great time. Love Dad

Maggie had pulled her phone from her pocket, and as she scrolled through her messages, she stopped dead.

"What's wrong, my love?" he asked.

"Nothing at all." When she lifted her face, it was beaming. "There's one from Janella. She's decided to go to school."

"That's wonderful. I'm so pleased to hear that."

"So am I. But she sent the message a couple of days ago, so she's probably wondering why I haven't replied."

"Well, you'd better do that now. Tell her congratulations from me."

"I will." Maggie smiled as she began typing her message.

Frank closed his eyes and thanked God for giving Janella direction, but a flood of other emotions broke upon him in waves. It was the right thing for her to do, he was sure of it, but it meant that she and Sasha would be leaving Goddard Downs, even if only for a time. His family was diminishing. Esther and Julian were gone, Joshua was living at Indigo, Caleb was in

Darwin, and now Janella and Sasha would be leaving. He needed a moment to process it all.

Maggie placed a gentle hand on his arm. "Are you alright, Frank?"

He nodded. "I'm fine." Tucking the tripod under his arm, he took her hand and continued towards the truck which was parked on the side of the Gibb River Road. A layer of red dust covered the bottom half of the cab and camper. Each time they passed another vehicle, it was like driving through a dust storm.

They climbed into the cab. He put the key into the ignition but didn't turn it. He sat with his arms resting on the steering wheel, staring at the road stretching into the distance. His heart was heavy. Although he was happy for Janella, he already felt a sense of loss. But why? The course was only two years, but something inside him warned that she might never return.

"Frank?" Maggie said gently, placing a hand on his shoulder.

Lifting his gaze, he placed his hand over hers and rubbed it gently. "I'm sorry, my love. It just feels as if everyone's leaving. It's for the best, of course, and I know Janella will thrive in Darwin. Both she and Sasha will. And it'll be good for Caleb to have his mother close."

Maggie smiled. "It's okay to miss them. And besides, they haven't left yet."

"Yes, but they'll be gone by the time we get back."

"We can always go and visit them. I wouldn't mind another trip to Darwin," she said, smiling.

"You're right as always, my love." He lifted her hand to his lips and kissed it gently. "But Goddard Downs won't be the same without her and Sasha."

"Nothing ever stays the same, Frank. You know that."

He nodded. "I do. As much as I'd like things to stay as they are, life isn't like that. I'm simply being selfish wanting her to stay. On a positive note, this is the first time I've seen her do something for herself."

"And it's time she did. I'm so glad she's decided to do it."

"So am I," he said, drawing a slow breath as he started the engine.

"You're over your tizzy, then?" Maggie asked, grinning.

"Tizzy? What's that?"

"You don't know?"

"I wouldn't ask if I did," he said, chuckling.

"And you call yourself an Aussie."

"I *am* an Aussie. I'm as Aussie as they come."

She reached out and placed her arm across his shoulders. "I know. I love that about you, Frank."

"You still haven't told me what a tizzy is." He turned and faced her.

"It's when you get wound up about something."

"Are you saying I was wound up?"

She shrugged. "Maybe."

He laughed. "You're incorrigible."

"I'm not." She laughed with him, lightening his heart. *Thank You, Lord, for Maggie,* he prayed silently.

The next stop was Tunnel Creek which they reached after an uncomfortable half hour on the corrugated Leopold Downs Road. Frank pulled into the small parking area and they had a quick bite to eat while reading the information board.

"Wow. I didn't know this is the oldest cave system in the state," Maggie said. "And you didn't tell me there are crocodiles in the water." She turned and faced him. "I'm not sure I want to do it now."

He chuckled. "They're just little freshies, love. They won't hurt you."

"But we have to wade through the water." Her eyes were wide.

"Hundreds of people walk through every day and come out the other side. Only one or two don't make it." The grin on his face made her laugh. She swatted him with her hand. "Stop making fun of me."

"I'm not, my love."

"Yes, you are."

He laughed with her. "I'm sorry. Come on. Let's do this." He held out his hand, and after a quick hug, they strolled back to the truck to grab their headlamps and change their shoes.

A short path led towards the cave, but they had to clamber over and between huge boulders to reach the entrance.

"That was a mission in itself," Maggie exclaimed, panting and leaning against a large rock while taking a sip of water from her bottle. "Are you okay, Frank?"

"Right as rain." He forced a smile and drew a slow breath. Truth was, he was struggling. It frustrated him because he'd been fit and active his entire life. But he'd get through this. He simply had to push harder and not give in.

After catching their breath, they entered the cave, pausing to let their eyes adjust to the darkness. The cave was cavernous, with little waterfalls tumbling over the ledges on the sides, the water trickling into the large pool below. Huge stalactites dangled from the ceilings.

The creek ran through the cave, and the only way to reach the other end was to wade through it. He faced Maggie. "Are you ready?"

"I guess so… I truly hope I don't come face to face with a crocodile, harmless or not."

"Hold my hand. We'll be fine." He reached out and grasped hers before they stepped into the water. At the beginning of the dry season, the water would have been much deeper. Now, it came only to his knees, but it was murky and dark, and the bottom was rocky.

"Are those eyes over there?" Maggie whispered.

Frank followed the direction she was pointing. His torch picked up two sets of eyes belonging to freshwater crocodiles. He couldn't lie. "Yes," he said.

"Crocodiles?"

"Yes, but they won't bother us."

She slipped her arm through his and clung tighter.

Halfway through the tunnel the ceiling had caved in, allowing light to penetrate the darkness. Small bats flitted in and out, and tree roots growing through the gaps looked like gnarled fingers of an old woman. Then it grew dark again.

Finally, light appeared up ahead. Emerging into bright daylight, Maggie's face filled with relief. "We made it."

"Yes, but we have to go back the same way." Frank chuckled as her face dropped. "It wasn't that bad, was it, love?"

"No. I just need to get over my fear of being eaten by a crocodile, that's all."

· · ·

LATER THAT DAY, after they'd set up camp at the Windjana Gorge campsite and were sitting around the fire after dinner drinking tea, Frank asked Maggie if she missed working.

She was silent at first and stared into the fire. He wasn't sure what had prompted the question. Now they were spending all day every day together, there was more time to discuss things they hadn't had time for before. Plus, he'd never asked her that question directly.

She lifted her gaze from the fire and faced him. "No. I loved working, and if it hadn't been for my job, I would never have come to the Kimberley on assignment, and I would never have met you, but there's a time and season for all things. That season of my life is over. I enjoy being able to help Serena with Oliver. I wouldn't have been able to do that if I was still working."

"If you want to go freelance and write the odd article here and there, I'll support you."

She nodded and smiled. "I appreciate that. I'll write a journal of our trip, but it will only be for us. I don't feel the need to work, per se. Unless I get a nudge from God, of course."

"Well, who knows what He's going to lead us into."

"*He* does, Frank." Maggie's eyes twinkled, and the little dimple on her cheek appeared.

He chuckled. "Yes, of course He does. I wonder when He's going to give us the heads-up."

"In *His* time, and not before."

"Right as usual, my love." He reached out and squeezed her hand.

CHAPTER 15

*R*eturning to Goddard Downs without Frank and Maggie there to greet her felt strange. Janella had driven the whole way from Darwin, stopping only to drop Jonah off at his home in Kununurra, and had arrived back at Goddard Downs late in the afternoon. They'd left early, just as dawn was breaking, to ensure she'd reach home before dark, and now here she was, pulling up in front of the homestead.

Having already told Caleb she'd be moving to Darwin to study, she now had to break the news to everyone else, especially Sasha.

She drew a deep breath and sent up a prayer as she got out of the Jeep. She wasn't sure what Sasha's response would be. The only place her daughter had ever lived was here, on the cattle station, and she was such a homebody. But she needed to spread her wings. Broaden her horizons. Make friends with girls her own age.

Was she simply trying to convince herself she'd made the right decision?

Perhaps. And yet, underneath the anxiety she felt over packing up and leaving Goddard Downs and moving to the city, excitement and anticipation were bubbling. God had opened this door for her, and although it was scary and even a little overwhelming, this was the path God was leading her down, and He'd be with her as she spread her own wings, broadened her own horizons, and made new friends. She'd already made two. Just yesterday, she'd met up with Kathy and Bill, the pair she'd met while taking the tour of the school, for coffee down at the jetty. It had been a balmy afternoon, but as she sat there gazing out at the azure blue of the harbour enjoying the sea breeze, she thought she could take more of that. It was vastly different to Goddard Downs where everything was familiar and safe, but the excitement that came with new beginnings welled within her. She didn't know what lay ahead, but God did.

"For I know the plans I have for you," declares the Lord, *"plans to prosper you and not to harm you, plans to give you hope and a future."*

Hope and a future. When Julian died, she thought her future had died with him, but now, she was convinced God had something waiting for her. If only Sasha would be onboard with all the changes.

"Mum!" Her daughter ran down the stairs and threw her arms around her, almost knocking her over. "I've missed you so much."

Janella laughed. "And I've missed you, too, honey." She kissed the top of her daughter's hair.

"How was Darwin?" Sasha asked brightly as they walked up the stairs together, arm-in-arm.

"Good. Caleb's doing well. And how have you been?"

Sasha shrugged. "Oh, you know…I've just been baking and doing schoolwork. Aunt Liv's been making sure of that." She chuckled.

"I'm sure she has." Janella sniffed the air. "Is that a roast I can smell?"

"Yes. We thought you'd like one for dinner."

Janella smiled. "You thought right." The roast smelled wonderful, and all of a sudden, her stomach rumbled. But before dinner, she had a task to do. "Come and help me unpack before dinner."

"Sure."

They headed to her bedroom, and as they began to unpack, she drew another deep breath. "Sasha, there's something I need to tell you."

Sasha's eyes searched Janella's face, her brows knitting together. "What, Mum?"

Janella sat on the bed and took her hand. "You remember that Jonah applied to go to culinary school?"

"Of course," she said, her expression perplexed. "He couldn't stop talking about it."

"Do you remember that I applied also, just to support him?"

Sasha nodded. "Yes."

"Well, I got accepted."

The expression on her daughter's face changed immediately. Her eyes popped and a grin spread across her face. "Really?"

"I did," Janella replied, laughing as Sasha threw her arms around her neck and hugged her tightly.

"Mum, that's great! That's better than great. Does Caleb know? Was that why you went to Darwin?" The questions came so quickly that Janella hardly had time to form answers before Sasha was onto the next one.

Finally, after she'd exhausted herself, Janella answered. "Yes, your brother knows, and yes, that's why I went to Darwin. I wanted to see the school for myself, not only for Jonah, but to see if I could fit in. I didn't want to accept the placement if I didn't think I'd like it or couldn't handle it."

"You can handle anything, Mum," Sasha said confidently.

Knowing that her daughter believed in her filled Janella with new excitement. She shifted on the bed and sat squarely in front of her, taking both her hands. "The school was wonderful. Jonah and I have both accepted. I know I should have talked to you first because this involves you as much as me, but I felt it was the right thing for all of us."

Sasha stilled as she looked into her mother's eyes. "You mean, we'd both be leaving Goddard Downs?"

"Yes. A few weeks before the term begins. We'll have to find a place for us to live and a school for you to go to."

"No more School of the Air?"

Janella shook her head. She was unsure how Sasha felt about that. Although she didn't actually see her fellow students or teachers in person, over the years they'd built up friendships. They understood each other, since all the other students had similar experiences living in isolated, remote places. Would she be happy letting that go? Would she feel threatened going to a proper school? Wearing a uniform? Making new friends?

Janella needn't have worried. The light that exploded in Sasha's eyes at the news was answer enough. How had she not realised her daughter was so keen to go to a proper school? "You mean it? I'd get to attend secondary school? A *real* secondary school?"

Once again, her daughter tossed her arms around her neck as Janella laughed. Sasha's excitement was contagious. "I take it you're okay with it?"

"Okay with it? It's wonderful. I've always dreamed of attending a normal school with other students—and I'll get to be near Caleb. Plus, you'll get to do something you love, Mum. What's not to like about that?"

"You aren't nervous at all?"

Shaking her head vigorously, she jumped to her feet. "Can I go tell my friends? They'll be so jealous when they hear I'm going to a real school."

Janella stood as she laughed. "Not yet. When was the last time your hair was done properly, young madam?"

Sasha grimaced. "Last time you did it."

"Well, sit down and let me fix it before dinner. I won't let you sit at the table looking like a bird's nested in your hair."

"Sorry," Sasha said with a sheepish grin while easing herself into the chair in front of Janella's dressing table.

"Pass me the brush," Janella said, holding her hand out.

Sasha passed it and Janella began brushing the knots out. Sasha's hair had grown so long but she refused to have it cut. Janella did her best to braid it into a neat style most days, although Sasha would be happy to simply wear it in a ponytail.

"Mum, do you think I could bake treats to sell?" The question came out of nowhere, taking Janella by surprise.

"Sell? Why would you want to do that?" she asked, lapping one strand of hair over another.

"To help."

Janella was confused. "Help with what, Sasha?"

"With school. I know you have to do everything yourself now that Dad isn't here. I want to help by earning some money."

The melancholy in her daughter's voice tugged at Janella's heart. "Sasha, honey, you don't have anything to worry about. We're fine."

"I've seen those shows on television. The father dies, and the mother's left to do everything herself, and it's hard. I don't want things to be difficult for you, Mum. Not if I can help. I've been working on recipes the entire time you've been away. I want you to try them, and then, if you like them, I'll sell them to some of the hands on the station, and maybe at Indigo Downs as well. And when we move to the city, I could sell them there, too."

Tears sprung to Janella's eyes. She shifted to the side and took her daughter's hands, studying the long, slender fingers and soft skin. Sasha worked so hard already, but taking care of the family wasn't her responsibility, it was Janella's. "Sweetheart, that's so sweet and thoughtful, and I appreciate you wanting to help, but it's okay. Dad left us well-looked after, so we don't need to worry about money. We're going to be just fine."

"But you never buy new clothes."

"No, but I might start."

"Really? Can we go shopping in Darwin? Just you and me? I'd love to get one of those new outfits Marcia got when she went shopping with her mum. I wouldn't want to look out of place. After all, it's not Kununurra, it's Darwin. It's more fashionable."

"Sure." Janella chuckled again. "There's a whole new world waiting for us, Sash." She smiled as she returned to her place behind the chair and parted out another section of her daughter's hair. She continued braiding as Sasha pumped her with questions.

"When can we start looking for schools? I want someplace near Caleb. Do you think there'll be a school near his? Does his school take my year level? Could I go to school with him? That would be great. I've always wanted to go to a secondary school and have my big brother look after me. It'll be just like on a sitcom."

Janella suppressed a chuckle. "Do you think this is Neighbours or McLeod's Daughters?"

Sasha looked over her shoulder and grinned. "Something like that."

Janella shook her head and laughed. "I'm so relieved that you're excited about this move, honey. I was worried you wouldn't want to go."

"It's not that I don't like it here, Mum. I love it here. It's just...there seems to be so much else out there that I don't know about, and I've never seen except on the telly. I guess I want to know more about lots of things." All of sudden, she turned her head and looked up, her face stricken. "What about grandpa? Does he know about us moving?"

"He does. Are you worried about him?"

"I just realised that he might be sad if we go," Sasha answered solemnly. "I know he misses Dad, and I wouldn't want him to be sad because we're gone too."

"Your grandfather's already given his blessing on this. In fact, he encouraged me to go after it," Janella said.

"Did he?" Sasha asked, her expression brightening.

Janella nodded. "He did, and he said that we'd have all the support he can give us. He thinks I'll do well."

"You will, Mum. I know it. I'm going to miss him, though."

"As will I, but it's not forever, and perhaps he and Maggie can visit us."

"That would be nice."

"It would," Janella said, nodding. "Now, turn your head back so I can finish this braid. It'll take all night if we keep going at this pace."

Sasha giggled and turned her head. Janella continued to braid. They were going to face some changes in their lives, things she couldn't begin to anticipate, but she was ready. Whatever lay ahead, God would be there with her. He wouldn't have opened the door if He hadn't already prepared the way for her and her children. It was scary and exciting at the same time. She'd relied on Julian for so long, deferring to him in every decision other than what to cook. Making a decision without him felt strange, especially a decision as monumental as this one.

She continued to braid as Sasha talked. She didn't speak, just let her daughter express herself while she listened attentively. Like Caleb, Sasha was growing up and changing. The little girl she was before her father died was gone.

The more Janella thought of it, the more benefits she saw in moving away for a while. She'd have to stand entirely on her own for one thing, and though it was nerve-wracking, it was also exciting. She'd never been solely responsible for their family before, and though she knew she could do it, it was still foreign territory to her. She loved being married. She loved having a husband to talk things over with, to arrive at decisions together, to bear each other's burdens, to support one another. Julian used to tell her that she allowed him to be the man he wanted to be, and even when he messed up, she stood by him and encouraged him. But he also made her better, although she wasn't sure he'd known that.

On the outside, apart from gaining a little weight and growing a few grey hairs, she hadn't changed that much since her teenage years when she and Julian had fallen in love, but marrying him and having his children had changed so much for her. Being part of the Goddard family had contributed. With him and his family, she'd found love, acceptance, and a place for herself in their midst when it may have otherwise been difficult anywhere else. No one ever looked down at her at Goddard Downs. No one saw the colour of her skin over who she was. The Goddards were some of the most loving, caring, and accepting people she could ever have wished to know, and they'd helped her see that the prejudices of the world didn't have to rule her or her thinking. Julian helped her to find a way to love past the hurts of her childhood and the instilled doubts she was still overcoming. Goddard Downs had done far more for her than anyone knew. It was going to be strange leaving, but she also knew it would always be 'home'.

But now, she had to tell the family that she and Sasha

would be moving to Darwin. Although perhaps she should wait a while. They had enough going on without her dropping this bit of news on them. But could Sasha keep it a secret? Somehow, Janella doubted it.

CHAPTER 16

*S*natching glances of her husband as they drove along the coast to their next destination, Maggie couldn't help but grin. The Dampier Peninsula was a spectacular stretch bordered by glistening blue water and white sandy beaches framed by ochre-coloured rock formations.

She leaned forward in her seat, camera trained in her hands as she snapped photo after photo, watching as the sliver of blue grew larger and larger. The vegetation became more vibrant, and the dusty road gave way to orange headlands jutting out from the coast like fingers grabbing at the water. The earth beneath them changed too, becoming paler in colour, with patches of yellow, until finally it was all sand and the sea lay before them like a canvas.

"Is that a crocodile?" She gripped the door handle as a dark figure slid into the water.

Frank peered over the steering wheel in the direction she was looking. "It might be. The lady at the store told me that some saltwater crocs live in the waters near here and to watch out for them if we decide to stop."

Maggie nodded. She would have loved to get a close-up photo of a crocodile, but it was too far away. She was tempted to ask Frank to veer off the path so she could get a closer look, but she wanted to get to Cape Leveque more than snap a photo of a croc. Instead, she leaned her head against the door as the wind blew against her face. It was warm and gentle, like a caress.

"What are you thinking?" Frank asked.

Maggie smiled broadly. "I'm not. I'm feeling."

He chuckled. "I don't think I've heard that before."

"That's because I've never said it before. I've never *felt* it," she replied, turning to her husband. "I've been feeling...I don't know how to describe it. But it's like I'm feeling everything. I think I'm finally understanding what true joy is."

"I know what you mean," he replied. "Since we left home, everything seems more vivid and real than before."

"Exactly. But it's strange. Nothing's changed, but it feels as if so much has. Or am I just being silly?" She laughed.

He shook his head gently. "You're not. Since we left home, I've been feeling it too. The longer we're away, and the more we see, the more at peace I'm feeling."

Maggie smiled. Whatever the Lord was doing in their hearts, He was doing it in them both. From the moment she married Frank, she knew her life would change, and with each passing month and year, it was only growing better. She couldn't imagine there could be more than this, but she could feel it.

Oh Lord, what are Your plans for us? I know they are only for our good, but what are they? What do You have in store for Frank and me? I feel as if I want to cry now, and I don't know why. Not tears of sadness, but joy. So much joy. Father, I've never felt like this, as if I'm walking into a new season. But what season could I be walking into? I just feel as if there's something so great and wonderful on the horizon, and I'm filled beyond measure by the hope of it. Oh Lord, how wonderful You are. How great. I wish I had words to give You the thanks You deserve. I wish I could convey the love I feel from You at this moment, travelling with my husband and seeing the glory of Your creation. Words are not enough to describe. Thanks are not enough to give, but I give You thanks all the same. Thank You, Lord, for loving us and bringing us to this place. I know that whatever is to come will be even greater than what has passed, for You said in Your Word that our latter days will be greater than our former. I do not know how You can surpass what You've already done, but I know You will. Thank You for what has passed, and thank You for what is to come. In Jesus' precious name. Amen.

The moment they stepped onto the sand, the wind whipped through her hair, sending a curtain of silver before her eyes. Maggie quickly turned in the direction of the gust to get the hair out of her face. "A bit gusty," she commented as Frank came around the front of the truck to stand beside her.

"A bit, but can you smell that freshness?" He inhaled deeply, closing his eyes and raising his face to the sky. Maggie watched him with an amused grin. Her husband had more of the sentimental in him than he knew. She took his hand and joined him.

She enjoyed photographing the orange shores that melted into the azure waters. It was truly stunning, better than any photo she'd seen in the advertisements. "Photographs don't do this place justice."

Frank smiled. "No, they don't. Let's find our camping spot and then you can take some more shots."

She nodded. "Sounds good."

They climbed back into the cab but stopped when they reached the headland to gaze out across the sea. She'd never seen a sea this colour before. It was a bluey-green, and so, so clear. It was absolutely gorgeous. Stunning.

Their campsite was at beach level, so after driving down the winding, bumpy track, they located the site and set up quickly. They were becoming experts and could do it in ten minutes, and that included erecting their awning, setting up their outdoor table and chairs, and putting out the solar panels. They worked like a well-oiled machine as they went about their specific jobs.

Maggie grabbed the makings for sandwiches and set everything down on the table. A more picturesque dining location she couldn't imagine, and with the way they'd parked the truck, they were out of the wind. It was glorious. She sat down and started cutting up a tomato as Frank joined her, smiling broadly as he eased back in his chair. "You know, this could be even better than the resort in Broome. What isn't there to love about this place?"

"Not much. In fact, it's a perfect place for a second honeymoon." She waggled her eyebrows.

His face lit up. "We could cancel our booking at the resort."

"Hmmm... let me think about that... Ah, no. The resort can be our third honeymoon."

His grin widened. "I like the sound of that."

"I'm sure you do." She chuckled as she handed him a knife. "You're on bread buttering."

"I can do that." He leaned forward in his chair and pulled the bread from the packet.

After a leisurely lunch, they strolled along the shore to an outcropping of rocks, all the while keeping a lookout for crocs. The reptiles were rarely seen in this area, but still, they needed to be watchful.

They stayed at Cape Leveque for three days, enjoying long walks on the beach and afternoon siestas under the shade of their awning before dinner around a campfire. After all the driving and hiking, it was the perfect place to recharge and refresh.

But Broome was calling. It was the one place where they had to be on time. It was an easy two-hour drive from Cape Leveque, but on the way down the peninsula, they called in at the Willie Creek Pearl Farm.

The instant she walked into the store, Maggie instantly fell in love. Pearls were her favourite piece of jewellery, and the store had so many.

"See anything you like?" Frank asked, sidling up behind her and slipping his hands around her waist. When he kissed her on the cheek, she felt her cheeks blush. "Frank, not here."

The shop attendant, an indigenous man of medium height and a jolly round face, grinned and quickly averted his gaze.

Frank backed away and stood beside her, draping his arm across her shoulders as she studied the contents of the display cabinets.

The pieces were stunning, all unique and highly crafted. "What don't I like?"

"Pick whatever you want, my love."

She looked up at him. "I don't need anything."

"I know, but I want to get you something special." She could hear the love in his voice.

"But you've already given me so much."

"Maggie. Choose something."

"Okay."

Half an hour later, they were once again in the truck heading for Broome. Maggie admired the gorgeous pearl ring on her finger. A stunning, cultured pearl set in a white gold band. She couldn't have asked for a more perfect gift.

ARRIVING at the resort at Cable Beach, Broome, they parked the truck in the outdoor carpark, since they needed to keep the fridge running. Frank placed a solar panel on the roof, and after securing it, plugged it in. "Should be right as rain." He tapped the side of the truck.

"I hope so," Maggie said. "We've still got Goddard Downs' beef in there." They'd need to stock up on other food items before they left Broome, but they'd vacuum-sealed as much steak as they could fit in the fridge before they left, and they still had plenty left.

"Trust me, love. It'll be fine. Now, let's grab our bags and check in." Opening the camper door, he stepped inside and passed their pre-packed bags out to her.

"It seems strange leaving the rig here and going into the resort. It's been our home for the past two weeks," she said, taking the bags from him.

"I did tell you we could camp."

"I know. But I'm looking forward to having a long shower and sleeping in a proper bed."

"And what's wrong with the bed in the camper?"

"Nothing at all. Other than being a little squishy."

"And what's wrong with that? We get to sleep closer to each other."

"It's fine until you start snoring."

"I don't snore."

She raised a brow. "Really? You snore like a freight train some nights."

"I'm sorry, love. I didn't used to. Maybe I should see a doctor."

"No, it's okay. It doesn't bother me that much."

"Good. But let me know if it does."

"Okay. But that aside, I'm also looking forward to not having sand and dirt in our bed for a few nights. That red dust gets into everything."

"I know it does. It's part of living in the top end, love. You know that."

"I do."

They reached the resort's entrance and joined the check-in line. Three other couples stood in front of them. "It's just as gorgeous as I remember from our honeymoon," Maggie whispered.

"And you're just as gorgeous as I remember, too." His eyes twinkled as he kissed her on the cheek.

"Frank..."

"I know. I'm sorry. I'll behave myself."

She chuckled as she rested her head on his shoulder. While they waited, they people watched. Families with children strolled by licking ice-creams, and a group of singles laughed as they headed to the bar. An elderly couple approached the concierge and asked a question before heading off in the direction he pointed. The resort had a tropical, laid back feel. Dotted through the reception area, tall palm trees stretched high into the atrium, creating a canopy of green. Baskets filled with lush green ferns hung from timber beams, and the sound of water trickling down a waterfall into a tropical fishpond completed the scene.

As they stood waiting, Maggie couldn't help but overhear the conversation the couple in front was having. They were in their late twenties or early thirties. She was blonde, while he had dark hair, and they were both dressed casually in shorts and T-shirts.

"This place is wonderful, Michael," the woman said. "We picked a great place to honeymoon." She was smiling brightly, her blue eyes reflecting her excitement, while her husband gazed at her adoringly.

"I wasn't paying much attention to the building. I was paying more attention to you," he replied, kissing her on the top of her head.

Her cheeks blushed a rosy shade of pink. "Michael."

"What? Can't I say that? You're my wife, after all. We waited five years for this."

"I know. It's just..." She couldn't finish her sentence. Her gaze darted around as she clung tighter to him.

Maggie smiled as she squeezed Frank's arm to get his attention.

He leaned down as she nodded to the couple and whispered, "Newlyweds."

He glanced at the couple and grinned. "He looks as anxious as I did when we came here for our honeymoon."

"Frank," Maggie said, smacking his arm lightly.

He chuckled. "What? I'd just married the woman I love. Wasn't I supposed to be anxious?"

Maggie felt her own cheeks warm. "Frank, you're incorrigible."

"No. I'm in love. As much now as ever before," he replied, gazing into her eyes.

She smiled. "I love you, too. Happy second honeymoon. Sorry, third." She winked as the woman in front turned around.

"Are you on your honeymoon, too?" she asked.

Maggie chuckled. "Kind of. Our second."

"This is our first."

"Jan, don't disturb them," her husband whispered.

"It's no trouble," Maggie assured. "When did you get married?"

"This morning. We flew here from Perth."

"Congratulations," Frank said. "Marriage is a wonderful institution."

"It is," the woman replied. "I'm Jan, by the way. This is my husband, Michael."

"Nice to meet you," Michael said as he extended his hand.

Frank took it. "A pleasure. I'm Frank, and this is my wife, Maggie."

"Nice to meet you," Maggie said, shaking Jan's hand first and then Michael's.

"Did you fly here, too?" Jan asked.

"No, we live in the Kimberley, so we drove. We live on a

cattle station, but we came to this resort for our first honeymoon, and since we're taking a road trip, we wanted to come here for old-time's sake."

"A cattle station? My great-grandparents used to own a cattle station in the Kimberley," Michael said.

"Is that so?" Frank said. "What were their names? Maybe I know them."

"The Emersons."

"Not Joseph and Amelia?"

"Yes. So, do you know them?"

"I do," Frank replied with a chuckle. "I used to visit their station when I was a boy. They were friends with my parents."

Maggie watched the exchange, and Jan listened as well, smiles spreading across both of their faces as Frank and Michael recounted their memories.

Jan drew closer. "Listen to them. It's like they're old friends."

"Mm-hmm. How long are you honeymooning?" Maggie asked.

"A week. We wanted to stay longer, but we're scheduled to go on a mission trip soon, and we still have a lot to prepare for."

Maggie's ears pricked. "A mission trip?"

"Yes, to the Sudan. It's the trip of a lifetime. I've always wanted to go, but Michael didn't want us leaving until we were married. He's been on several trips before, but this is the first time we'll be going on one together."

"That's wonderful," Maggie said. "I've met a few missionaries in my time, and I've always admired the commitment it takes to follow such a calling."

Jan's expression brightened. "I'm so happy to hear you say that. Most people think that being a missionary is just something good to do, but as you said, it's a calling, something the Lord puts on your heart."

The line moved forward quickly. There were three reception desks, each occupied by a female employee dressed in red. "You're up next," Maggie said, "but I'd love to hear more about your mission trip. If you and your husband aren't doing anything for dinner, would you like to join us? I know you probably want to spend time alone, being your honeymoon and all, but if you have time, I'd love to talk with you more."

Jan looked at her husband. "I'll talk it over with Michael. I'm not sure what he has planned. He likes surprises, so I'm sure he has something up his sleeve."

"That's wonderful," Maggie said with a grin. "My husband's the same. Why don't you check with him and then call our room and let me know? Reception can connect you."

"I'd like that," Jan replied. "I'll be sure to let you know. Michael, we're next."

"Sorry?" He was still engaged in a deep conversation with Frank, and both seemed oblivious to what she and Maggie had discussed.

"I'll tell you in a minute," Jan said. "It's our turn to check-in." She took her husband's arm and directed him to the desk, looking back at Maggie with a smile and mouthing that she would call.

"What was that all about?" Frank whispered as they shuffled forward.

"Just making dinner plans," Maggie answered.

Frank's brows arched. "Dinner plans?"

"Jan and her husband are going on a mission trip. I asked them to join us for dinner if they have time. I hope you don't mind."

"Not at all, but they're on their honeymoon. I'm sure they don't want to spend their first meal together with us."

Maggie shrugged. "We'll see."

"I can't believe he's Joseph and Amelia's grandchild," Frank mused. "I must have seen him at some point when he was young, but I don't remember him. He had a lot of questions about the station. I was telling him what's been happening and about the people who own the station now."

"What happened to the Emersons?"

"They passed away a few years ago, and the property was sold," he answered, setting their bags in front of the desk before addressing the clerk who'd just waved them over.

"Didn't the family want to keep it?"

"No." Frank said, shaking his head. "The children moved away a long time ago, and it was just Joseph and Amelia and the hands. It wasn't like us at Goddard Downs, where everything is run by the family."

Maggie nodded in understanding. It was unfortunate, but she understood. Their way of life wasn't for everyone.

MAGGIE SAT on the edge of her seat as she waited for Jan and Michael to arrive. She was overjoyed when the young woman had rung their room to say they'd join them for dinner that night. Maggie couldn't help but think that something was about to happen. She couldn't take their meeting as purely coincidental. There had to be more. Nothing about this trip so far had been arbitrary.

"There they are," she said as the couple walked in. She raised her hand and waved to get their attention.

Jan smiled and waved back. "Sorry we're late," she said as they approached the table.

Frank and Maggie stood to greet them. "It's no problem at all. We weren't waiting long."

"Have a seat," Frank said, extending his hand. Michael pulled a chair out for Jan before sitting.

"Thank you for inviting us. Jan insisted we come," he said.

She grinned. "What can I say? I had a good feeling."

"I did also," Maggie confirmed.

The two women smiled at one another. A waitress brought them menus and poured water into four glasses as they talked. The dining room was cosy but tropical with dark timber floors, cane furniture, and loads of green luscious plants.

The meal was wonderful, but the conversation was better. Maggie learned so much about life as a missionary—the joys, the heartaches, and the blessing of watching someone who'd never known Christ accept Him into their heart. Listening to Michael speak was invigorating. Frank seemed entranced. There was a light in his eyes as he sat with his back straight, his gaze fixed on Michael while he spoke of travelling to Asia and the Middle East. He'd seen a lot and experienced more.

"You're truly blessed," Maggie said when he finished another story.

"That's quite a life you've had," Frank said. "And to think you've just begun. And now that you have your bride at your side, I can only foresee more wonderful experiences."

Michael smiled, draping his arm around the back of Jan's chair. "They've already begun. Marrying her is the highlight of my life. I waited so long, and finally I can call her my wife."

Maggie looked at Frank as his hand clasped hers. "I know what you mean. I felt the same when I married Maggie."

She patted his hand. "Marriage is a wonderful adventure. A lifetime adventure as two become one. There'll be plenty of things to test the vows you made today. Some good and some challenging. You have to be resolute that no matter what happens, you'll stand for each other."

"We do already," Jan said, smiling.

"If you'd allow us," Maggie said, "Frank and I would love to bless you with a gift."

Obviously curious, the young couple glanced at each other before Michael replied, "Of course."

Nodding, Maggie deferred to Frank.

He pulled a small envelope from his top pocket and slid it across the table. When they'd arrived in their room and Jan called to say they'd join them for dinner, they'd immediately prayed about it and were moved to give the couple a gift to start their married journey.

"This is from us. May it bless you wherever you go," Frank said.

Michael studied the contents of the envelope and blinked. "But you don't know us. Why would you do this?"

"We prayed about it, and we're sure that this is what God would have us do, to bless your marriage and your work," Maggie said.

"We'd love to pray with you if you'd allow us," Frank added.

"That would be wonderful," Jan replied. "And thank you. This gift is so generous and kind."

"You're more than welcome," Frank said.

The four clasped hands at the table, indifferent to those around them. Frank raised a prayer of thanks to God and a blessing on the new couple. "Father, we thank You for creating marriage as the ultimate representation of Your love for Your church. As this couple walks the long road of love, marriage, and life together, we pray that they will always know Your love, protection, and faithfulness. We ask that You make their way straight and their course bearable as You take them through each season of life. As they go about fulfilling Your mandate to spread the good news of salvation, I pray that souls may be won, lives changed, and that they be blessed for the efforts they make for Your kingdom. May You continue to uphold them with Your righteous right hand and give them peace wherever they go. In Jesus' precious name. Amen."

"Amen," Maggie said in unison with Jan and Michael.

"Thank you again." Jan smiled at them both. "Your prayers mean a lot."

"We meant every word," Frank replied. "We wish you the very best."

Michael laughed. "God never ceases to amaze me. We came here to spend a week together and never expected anything like this."

"Neither did we," Maggie agreed. "But God always has a plan. We were here to have a honeymoon, but He wanted to bless You with a gift. We're just the people He chose to deliver it."

"God looks upon your efforts, and He knows your heart. He won't forsake you," Frank added.

Jan sniffled. "Thank you. You have no idea how much this means."

"Things have been difficult for us with getting everything together for the mission trip," Michael said softly. "Then you give us this gift. It's going to help so much."

Maggie smiled. It was a large gift in the eyes of some, but two thousand dollars was something she and Frank had and were more than willing to give. Money was a tool by which they could build people, lives, and the kingdom of God. What better use could there be for it?

"We hope it will help with your ministry," Maggie continued.

"God bless you both," Michael replied.

Maggie smiled. "Should we have dessert?"

CHAPTER 17

*a*lone in the kitchen in the pre-dawn gloom, snacking on cookies and chips because he couldn't sleep, Sean flexed his hand. He'd expected to feel euphoric now the cast was off. Instead, he felt strange. It had only been a few days since the doctor had removed it, but the arm didn't feel like his at all. Each time he looked at it he thought it belonged to someone else, as if a transplant had taken place underneath the plaster.

The doctor had warned him before it came off, but even so, his heart constricted when he saw that his strong, brown arm had been swapped for an insipid, pathetic imitation. The doctor had also cautioned him to take it easy. The arm was weak and would need time to regain its strength.

Sean flexed his hand again and swore at it. There was only one thing to do. Get to work and pummel the stupid appendage into submission. His arm would simply have to do what it was told.

He released a heavy sigh and finished the packet of chips. When the lights came on and Janella walked in, he blinked. *What time was it?*

She looked startled. "Sean. I didn't expect to see you here."

"Me either. Couldn't sleep," he mumbled.

She looked at him sideways. "What's the matter? Are you feeling alright?"

He shrugged. "Yeah. I'm fine," he lied.

"You don't look it," she challenged gently. She rested her hip against the counter. "You can talk to me, you know."

He looked up and frowned. In all the years he'd been on the station, only his uncle and Joshua had said that to him. Janella had never been cold or distant, she'd always been kind, but she was always busy.

Her brow wrinkled. "I mean that. You can talk to me."

He gave a nod and pushed to his feet. "Thanks, Janella. I'll remember that."

"Make sure you do. I'd chat now, but I've got to get break-fast going."

Exactly. "I'd offer to help, but I'm no good at that sort of thing. I can do beans in a can, but that's about all," he said.

"I'll remember *that*." She laughed as she crossed the floor and started to pull ingredients out, setting them on the counter before tying an apron around her waist.

"Don't bother cooking for me. I've eaten enough." He tossed the empty chip packet into the bin. "Plus, I'm heading over to Indigo this morning."

"Really? That's good. I can pack some food for the drive if you like."

"Nah, I'm good. I'm sure Josh will feed me when I get there."

"Okay. Safe travels."

"Thank you." He gave a smile and left the room. He was tempted to grab an hour or so of sleep before he headed out, but the sun was up, and he had a four-hour drive ahead of him. Sleep would have to wait.

He headed to his room and gathered his things. He still wasn't one hundred percent sure that Stella would welcome him, although Joshua had assured him she would. He figured he may as well go, because once the bridge started, there'd be no time for gadding about. Grabbing his keys from the nightstand, he headed out.

As he turned the key in the ignition of his truck and the engine roared to life, adrenalin surged through him. He put it into gear and slammed his foot down. For too long he'd been a passenger. How good it felt to be back at the wheel!

The trip didn't take four hours. He turned into the gates at Indigo Downs three and a half hours after leaving. He knew the roads well and enjoyed the buzz of being behind the wheel again. Some might say he was speeding. He'd say he was simply driving to conditions.

The gate, or what remained of it, was shut. He stopped the truck and jumped out. The gate was hanging, the hinges loose on the post. He carefully manoeuvred it open, forcing his pathetic excuse of an arm to do the work, climbed back in, drove through, jumped out again and closed it, then got back in again. If it hadn't been drummed into him how important it was to leave gates the way they were found, he wouldn't have bothered.

As the truck trundled along the dirt track towards the homestead, the state of disrepair shocked him. The sheds were leaning and only just standing, the holding pens were falling apart, and the equipment had seen better days. What was his cousin thinking, taking on something like this? The maintenance at Goddard Downs was nothing compared to what needed to be done here. He hoped Joshua hadn't bitten off more than he could chew. He also hoped his cousin had found some good help. Again, Sean felt a sting of rejection. Before, he would have been Joshua's first pick to help in his endeavours. He pushed the thought aside. He wasn't there to wallow; he was there to visit his cousin.

The homestead was much smaller than Goddard Downs'. What was left of the paint was peeling off, and the stairs appeared rickety and potentially dangerous. He was surprised Joshua hadn't made them safe.

Pulling up out front, he turned off the engine and climbed out, slamming the door behind him to announce his arrival. He felt strange standing there, a visitor to his cousin's home.

"Sean!" Joshua's face lit up as he opened the front door and carefully navigated the steps.

"Hey!" Sean replied with a grin, stepping forward to embrace his cousin. They patted each other on the back before parting.

"Glad you could come. What do you think of the place so far?"

Sean could hear the pride in his cousin's voice. He didn't blame him. He'd be proud if he owned his own station, even a rundown one like this. The place held potential. The location was great, and everything could be fixed in time.

He shoved his hands in his pockets. "It's uh... it's great!"

"Sean!" A female voice, sounding very much like Elizabeth's, called out from the verandah.

He peered over Joshua's shoulder and his eyes widened. It *was* her. "I...I thought you'd gone home."

She grinned and flicked her hair over her shoulder. "No. I'm still helping Stel turn this place into a home. There's a ton to do."

"Sorry, mate. I should have told you Liz was still here," Joshua said, grinning.

"Well, I'm glad you've got some help. Sure looks like you need it." Sean's gaze shifted to the stairs as he raised an eyebrow.

Joshua ran his hand across his hair. "Yeah. But you should see the inside. Between Liz and Stella, this place looks like a palace."

Sean struggled to believe that, but he soon discovered Joshua wasn't lying. The inside of the homestead more than made up for what lacked on the exterior. Each room had been freshly painted, and there were rugs and drapes in colours and textures, the likes of which had never graced the floors and walls of Goddard Downs. He had no idea Elizabeth and Stella had such an eye for interior design.

He glanced around. *Where was Stella?* Had she disappeared because he was coming? "Where's Stella?" he finally asked.

"She had to go to Kununurra. She'll be back a bit later. Hey, take a seat, mate. Can I get you anything? A drink or something to eat?" Joshua asked.

"I'm good, thanks," Sean replied as he took a seat at one end of the couch.

Joshua eased his tall frame into a large lazy boy and crossed his legs at the ankle.

Elizabeth flopped onto the other end of the couch, folding a leg beneath her. She wore brown knee-length shorts and a green top, and her hair was down and tousled and smelled like something floral. It was all he could do to keep his eyes off her.

She smiled, wagged her eyebrows. "So, what's going on? Did you do what I suggested?" she asked boldly. Her candour never ceased to amaze him. She was fearless in her speech. If only he could be as bold.

Joshua chuckled. "You're very blunt, aren't you, Elizabeth?"

"I don't believe in wasting time. We can't be sure of anything, so it's best to get things out of the way and dealt with sooner than later." She flashed a brilliant smile and eyeballed Sean. "Well, did you?"

He looked to his cousin for help, but none was forthcoming. Instead, Joshua sat there, grinning, the smirk on his face a tell-tale sign that he was butting out and leaving him to handle the matter on his own. "Yes, Sean. Did you do what Elizabeth suggested?"

Sean shot his cousin a sarcastic look. More than anyone, Joshua should know he wouldn't do what Elizabeth had suggested, even if it made sense to be more assertive. There was too much room for things to go wrong, and him winding up worse off than he was now. Everyone would think he'd taken some kind of drug if he tried putting himself out there. He was better off staying in the background. Being a nobody. It was easier to leave things as they were.

"You didn't." Elizabeth sighed with disappointment.

Joshua pushed up from his chair. "I'll leave you two to

discuss this. I have a few calls to make. I'll show you around the rest of the station later." He nodded to Sean, a grin still on his face as he left the room.

Sean stared at his cousin's retreating back with narrowed eyes. He didn't need to leave him alone with Elizabeth. Drawing a deep breath, he faced her. She was sitting with her arms folded over her chest, still eyeballing him.

"So...how are you enjoying your stay?" he asked, clearing his throat.

"It's great here. I love it. But you're avoiding my question." She lifted an eyebrow and pinned him with her gaze.

Unable to help himself, Sean laughed. "How do you do it?"

"Do what?" she replied, frowning.

"Live with so much energy. You're exhausting to watch. You know that, right?"

Her eyes grew wide. "I don't know what you're talking about. I'm just being me."

"Then I don't know how you do it. It must take every bit of energy in your body to be you, as you say."

She laughed lightly. "I'll take that as a compliment."

"I didn't mean it otherwise." A smile tugged at his lips. He didn't know what it was about her, but she possessed the uncanny knack of making him happy when he felt anything but.

She sat forward and rested her elbow on the couch's arm. Her voice lowered and her expression grew serious. "Sean, I know it's not my place, but I'm going to say this anyway. Life isn't going to serve itself up to you without any effort. If you won't take the leap of faith, you'll never see how faithful God can be."

He snorted. "God?"

"Yes, God," she stated firmly. "Why is it so difficult for you to believe in Him? He believes in you."

His mind went blank. He always had so many reasons why he couldn't and wouldn't believe in God, but for some reason, he couldn't think of any.

"You want to believe in Him, you just don't know how. Isn't that right?" Her brows quirked before the beginning of a smile tipped the corners of her mouth.

Again, he found himself at a loss for words.

She chuckled and unfolded her legs. "When you decide you're ready to acknowledge that your life isn't what you want it to be, and that there might be a way for it to be better, I'd be happy to help you."

"Liz," he said, reaching out and grabbing her hand.

Her eyes widened.

Their gazes held and something passed between them. He didn't know what it was, but boy, did her hand feel nice. Soft, smooth. His gaze travelled over her face and searched her eyes. "Feel like showing me around the station?"

She blinked. "Sure."

Gulping, he released her hand and pushed to his feet.

On their way out, they found Joshua hunched over his desk with the phone to his ear. He didn't even notice when they tried to get his attention from the doorway. Instead, they left him to his work and headed outside.

It was supposed to be the grand tour, but Sean saw less of the station and more of Elizabeth. Listening to her, he learned that Joshua and Stella had everything organised and planned down to the tiniest detail. Apart from the repairs that needed to be done, they were going to build larger holding pens to manage the new herd when it came, build a new workshop, and extend the house. That he hadn't been invited to be a part of Indigo's transformation saddened him.

"And here's where we're thinking of making a vegetable garden," Elizabeth said finally. The tour had taken them around the primary areas within walking distance of the main house.

"I'm sure it'll all be great," Sean said, trying to hide his jealousy.

"I think so. Stella's been wanting to make these changes for years, and now she's finally getting to turn this place into what she always wanted it to be. I'm happy for her. She's found her happiness."

Sean searched Elizabeth's face, noting the whimsy. The question jumped out before he had thought to retract it. "Have *you* found your happiness?"

The question seemed to take her by surprise as she looked at him mutely, blinking several times.

"Liz?"

After a moment, she replied, her tone serious. "Happiness is fleeting. You can have it today and not tomorrow, but when you have true joy, the kind you get from knowing God, it truly doesn't matter whether you're happy or not. Happiness comes from external things. True joy comes from within, and you can experience it, regardless of your circumstances."

Her words somehow resonated with him. It would be nice to know that whatever life threw at him, he could still feel joy inside, but it wasn't his reality, and it didn't answer his question. "You have a way of avoiding personal questions."

"I do?"

"Yes, you do." Sean nodded. "You said the same about me."

She chuckled. "Some things aren't about me."

"This is." He held her gaze.

She cocked an eyebrow and grinned. "Is it? I thought we were talking about you."

"You know what I mean."

"I do, but I repeat. This isn't about me. It's about you. Until you figure out what you want and make the efforts to get it, you'll remain in this state of limbo. You aren't stepping forward, but you know you can't go back, either." She angled her head. "You do know that, right?"

The question made him pause, but finally, he nodded. "Yes, I know I can't. My years on the rodeo circuit are over, and not just because of this." He rubbed his arm. "It's not what I want anymore. I just haven't figured out what it is I do want."

"Then you need to figure that out." She released a heavy breath and then smiled. "Come on, we'd better go in before Joshua starts looking for us."

CHAPTER 18

rank and Maggie's time in Broome passed far too quickly. During their week there, they'd taken leisurely walks along Cable Beach, enjoyed the glorious sunsets, took a camel ride, and dined at their favourite restaurants, but all too soon it was time to hit the road again. There were still plenty of other places waiting to be explored.

"I truly hope things go well for Jan and Michael," Maggie commented as they headed down the National Highway towards Port Hedland.

"I'm sure God has His hand on them," Frank replied, shifting down a gear to pass a large caravan towed by a large 4WD.

Maggie nodded and settled back in her seat. It was almost a ten-hour drive to their next stop, the Karijini National Park. "I think I'm going to take a short nap. Wake me if you see any wildflowers."

"Sure will." He squeezed her hand and then did his best to keep his eyes on the road. Unlike the Gibb River Road, this highway was sealed, but it was ever so boring. He could easily nod off. Not that he was tired. When he woke that morning, he felt invigorated and ready for anything, but a road like this would test anyone.

As Maggie slept peacefully, he embraced the silence and allowed his thoughts to wander.

They were only two weeks into the trip, but so far it had been perfect. Better than he could have imagined or hoped for. The Lord was blessing them in so many ways with the places they were seeing and the people they were meeting, but more than that, he and Maggie were growing closer. He hadn't thought he could love her any more than he did, but this trip was proving him wrong. He was falling deeper and deeper in love with her.

He glanced at her and smiled before turning on some country music to keep him awake. Kenny Rogers and Dolly Parton. Nothing better for a road trip. Soon, beads of sweat formed on his brow as morning turned to midday. It was a bright, cloudless day, the kind that scorched your skin and made your throat dry. He sipped some water from his bottle and cranked the aircon up. He'd rather have the windows down, but it was simply too hot.

Sometime later, he heard the change in Maggie's breathing, the soft hum of her stretching as she woke. "Had a good nap?" he asked, glancing her way.

"Great." She pulled up in the seat and smoothed her hair before reaching for her water bottle and taking a sip from it. "It's hot, isn't it?"

"Yep." Frank nodded. "The temperature tipped an hour or so ago."

She turned the blower on her side further in her direction and fanned herself with her hand. A short while later, she asked if she could change the music.

He cocked a brow. "You don't like Kenny and Dolly?"

"I didn't say that."

He chuckled. "You didn't have to. What would you like to listen to, my love?"

"How about some seventies soft rock?"

His eyebrows lifted. "Not Abba?"

"What's wrong with Abba?"

He shrugged. "Nothing, I guess."

"I actually like Abba," she said. "But I'm happy with some Fleetwood Mac or Billy Joel if that's more to your liking."

"Okay. Put on whatever you want."

"Thank you." She grinned playfully as she chose a CD from the case and inserted it into the player. Soon, she was bobbing her shoulders up and down and singing along to her favourite tunes, including some Abba songs. Despite himself, he joined in. It was like they were a young couple belting out the latest hits.

They stopped for a quick lunch at Port Hedland and then turned south on National Highway 95. Frank felt a little weary, so Maggie drove the last four hours to Karijini. She hadn't driven up until then, but he had full confidence that she'd manage the rig like a pro.

He was dozing when she tapped him on the arm. "Frank, there's someone walking along the road up ahead."

Straightening, he leaned forward and squinted. She was

right. A man dressed in muted colours carrying a haversack on his back was walking along the road in the direction they were travelling. "Slow down, love," Frank said. "Maybe his car broke down."

"I don't recall seeing one," she said, shifting down a gear. "Do you think he needs a ride?"

Frank rubbed his beard. Picking up strangers wasn't the safest thing these days. Once upon a time, people could be trusted, but now, things were different. People weren't as kind or honest.

Help him.

The voice was so familiar, like that of a good friend. Frank couldn't help the hint of a smile that spread across his face at the sound of it. He glanced at the man again, his decision made. "I think we should stop."

"I think so too," Maggie agreed. She continued on at a snail's pace until they drew level with the man, finally stopping just ahead of him. A wide-brimmed hat covered his eyes and half of his face as he trudged along.

Frank wound down his window and called out, "Excuse me."

The man walked to the window and looked in. Frank could see his eyes now. He was much younger than Frank had first thought, perhaps in his thirties or early forties, though he looked worn and weary. His clothes were covered in dust, and his cheeks were red from the heat. His lips were visibly chapped. "Yes?" he said.

"My wife and I are wondering if you need a ride."

The man narrowed his eyes, his gaze vacillating between

the road ahead and Frank. "I don't know. I think I'll be fine. Why do you ask?"

The question took Frank aback. "Why?"

"Yes, why? I've been walking this road for a long time. Plenty of vehicles have passed me, and not one of them stopped. Why did you?" The man shifted the weight of his haversack from one shoulder to the other. It was bursting at the seams and had been patched several times, and if Frank wasn't mistaken, one of the straps was shorter than the other.

"We just want to help," Maggie said, leaning across Frank. She smiled at the man. "You look as if you've been walking a while. Did your car break down?"

He shook his head. "I've been walking for a few months now. I'm on my way south, but thought I'd stop in at the National Park. They say it's beautiful."

"We've heard that, too," Maggie said.

Frank refocused his attention on the man. "We're headed that way. Why don't you jump in? Out here's a lonely place, and the sun isn't making it any easier."

Lifting his hat, the man wiped his brow with his arm. "It's a tempting offer."

Frank waited. If the man was going to join them, then it was up to him. He'd been obedient; the rest was up to the stranger. As he waited for the man's response, questions rolled around in his mind. *Why had God prompted them to stop? Was this one of those moments that could determine someone's future, either theirs or the stranger's?*

He watched the man carefully. Indecision and curiosity reflected in his eyes as he contemplated their proposal. Frank suspected he had similar reservations as he did about riding with strangers, but if this was of the Lord's doing, he was sure that the Lord would move him to accept, just as He'd instructed Frank to help.

"Why not," the man said with a small chuckle. "This is the hottest winter's day I've known."

Frank laughed. "We don't get winter up here, mate."

The man grinned. "Yeah, I know. I was just kidding. My name's Richard, by the way." He extended his hand to Frank through the window.

Frank shook his hand. "Nice to meet you. I'm Frank, and this is Maggie, and we have plenty of room. Your pack can go in the back."

Frank got out and opened the camper so Richard could place his pack inside. "You'll have to sit up front with us. There's only the one seat, but it's big enough for the three of us."

Frank closed the camper and climbed back in the cab, shuffling across the seat until he was beside Maggie.

Before he got in, Richard took his hat off and tapped it against his trousers. A small cloud of dust floated away on the breeze before he climbed in and sat between Frank and the door.

"Would you like some cold water?" Frank offered as Maggie put the truck into gear and pulled back onto the road.

"I'd love some," Richard said. "I haven't had cold water in weeks."

Frank lifted the small cooler onto his lap and poured some into a spare bottle and handed it to him.

"Thanks. You're too kind," Richard said before taking some greedy mouthfuls, a dribble of water leaking down his chin. He wiped it with the back of his hand and continued to gulp from the bottle until it was empty.

"Let me refill it," Frank said.

They'd driven only a short while before curiosity got the better of him. "You said you've been walking for months. How many, exactly?"

"This would be month six," Richard replied. "I'm planning on walking right around the country."

"Why?" Maggie asked, a little too sharply.

Frank glanced at her, and she quickly softened her tone. "What I mean is, how can you take such a long time to walk around the country. What about your family? Work?"

"I don't have any," Richard replied solemnly.

There was a story there, and a sad one, too, if his expression was anything to go by.

"I'm sorry," Maggie said.

"It doesn't matter. It was a long time ago."

"Is that why you decided to take this trip?" Frank asked.

"Something like that."

Frank didn't press further. No matter how much time had passed, whatever wound Richard had suffered, it was still very raw. It would do no good to force him to speak about it, although Frank had the feeling that he wanted to share. Was that why the Lord had put them together for this part of the journey?

FRANK AND RICHARD chatted the whole way. Maggie sensed that their meeting hadn't been random, but orchestrated by

God Himself, and so as she drove, she also prayed for them both. She prayed for wisdom and sensitivity for Frank, and an open heart for Richard. He hadn't revealed much about himself. Instead, he'd talked about the places he'd been to and the places he hoped to see, but underneath his bravado, she sensed an ache deep in his heart.

Arriving at the Karijini National Park two hours later, she knew instantly it was one of those places that would stay with her forever. Like an oasis in the middle of a desert, the red, layered cliffs lining the spectacular palm-filled gorges, and the vast open plains covered in yellow-flowering cassias and wattles, northern bluebells and purple mulla-mullas, took her breath away.

They found the campsite, a large area dotted with picnic tables and gas barbecues. With very little shade available, they chose a spot that looked across the carpet of wildflowers. Maggie couldn't wait to get her camera out.

Richard had a small tent which he set up not far from their camper. A little later, after they'd stretched their legs and organised their site, Frank stood beside him, arm around his shoulders, as they raised their glasses against the most gorgeous sunset Maggie had ever seen while she took snaps.

Richard joined them for dinner, and then at the campfire he'd helped Frank make. He seemed hungry for company, but Maggie sensed he wouldn't open up with her around, so after a short while, she yawned and excused herself. "I'm a bit tired. If you two don't mind, I think I'll turn in for the night."

"That's fine, my love. I think I'll stay up a bit." Frank gave a knowing nod, as if he'd read her mind.

"Good night, Maggie. Thanks for dinner." Richard smiled as she stood and folded her chair.

"You're more than welcome." She returned his smile.

After she stepped inside the camper and closed the door, she offered up another prayer for the two men sitting outside.

～

"I DON'T THINK I could ever tire of gazing at the night sky," Frank said, looking up as a star shot across the vast, inky darkness. With no city lights to compete with, the stars glittered like diamonds.

I agree," Richard said. "It blows your mind, doesn't it?"

Frank nodded. "It certainly does."

"My wife used to like looking at the stars."

"Oh?"

Richard sighed heavily. "Yes. Penelope was fond of camping. She was always taking photos, just like Maggie. She reminds me of her." His voice sounded wistful and sad.

Frank took a deep breath. This is what he'd been waiting for. A small crack in Richard's bravado. "When did she pass away?"

Richard raked his hand over hair. "Five years ago. She was in a car accident with our two children. A young, foolish boy, who thought that drinking and driving was no big deal, assumed he could get home safely after having a skinful." Richard stared into the fire. "He did go home a couple of days later with just a few bruises and a broken arm. My family didn't come home at all."

"I'm sorry to hear that. I can't imagine how painful it must have been."

"You get used to it," Richard replied, shrugging.

"Do you?" Frank asked.

Richard lifted his gaze. With just the flicker of flames providing light, it was difficult to be sure, but Frank thought his eyes were moist.

"No, I suppose not," he finally said.

Frank reached out and squeezed his knee.

They sat in silence for a few moments before Frank prodded further. "So, when did you decide to quit your life and start travelling?"

"The day after they died. My life had no meaning without my family. What did I have to live for?"

It was then that Frank noticed a scar peeking out from beneath the cuff of Richard's shirt. He couldn't imagine the despair that would drive someone to such a desperate act. Losing Esther had been difficult, but he'd never thought of ending his life. He still had too much to live for.

"There's always something," he said gently. Leaning forward, he carefully contemplated his next words before uttering them. "I lost my wife a number of years ago, but I still had my children and our station. Then I met Maggie, and I fell in love again. I never imagined I would, but when she walked into my life, it was as if God was saying, *I'm returning to you what was lost.* Like He did with Job."

Richard's response was hard, bitterness making his words sharp. "Don't speak to me about God. There's no such thing."

Frank straightened. "But there is. *He* is."

Richard scoffed. "Then where was *He* the night my family

died? Where was *He* when their lives were snuffed out? Tim was only four, Rebecca, one. Didn't they deserve the chance to grow up? And what about my wife? Didn't she have the right to see them grow into adults? I used to think that God was real, but after they died, I knew that He was just something people made up to make life easier to bear. But life isn't easy, and anything can happen for no reason at all. It's all chance. Nothing more."

Richard's voice had risen considerably, and a moment later, Maggie appeared at the door. "Is everything okay?"

"Everything's fine. Go back to bed, my love," Frank assured, rising to his feet and walking to the door. He kissed her forehead. "Get some rest. Richard and I are just talking."

"Are you sure?" she whispered.

He nodded and glanced in Richard's direction. He was drinking from his cup, his gaze fixed on the fire. "I'm very sure. I'll talk to you when I come in," he whispered back.

"Alright." Maggie was hesitant, but she turned and went back inside, closing the door behind her.

Frank returned to his seat. "God isn't to blame for their deaths," he said gently.

"Isn't He?"

"No, just the way He wasn't to blame for my late wife's or my son's death, just over a year ago."

Richard was silent for a moment. "How did they die?" he finally asked, his voice calmer.

Frank took a deep breath. "Esther drowned while saving our grandchildren. Julian died last year in a car accident."

"Drunk driver?"

"No. An angry one."

"And what happened to them? Nothing, right? And you say there's a God," Richard scoffed once more.

"The person responsible died."

"I bet you were glad."

Frank took a deep breath, a small sad smile on his face. "Actually, no, I wasn't. I could never be happy about someone's death."

"Not even when they killed your son?" Richard sounded confused, and there was a hint of disbelief in his voice.

"Especially then," Frank explained. "The person responsible was my son. He chose to get behind the wheel in a rage without any consideration for the turbulent weather we were having or our pleas for him to have restraint, and it resulted in his death. God didn't make him die. God gave him free will to make his own choices. He gives that to us all. And being a gentleman, He allows us to make our choices, but He's always there when we're ready to ask for help or guidance."

Richard shook his head. "And you really believe that?"

"I do," Frank replied. "I've lived long enough to know that God always comes through, even in ways we never expect. Because of the death of one of my sons, the other finally got his life together. This year, he got married, bought a station, and allowed our family's station to enter into a contract that will support us for a long time to come."

"So, you're saying that was God's plan all along, to kill your son so you can have all of that?"

Frank sighed, shaking his head. "No. You're missing my point. Julian made a choice, but God was able to turn that choice into something good, even though it didn't appear to be something good at the time. The Bible tells us that what is meant for evil or harm, God uses for good."

Richard set his glass down and got to his feet. "I think that's enough for me, Frank. I'm sure you meant this to be helpful, but I don't need it. I think I'll turn in."

Frank remained in his seat. "Okay. Good night, Richard."

He gave a short nod. "Good night to yourself."

"Richard," Frank called out as Richard headed towards his tent.

"Yes?" The younger man looked over his shoulder, his expression blank.

"You may not believe it, but God has a plan for your good. You just haven't begun to see it yet."

He didn't reply. He looked at Frank for several seconds before turning away and disappearing into the darkness.

Frank's heart was heavy. Had his words made any impact at all? Had he said too much, or too little? He'd hoped for another experience similar to what he'd had with Michael, but his talk with Richard hadn't gone that way. He'd been convinced that Richard would be open to hearing about God, especially since he was convinced that God had prompted them to stop and offer him a ride. *God, what are you up to?*

He sat around the fire a little longer but finally put it out and went inside. Maggie was waiting up for him.

"Everything doesn't always go as we expect, but God has a plan," she said when he told her what had transpired.

He nodded as he sat on the bed and pulled his socks off. "You're right. It's not up to us to convert people. We simply have to share our story. The rest is up to God."

"Yes. And you don't know what seeds might have been

planted in Richard's heart. You did what you felt led to do, and that's all that matters. Would you like to pray for him?"

He nodded. "That would be great."

They joined hands and Maggie began. "Dear Lord and Heavenly Father, we bring our friend Richard to you. Thank You that Frank was able to share with him about You, and we pray that his words might take root in Richard's heart, and that over time, he might ponder them and begin to look to You for healing and purpose. Lord, we thank You that you've opened our spiritual eyes and we have complete assurance of Your faithfulness, mercy and love. We trust that Richard's spiritual eyes might also be opened that He can see You and know with assurance that You love him and have a plan for his life, and that the loss of his family doesn't have to be the end of his story, that You can use this devastating loss for good if he allows You to. We pray these things in Jesus' precious name. Amen."

Frank squeezed her hand and smiled. "Thank you, my love. That was a beautiful prayer."

She returned his smile. "You're welcome. Now, come here, and let me give you a hug."

He chuckled as she slipped her arms around him and held him close. She knew exactly what he needed.

When they got up the following morning, Richard was gone. The only tell-tale sign that he'd been there at all was a note tucked into their door. Frank pulled it out and read.

Thank you for last night. I don't know where I'm headed, but maybe one day I'll meet God on the road. Take care. Richard.

Frank smiled as he tucked the note into his pocket. He'd

done what he'd been asked. It was now up to God to move Richard's heart and Richard to let Him in.

THE CORAL COAST was beautiful no matter where she looked. Maggie couldn't stop taking photos as they drove along this amazing stretch of road. The ocean was such a gorgeous colour, and there were so many places to stop at and simply take in the beauty of God's creation. Towns were few and far between, but they stopped at each for a day or two to explore and enjoy what was on offer. At Coral Bay, they snorkelled in the clear turquoise waters over the Ningaloo Reef. At Monkey Mia, they swam with dolphins, and when they reached Carnarvon, they lounged in the coral lagoon, enjoying the warm water with fellow travellers. On the second day there, they headed to the farmers' market where Maggie picked up jars of jams and homemade vinaigrettes to take back home, while she enjoyed chocolate-covered frozen mango as they strolled around. Frank enjoyed the homemade ice cream. That night, as they strolled along the one-mile jetty, holding hands and looking out over the ocean, Maggie couldn't help but feel a sense of peace.

"And Adam and Eve walked with God in the cool of the day," she said jokingly.

Frank took a deep breath. "You can feel Him here."

Her skin tingled with the thought. "What would it be like to walk side-by-side with God? I think it'd be exciting. I'd probably cry the entire time. I'd be so overwhelmed."

"Me too." Frank chuckled. He stopped and leaned against

the white rails, pulling her close. "But right now, you're here, and I can't think of better company."

She gazed into his eyes. Her husband's words had a way of making her cheeks warm and her heart flutter. "Frank Goddard, you are quite the man, do you know that?"

"I have an inkling," he said with a grin. "But I'm happy you think so."

"I do," she replied.

He pulled her closer, tucking some errant strands of hair behind her ear as he looked deeply into her eyes. "I love you, Maggie. With all my heart."

"And I love you right back."

CHAPTER 19

*W*hen Frank and Maggie entered Perth, the capital city of Western Australia, they felt like hillbillies. With its busy freeways, tall buildings and traffic, the city was such a contrast to the wide, open countryside they'd enjoyed over the past four weeks, so they were glad they'd chosen to stay near the coast rather than in the centre of the city.

Maggie helped Frank navigate the busy roads and freeways until they finally arrived at the caravan park at Gwelup. After the amazing campsites they'd been used to, the park felt cramped and confining, but it was simply a base to explore the city from.

It was Maggie's birthday, and Frank had booked a table at a restaurant in the city that Michael had told him about. Their dinner reservation was for seven. Thankfully, Maggie had packed an evening dress just in case something like this happened.

Her dress was black, with a V-neck and bodice that hugged her form and reached to her calves. The sleeves stopped at her forearms, and a tiny band of pearls marked the cuffs and hem. She enhanced the look with the ring Frank had bought her. She couldn't decide whether she should wear her hair up or down. Eventually, she decided on wearing it up. Finally, she was ready, but it wasn't quite time to leave.

She sat outside the camper and waited for Frank. He'd gone to the bathroom, but she expected him to be back already. Since when did a man take longer than a woman to get ready for an evening out?

The sun was already setting, and the sky was taking on a dark orange hue.

More time passed. Maggie grew anxious. Where was Frank? He should've been back by now. If he didn't get back soon, they'd be late.

He finally appeared, looking dapper in his dark suit and tie. Grinning, he presented her with a bouquet of red and white roses. "For you, my love. I'm sorry I took so long. The nearest florist was farther away than I thought."

Overwhelmed, Maggie took the bouquet and held it to her nose. "Frank, these are beautiful, but you didn't have to."

"No, but I wanted to. Now, if you'd put the flowers in water, our chariot awaits."

"Chariot? You mean, we're not taking the truck?"

"Nope. We're travelling in style tonight. I booked a limo."

Maggie blinked. A limo? "Oh, Frank. You really are spoiling me tonight."

He chuckled. "That's my plan." His eyes twinkled as she stepped closer and kissed him on the lips.

ELEGANT DIDN'T BEGIN to describe the restaurant. The carpet was thick and luxurious, complementing the rich, brown furniture and crisp, white tablecloths. Nearly every table was occupied, and the low murmur of voices and the clinking of silverware blended with the background music.

They were shown to their table which was right beside the window, giving them a spectacular view of the city and river. "This is the best table in the restaurant," Maggie leaned forward and whispered.

"I wonder if Michael had anything to do with it," Frank answered.

Maggie chuckled. "You never know. This trip has been anything but predictable."

"That's for sure," Frank said, sipping some of the water the waitress poured. He opened his menu and Maggie did the same.

Everything on it sounded mouth-watering. They made their selections, and the waitress came to take their order. They both had a salad as starters, then Frank chose the pork belly with smoky eggplant and confit tomatoes., while Maggie had the grilled fish with fried chat potatoes, tomato relish, and house-made parsley sauce. They shared a dessert.

"That was delicious," she commented, dabbing the corners of her mouth with the napkin.

Frank leaned back in his seat. "I second that." His brow furrowed a little and he rubbed his chest.

"Heartburn again?"

"Yes, some kind of indigestion, I think. I should have eaten something a bit more substantial earlier on. I saved up for too long." He grinned.

She leaned forward, reaching across the table for his hand. "Do you want to get some peppermint tea? It'll help."

He nodded. "That sounds great."

"I'll get the waitress."

"You don't have to, I can do it," he insisted. He raised a hand to get the waitress's attention.

Maggie rubbed his hand with her thumb and looked him in the eye. "I think you should get someone to check out your heartburn. It might be acid reflux." She'd wanted to talk to him about it for a while, but this was finally the right time. "I know you think it's nothing, but it's persisted for a long time now. I think you should see a doctor."

"I've already made an appointment, my love. I plan to go once we get back home." He coughed lightly, raising his fist to his lips and the other hand to his chest.

"Frank?" Maggie watched as her husband's expression changed from discomfort to one of pain.

"I don't feel so good," he said, his voice strained.

She got up and hurried to his side, her heart racing. She looked around to get someone's attention.

The waitress was already on her way and arrived a moment later. "Is everything alright?"

"My husband's not feeling well," Maggie said, trying to stay calm.

The young woman immediately became concerned and bent down to question him, but he could barely speak.

"Maggie," he groaned, trying to stand.

"Frank, sit down. I don't think you should be standing." It was too late. He was on his feet, but the next second, he fell. She watched in horror as her husband's face contorted in pain and his knees buckled beneath him as his body slumped to the floor.

"Frank!"

MAGGIE COULDN'T HEAR anything the people around her were saying. Her heart was beating so quickly she could hardly breathe. Her hands were trembling, and tears filled her eyes as the doctors and nurses wheeled the gurney with Frank on it behind the doors that she wasn't allowed to enter.

"Ma'am? Ma'am? I need you to help me. I need you to answer a few questions," a nurse with a clipboard said. "Please, follow me over here where you can take a seat."

Maggie couldn't think. She simply followed instructions, her mind drifting to the last time she'd found herself in a hospital under such upsetting circumstances. Serena had been the patient then, fighting for her life after the explosion in Paris. Now, it was Frank.

"Miss?"

"Missus," Maggie corrected. "Mrs. Goddard. My name's Maggie."

"And your husband?"

"Frank," she answered shakily. "Is….is he okay?"

"The doctors are with him now, Mrs. Goddard. They're taking care of him," the nurse assured.

Maggie nodded, but tears still trembled on her eyelids.

The nurse passed her some tissues.

She wiped her face and then began filling out the form. When she handed it back to the nurse, she glanced at the closed doors. It had been a while and no one had come to speak to her. "Does it usually take so long to get some news?"

"It isn't about time," the nurse explained. "A doctor will be out as soon as your husband is stable. There's just no knowing when that will be. I'm sorry."

Maggie nodded. She had no choice but to wait.

And wait.

While she waited, she put her face in her hands and poured her heart out to the Lord.

Who is like You, Lord God Almighty? You're the author and finisher of all things, and life and death are in Your hands. But I come before You humbly, asking for mercy. Lord, please spare my husband. I don't believe you brought us this far to have it end with Frank not making it. You took us on this trip. You brought us to this place. You wouldn't do that to end it here, so far from home and everyone we love. My husband loves You, and though we both wish to see You one day, not yet. Please, not yet. She blinked back fresh tears. *I'm not ready to lose him yet, Lord. I wish I could be braver, but I'm not.* She swallowed hard. *I need You, Lord. I need Your strength. I need You to save my husband. Touch the doctors' hands. Give them everything they need to save him, to find out what's wrong. They have their skill, but You are God, and God alone. What is beyond them, is not beyond You. I put my trust in You, Lord. I put Frank in Your hands. In Jesus' precious name. Amen.*

Finally, after what seemed an eternity, a woman in green

scrubs came out. Maggie's heart beat harder as she approached. *Did she carry good or bad news?*

"Mrs. Goddard?"

"Yes," Maggie answered, rising to her feet.

"I'm Dr. Greer. We've been able to stabilise your husband for now, but he's not out of the woods. We're running some tests to confirm exactly what happened and then we'll know what the next steps are."

Relief and fear simultaneously flowed through Maggie's body. Frank was alive, but only just. "Can I see him?"

"Not yet, I'm afraid. The tests will take some time to complete. Someone will come and get you once they're done."

"Thank you," Maggie replied. Her legs felt shaky, so she returned to her seat. She felt numb. How had this happened? They were supposed to be enjoying their three-month trip, not be in the hospital with Frank fighting for his life.

"Mrs. Goddard, is there anyone I can call for you?" the nurse asked, placing her hand lightly on Maggie's shoulder. "Your family, or someone close to you so you won't be alone?"

Maggie looked up blankly. She hadn't thought to call the family. Perhaps it was because they were so far away, and all she could think about was whether he'd be alright. She swallowed the lump in her throat. "Uh…our family. Everyone's at the station. There's no one nearby."

"Do you want me to call and ask them to come?"

"That's very sweet, but no, I'll do it," Maggie answered. "They need to hear it from me."

"Alright. I noticed you praying before. Hang in there. The Lord's with you."

Maggie smiled for the first time since she'd arrived at the hospital. "Thank you. I needed to hear that."

The nurse left, and Maggie was alone. She took her phone from her purse, her hands still trembling, and began to dial, but she didn't know who she was calling. She paused, tears once again filling her eyes as she finally thought of who to call.

She closed her eyes as the phone answered. "Joshua, are you sitting down? I have something to tell you."

CHAPTER 20

*W*as there a stampede? The sound of thudding woke Sean from what was a good dream. In it, he was at Indigo Downs, driving a herd of cattle to new grazing ground, but Joshua wasn't the owner. He was.

He rolled out of bed, groggy and disoriented. He'd stayed up all night with Sasha watching movies. She'd dragged him into a marathon of nineties teenage chick flicks, which he surprisingly enjoyed, though he'd never admit it. Alicia Silverstone was a crush of his back in the day, but that was another thing he wouldn't admit.

As he stood, the noise from the rest of the house didn't lessen. He glanced at the clock and frowned. It was one in the morning. What was with all the noise? What on earth was going on?

He quickly pulled on his jeans and headed towards the voices. He was met by a frantic-looking Olivia and an equally perplexed-looking Nate. He stopped him with a hand to the shoulder. "What's going on? Why's everyone up so early?"

Nate looked him in the eye. "Joshua just called. Something's happened to Frank. He's in the hospital in Perth."

Sean's heart faltered. "What...what did you say?"

"Something's happened to Frank."

"Like what?" Sean asked. Saying something had happened to Frank was so vague. *Had he suffered an accident? Was he sick?*

"We don't know exactly. Joshua said that Maggie told him he had discomfort in his chest at dinner last night, and then he collapsed. They rushed him to the hospital, but they haven't been able to identify the cause yet. They're running tests."

Sean couldn't speak. He couldn't imagine anything happening to Frank. His uncle was strong and healthy, the backbone of the station. Something couldn't happen to him. It just couldn't.

Olivia tripped and stumbled against a table. She uttered a word Sean had never heard her say before.

"Liv?" Nate called, rushing to his wife's side. Following, Sean stood silently as Olivia's complaints of pain turned to tears, then sobs.

"Nate, not my dad," she moaned against his shoulder. "Not my dad."

Nate held her tightly, stroking her hair as he comforted her. "It's alright, Liv. Your dad's a strong man. I'm sure that whatever's happened, he'll be fine. Wait and see. I'm sure that by the time we get there, he'll be as right as rain, and he'll be able to come home."

"What if that isn't the case? What if..."

"Don't think like that," Nate interjected. "You have to believe he'll be okay."

"He'll be fine," Sean said boldly, his gaze on Olivia.

Everyone in the room looked at him as Janella and David walked in. "Uncle Frank isn't the kind of man who just…" His words faltered, but only momentarily before confidence he hadn't felt before surged through him. "Uncle Frank will be back home soon, but until then, we need to make sure everything's in order."

"I don't…"

"I'll deal with everything," Sean interrupted. Olivia was in no position to handle anything. He'd never seen her in such a state, and he didn't like it. Janella also looked stricken, and he understood why. It wasn't that long ago she'd lost Julian, and before that, her mother-in-law. The family couldn't take another loss. *They won't.*

"Is Joshua coming?" Janella asked.

"He and Stella are going straight to the airport," Nate answered.

"I'll call the airline," Sean said. "You guys need to get to Perth as soon as possible. You should start packing." Everything happened quickly. It was as if there was a script in his head that he was following. He'd organised so many trips for Joshua and himself that he was moving on instinct now. His family needed him, and for the first time since his return to Goddard Downs, he was in a position to help.

Janella woke Sasha to tell her the news. His young cousin broke into tears and wept for not only her grandfather but her father, too. It was a pitiful sight. Her sorrow tugged at his heart and made his eyes sting, but he refused to give in to it. They needed him to be strong, and he would be.

By the time they'd packed, he had all of the arrangements made. E-tickets were booked and waiting for them at the airport in Kununurra.

"Sean, are you sure you're going to be okay here?" David asked. Oliver was asleep on his shoulder while Serena was helping Janella calm Sasha.

"I'll be fine. I know what I'm doing," he replied. "Besides, I can't help there. Uncle Frank and Maggie need you guys with them. Someone has to take care of the station while you're gone."

David patted his shoulder. "You're needed, too. You know that, mate."

Sean's confidence spiralled upwards. "Thanks, David."

"Don't mention it," he replied with a smile.

The family gathered in the living room. They were all in varying states of shock, dismay, and fear. It felt strange being the one who was steady under such circumstances. "Alright, let's go over everything. I've booked the tickets. Your flight departs at seven, which doesn't leave much time. The fastest way to get to the airport is by helicopter. Dan's ready to take the first load of passengers and will come back for the rest. You should make it in time."

"What about the children?" Serena asked. "Were seats booked for them as well?"

"I figured you'd take Oliver, but he doesn't need a seat. He'll sit on your lap."

She nodded, a look of relief on her face. "Thank you."

"What about Issie and William?" Olivia asked. She was

calmer now, although her nose was red, and her eyes were puffy from crying.

"I should have checked, but I thought they should stay here since you'll be at the hospital most of the time. Sasha can help with them, but I also thought that since Stella's cousin Elizabeth is still staying at Indigo Downs, she might come here and help. I took the liberty of calling and asking her, and she said, of course, she will. I'll do what I can, but I don't have much experience with children. They'll be fine with her."

"But I want to go," Sasha said, bursting into tears again.

Janella spoke to her quietly. Whatever she said worked because Sasha nodded her head and dried her tears.

"What about the construction?" Olivia interjected. "When we see Dad, he'll want to know what's going on."

"I can handle that, too," Sean assured her with a smile. "I've been a part of it from the start. I know what needs to be done. You don't have to worry, Liv. I can handle it. Tell Uncle Frank that when you see him. Tell him that things are being taken care of here."

His cousin was worried about her father, but she was also worried about the station. There was so much going on that needed overseeing. Usually, she would be the one to do that. She liked to be the one making sure everything was going to plan, but right now, nothing in her life was going as planned. She'd never expected to get a call saying her father was in the hospital in Perth, three-thousand kilometres away. None of them did.

Sean strode to the front door and opened it. "If no one has questions, the first group should be leaving."

CHAPTER 21

*E*lizabeth was a woman of her word. Within five hours of Sean calling for help, she'd driven through the night and arrived at Goddard Downs ready to care for William and Issie. Watching her was amazing. She stepped into her role without so much as the bat of an eyelid. The children took to her immediately as Sean had no doubt they would. People liked Elizabeth. Being warm and open was a gift she possessed. One he'd experienced the first day he'd met her. Her God-talk was a bit annoying at first, but that soon faded once he realised it wasn't a pretence with her. It was the real thing. *She* was the real thing. But what about him? Was he the real thing, or was he a fraud?

The morning after she arrived, he woke with a thundering heart, a nightmare having given him a fitful sleep. Blood throbbed in his ears. He'd never been responsible for anything of significance in his life. Now, he was in charge of the entire station and the construction of the bridge. It was a lot for anyone to handle, and despite his bold speeches, fear and reservation gripped him now.

He raked his fingers through his hair, his mind racing with everything he had to do. There was no time to waste. He had to be up and ready for when the men arrived with the pile driver and other equipment, and for the first morning in a long time, he was starving.

After a hot shower, he made his way to the kitchen for breakfast. Elizabeth was a good cook, much better than he imagined. He would even say she was on par with Janella, though her menu was different.

"Good morning, Sean," she said as he walked into the kitchen. She was sitting at the table with William on her knee as she, Sasha and Isobel ate their breakfast.

"Good morning. What smells so good?" He walked to the stove to take a look.

"I made mini bacon and egg quiches. I thought you might want something easy to take with you. There's also overnight oats in the fridge and some French Toast in the oven. I took the liberty of fixing you a flask with coffee and another with juice. They're on the counter."

Sean blinked. No one had ever taken care of him so thoroughly before. He almost forgot how to say thank you. "Thanks, Elizabeth. You didn't have to do all of this."

She grinned as she took a bite of toast. "It was no trouble. I wanted to make things easier for you. I know it's a big day."

He lifted his gaze and met hers. It was difficult to define what was in her eyes. Sometimes he'd seen hope in his uncle's eyes when he looked at him, but this was something different. Something deeper.

Don't think of it. Don't you even dare. This isn't the time, and she isn't the kind of woman who would ever consider it. Would ever consider you. She's far better than you and you know it. Don't do that to yourself.

He cleared his throat. "I should get going. Have you seen David?" he asked as he grabbed a small cool box from the cupboard and packed a bit of everything into it. Serena's husband was originally accompanying the family to Perth, but at the last minute it was decided he should stay because he was more familiar with the workers than Sean.

"I'm right here," David replied from the doorway. "Pack a few of those for me too, will you? I'm starved already."

"I fixed some flasks of coffee and juice for you, too," Elizabeth said.

Sean's heart sank. It had felt good thinking she'd prepared something special for him; now he knew she hadn't. *Keep your mind away from those thoughts. You're making something of nothing. Nothing is ever going to happen between you and her, so just get that out of your head.*

"Everything's packed," he said to David. "We need to get going if we want to be there to meet the men and get this thing started." They were due to meet the workers onsite at seven, and it was already twenty minutes to.

"Have a good one, Elizabeth," David said, taking the container from Sean and raising a hand to her.

Sean glanced in her direction as he headed out the door. "See you later."

"You sure will," she said, her mouth curving into a smile that sent his heart racing.

The walk to his truck was a silent one as he tried to focus

on what was important, but other thoughts still lingered. How was his uncle doing? And how about everyone else? It seemed strange that they were so far away.

But the most pressing question was whether he would make good on his promise to take care of the station. He could still see the look in his uncle's eyes as he spoke to him on the day he left. The responsibility was huge.

Reaching the truck, Sean squared his shoulders, pulled the door open, and climbed in. Uncle Frank believed in him. Trusted him. He would get this done. He had to. When his uncle came home, he would see how good a job he'd done and be proud of him.

Sean turned the key and headed to the site. He barely saw the scenery as he drove.

"You okay, Sean?" David asked.

"Yeah. Of course. Why'd you ask?"

"Your uncle's in the hospital, and now you're responsible for all of this. That could take a toll on a person."

Sean turned and met his gaze. "You don't think I can do it?"

"No, that's not it at all. I'm sure you can do anything you set your mind to. Frank wouldn't trust you to help run the station if he didn't think so, and if I've learned anything, it's that Frank has good judgment."

Sean didn't know what to say. David's words only made him more determined to make his uncle proud. There were few people in his life he looked up to, and even less who cared about what happened to him. His uncle was top of that list. If there was anything he could do to deserve his trust and confidence, then he would do it.

"You're sure about these guys, David?"

"Very," he replied.

"I want to get this done before Uncle Frank gets back," Sean said, his voice shaky.

"We can try. There's no telling when he'll be back home," David answered solemnly.

Sean didn't like David's tone. "He *is* coming back. And soon," he asserted. He said it with all the confidence he could muster, but was he lying to himself? He shifted gears and the truck leaped forward.

When they arrived at the site, all was quiet. The men weren't there, and a wave of panic washed over him. "Where are they?"

David checked his watch. "They're just late. They'll be here."

"How can you be so sure? We can't waste time on this," Sean said, his voice tense.

"I know these guys. I trust them. They don't fail. They don't know how to. Neither do I, mate. We'll get this done. Your uncle will be happy when he sees the bridge is finished, and you'll get the credit for it."

"I don't care about the credit. I want to get this done for him."

David leaned back in his seat and inspected his fingernails. "I want to see it done, too. Frank's been nothing but good to Maggie, and that means the world to Serena." He lifted his gaze and met Sean's. "Not just that, he's been good to me. If it wasn't for him taking the time to talk to me and help build my confidence and faith, I don't know that I'd be where I am now."

Sean pursed his lips. "He tried that with me, but I never took the time to listen." He drew a deep breath. "Maybe I should have."

"There's still time," David replied.

Sean narrowed his eyes. "I hope so."

"There is. I believe that. God isn't ready for Frank Goddard to go home yet," David affirmed with an assuring smile. He placed a hand on Sean's shoulder, and for some reason, it relaxed him.

"I wouldn't know what to do if he didn't make it," Sean admitted. "Uncle Frank is the one person who never lost faith in me. You don't understand what it meant to me when he let me come back to the station after everything I did. I was a real jerk about Joshua getting married. I threw a man-sized tantrum. I was so stupid, but he didn't care. He forgave me when others wouldn't."

David chuckled. "That sounds like Frank. From what I've seen of him, he keeps the Word of God close to his heart and it reflects in his actions. I would have expected him to forgive you."

Sean frowned. "Why's that?"

"Because the Lord says we need to forgive because we've been forgiven. It's a bit hypocritical to have God forgiving us what we've done, if we're not willing to forgive those who've done things to us."

"I guess," Sean said, lowering his gaze.

"Is there anyone you need to forgive?" David asked gently.

Sean's nostrils flared as he inhaled deeply. Did he have people to forgive? The better question was, who didn't he have to forgive? His father. His mother. Himself. The list was longer than his arm. He'd spent most of his life rubbing people the wrong way. It was how he got through life. He'd spent so much time pushing back, forcing people out, and he couldn't stop himself. Then Joshua got hooked up with Stella and everything fell apart. He'd pushed the last person who understood him right out of his life because he wanted something different than they'd planned. "I was a real jerk," he repeated in a whisper.

"Not anymore," David replied.

Sean met his gaze. "I think it might be too late to build bridges."

David smiled. "It's never too late. Seasons change in our lives, and we have to change with them. It simply makes it harder when we resist."

"Did you have to change?"

David nodded. "I did."

Sean blew out a long breath. "I feel like I've been stuck for a long time. I want things to be different, but I just don't know how to make that happen."

"It's not easy, but you can do it. I can help."

"Why would you do that?" Sean's brow knitted. David barely knew him. Why would he want to help him?

"Your uncle barely knew me, and he helped me find my way when I was confused. Why can't I do the same? Pay it forward."

"What do I have to do?" Sean asked, unable to hide the hope in his voice.

"Let go of your pre-conceived ideas and accept the hand that's open to you."

The wrinkles on Sean's brow deepened. "What hand?"

David smiled. "God's."

Sean would usually have laughed at such a statement, but he couldn't bring himself to. He was tired of laughing at comments like that. Everyone around him had their lives under control. He didn't, but the common denominator they all had was God.

"I don't think God wants to hear me," he said. "I've laughed Him off too many times."

"Sarah laughed when she was told she was going to have a baby in her old age. God didn't reject her. She remained faithful, and He kept His promise."

Sean grinned apathetically. "Sorry, I don't know the story."

David smiled. "You should check it out sometime, and while you're at it, check the Book of Hebrews. It's all about faith."

"I don't have much of that," Sean admitted. He lifted his gaze to the horizon and saw a small cloud of dust. It was probably the team coming to work on the bridge; there wasn't any reason for anyone else to be arriving. He bit his lip. "You pray much?"

"A lot more than I used to," David answered.

Sean faced him. "Do you think we could pray for my uncle?"

David smiled as if he were expecting the question. "Of course."

"Let's do it. Let's pray for him. What do I do?"

Again, David smiled. "Close your eyes."

Sean glanced at the growing cloud of dust. It was getting closer. He closed his eyes, anyway. It was a strange feeling, a vulnerable one, to sit with someone and not see anything, to leave yourself exposed. Then David started to speak, and the discomfort he felt began to melt away.

"Lord, we give You thanks that today one of Your children

is coming to You on behalf of his uncle. Heavenly Father, we entrust You to take care of Frank. He's Your faithful servant, and we know You love him. We ask You to be with him, to heal him and bring him home to the station and his family, safe and well. Lord, I also ask that You give peace to Sean, and that You'll open the eyes of his heart that he might see You. In Jesus' precious name. Amen."

"Amen," Sean repeated in a whisper.

"Sean," David said, but the roar of engines interrupted him. The cloud of dust was no longer just a cloud. Heavy machinery and trucks emerged through it and stopped.

"They're here," Sean said, shoving the door open. He jumped down and slammed the door behind him, his heart thudding. He could do this. He'd show his uncle that he hadn't wasted his time believing in him. He'd prove to Uncle Frank that the time he'd expended on him wasn't in vain. He'd make him proud.

CHAPTER 22

*J*anella didn't like the hospital. The smell of antiseptic permeated everything from her hair to her clothing. She'd stood at the entrance for several minutes before forcing herself to go in, a prayer on her heart with every step she took. She wanted to see Frank and prayed that all would be well. Still, in the back of her mind was the lingering memory of the last time she'd walked into a hospital and the tragic results. The memory would have consumed her if not for Olivia. Her sister-in-law was beside herself. Janella had never seen her like this before, but she supposed everyone had a breaking point. Janella always presumed that through the loss of her mother and her brother Julian, Olivia had done her best to remain strong for her father, but now that his life was at risk, she was crumbling.

"Liv," Janella said, moving to stand beside her and placing a comforting hand on her shoulder. "He's going to be all right. I know he will."

Olivia placed her hand over Janella's. "Nella, I..." She was unable to finish her words.

That was something Janella had never witnessed before. A speechless Olivia was a rare thing.

Maggie, who sat nearby, looked over with puffy eyes and a red nose. They probably all looked the same. Janella had cried her tears on the way there, but once she arrived, she collected her emotions. She steeled herself for whatever they had to face. Whatever lay ahead, they would get through it together as a family. They needed to be strong for Frank. He needed them and their prayers. Tears could only do so much.

"Frank is a strong man, and he'll get through this. Whatever it is," she assured Olivia.

Olivia squeezed her hand tighter. "Nella, I can't lose Dad, not after Mum and Julian. I just...I can't," she whimpered. A second later, her shoulders shook, and fresh tears rolled down her cheeks.

"Liv," Nate called out as he hurried towards them. He'd gone to check on Frank's condition with the nurses and was now returning from their station around the corner.

Janella held her breath but he had nothing to share. He focused his attention on his wife. Cupping her face in his hands, he looked her in the eye. "Don't do that to yourself. Your dad's going to make it."

"Nate," she sobbed as she leaned forward and hugged him tightly.

Janella stepped back. It was good that Olivia had her husband there. She would have given anything to have Julian with her now. Her husband had been strong and supportive.

He'd always been in control and took on the brunt of things himself.

Tears stung her eyes, but she held them in. There was no bringing Julian back. *And tears won't help Frank.*

"Mrs. Goddard?" A female doctor in a long white coat stepped into the waiting room and looked around.

Maggie stood immediately. Janella rushed to her side, eager to hear what news there was on Frank's condition.

"Dr. Greer, how's Frank?" Maggie asked, her tone anxious.

"We've completed our tests and he's resting comfortably," the doctor replied. She smiled at Maggie and then glanced at Janella and the others who'd joined the group before she returned her focus to Maggie. "We've determined the cause of your husband's complaints."

Maggie stepped closer. "Yes. What…what is it?"

"He has a defective heart valve. He's going to need a replacement," she explained. "And quickly."

Maggie was quiet for a moment, only the blinking of her eyes indicating that she was even listening. "How soon?"

"As soon as possible," the doctor replied. "There are some decisions you'll need to make when he comes fully around."

"When will that be?" Maggie asked.

"A few hours, perhaps. He's drifting in and out of sleep at the moment. The condition makes him tired."

"Yes," Maggie said. "When we were hiking, he was really tired. He seems to have been tired a lot recently, and he's also been complaining about his chest. I thought it was heartburn. We both did. He was making plans to see a doctor when we got home."

"Why didn't you say anything?" Olivia asked through tears, her tone accusatory.

Maggie looked at her sadly. "We thought it was nothing."

Olivia was on her feet. "But it wasn't," she cried. "It wasn't."

"All right, Liv. This isn't helping," Nate said, standing with Olivia and holding her close.

She looked at Maggie as more tears rolled down her cheeks. "Maybe there was something that could've been done before now."

"He wouldn't have known what was wrong until he sought medical treatment," Dr. Greer said. "There's no way of identifying heart failure without proper medical investigation. It can easily be seen as simple fatigue, or heartburn, or atypical chest pain—a very common occurrence. There was nothing anyone could have done to prevent this."

"Okay." Maggie nodded. "What happens now?"

"Your husband will need a replacement valve. There are several options to choose from, both organic and inorganic. An organic replacement will require a new valve being put in every ten years, while an inorganic valve can last for the rest of his life."

"You mean if he gets the organic one, he'll have to have heart surgery again?" Maggie asked.

"Yes. Approximately every ten years for the rest of his life."

"That seems a lot," Joshua said, stepping closer.

"It can be, but some individuals prefer to have a valve crafted from living tissue rather than synthetic. It's a matter of preference," Dr. Greer answered. She turned back to Maggie. "We'll go through the options at another time when you and your husband can be together and I can give you more details. In the meantime, you can go in and see him."

Maggie smiled. "Thank you, Dr. Greer. God bless you."

"It's my pleasure. I'll check in with you a little later." She gave a nod and walked away, leaving the family standing together in shock.

Maggie was quiet. She lowered herself into a nearby seat and clasped her hands in front of her. "How can this be happening? We were having such a wonderful time travelling. I don't understand."

"It's okay, Maggie," Janella replied, rubbing her back. "We don't always know why things happen, but God can make all things work for good, and ultimately, He's in control." She tried to sound confident as she sat beside her.

Maggie nodded. "I know He is. I just don't understand how this happened. Frank was fine. He was a bit tired, but it wasn't serious. We never thought it would be something like this."

"At least we can see Dad," Olivia said with a sniffle. She looked at Maggie. "I'm sorry for my outburst. I was really upset."

"It's fine, Olivia. It was a shock for all of us," Maggie replied with an understanding smile. "But we have more important things to think about right now. Your father needs us to be strong. He needs our prayers more than anything else. I think we should do that before any of us see him."

"I agree," Joshua added. "Dad doesn't need to see us worried. He would expect us to go to God about it, just like he would."

"You're right," Olivia agreed, blowing her nose. "Let's pray for Dad."

The family formed a circle as they stood in the long, white corridor of the hospital. Clasping hands and bowing their heads, they prayed in unison for Frank, each one expressing their love for him and their desire for his healing.

Once their prayers were said, Maggie and Olivia were the first to go in to see Frank while the rest of the family waited in the corridor. They sat together quietly, but Janella couldn't sit. She was too anxious, so instead, she paced. Back-and-forth across the corridor she walked with her arms folded over her chest and chin dipped.

Being there revived all the feelings she'd hoped to have put aside. The days she'd spent at Julian's bedside praying for him to recover flashed vividly across her mind. The hours spent in that sterile place, the beeping machines, the announcements over the PA system, and the myriad of nurses who came in to check on him every half hour. Julian was surrounded by people with skill and experience, but they couldn't save him. Once God decided his time was up, there was nothing anyone could do.

Lord, I don't know Your thoughts for they are far above mine, but I pray that this time You will answer our prayers and save Frank. I know that You never do anything out of spite but out of love and justice. You wanted Esther and Julian with You, for their passing served a greater purpose in bringing this family together. But Lord, I can't see how Frank's death would help. I don't think it would, but not my will, but Yours be done.

Tears stung her eyes, and before she knew it, they were rolling down her cheeks. She took a ragged breath and tried to blink them away, telling herself not to cry, but it was useless as thoughts of her late husband overwhelmed her.

"Nella?" Joshua called. He stood and walked towards her.

"Yes?" she answered, wiping her eyes with the back of her hand.

"Come here," he said, pulling her into a hug. He held her firmly as her body began to shake, and the tears she'd suppressed surged forward.

"I'm sorry," she apologised. This moment wasn't about her. She almost felt selfish allowing Joshua to comfort her.

"What are you apologising for? You didn't do anything," he replied, stroking her hair.

"I shouldn't be crying like this," she said. "We need to be strong."

"It doesn't mean we stop feeling," he replied. "Dad wouldn't want that. He'd want us to feel and let it out in a healthy way. You've spent so much time trying to hold in everything since Julian died. You threw yourself into work and your kids instead of letting yourself grieve. I guess we all did that in one way or another. It works for so long, but it can't last forever."

She hugged him. "Oh Josh, I'd hoped to never come into a hospital again," she admitted. "I can't stop thinking of Julian since I got here. He was in so much pain. His body was so broken after the accident, but he held on until you came. He held on until you two made things right between you."

"That, he did," Joshua said, and Janella could hear the sadness in his voice. When she looked up, a small smile was on his face. "I'm glad we were able to settle things between us, to be brothers again, even if it was only for a short while. I'm also glad we're with Dad now."

"He isn't going to leave us, Josh. I know he isn't. God's plans are greater, and though I don't understand them, I believe that taking your father isn't a part of them." She stepped back to look him in the eye. "God is faithful, and His love is everlasting. I'm sure He has a plan."

Joshua nodded. "I know He does. I'm going to keep faith that He will see this to a happy end. Maggie needs Dad. We all do. We aren't ready for him to go, and the doctor said that with the surgery, he'll be fine." He smiled. "Besides, Dad can't go until he meets his new grandchildren."

Janella's eyes widened. "Are you and Stella expecting?"

"No." He chuckled. "But someday, maybe soon. He can't leave until then. Not yet." He hugged her again, and Janella rested her head on his chest. She was glad for Joshua, for his friendship and love. She needed that now. He represented that friend who was closer than a brother, as if the Lord Himself was hugging her. However, there was something that Joshua's hug wouldn't solve.

Now that they knew Frank's condition, she could imagine what his recovery would be like. Heart surgery was no walk in the park. He may be unable to function for some time, and even then, it may not be to the level he was accustomed to. She couldn't leave Goddard Downs now. It was impossible. With Frank incapacitated, everyone would have to wear multiple hats until he was back on his feet. They all had to pull their weight, and that meant she needed to be there, in the kitchen, making sure everyone was fed and taken care of in the only way she could. Leaving now would be selfish. Frank had been there for her for so many years. She would be there for him now.

Joshua left her a few minutes later and returned to Stella. They looked happy together, even in this period of stress. Janella took a seat and watched them for a while before her thoughts began to once again overwhelm her.

The decision to stay at Goddard Downs wasn't a difficult one to make. Despite her desire to pursue her certificate at culinary school, some things were more important, namely, Frank and the family. She'd have to console Sasha, who would be very disappointed. Her daughter was so looking forward to moving and starting a new school in Darwin. She was sorry she'd have to let her down, but it couldn't be helped. She was sure, once Sasha knew her reasons, she'd accept that she'd have to continue with the School of the Air until she could attend boarding school, like Caleb. The thought of her son made her stop. She hadn't called to tell him what had happened to his grandfather. She'd wanted to wait until they had something more definitive to tell him. Now, she'd have to make that call. She checked her watch. He'd be in class. She'd have to wait until the afternoon to call him at the dorms. Unsure as to how he would take the news, she could only pray that he'd take it well.

Lord, please let Caleb handle this news. He and Sasha shouldn't have to deal with so much at their age, especially after experiencing what they did with their grandmother, so I ask for a special measure of protection over them both. I know You have them in Your hands, and that You'll take care of them, but Father, please give them peace. I wish You could hold me and hug me and tell me everything will be all right. I need Your comfort, Lord.

As if answering her prayer, a wave of calm settled over her

as she sat alone, staring at her clasped hands. Come what may, she would trust the Lord. If He wanted her in Darwin, He would make the way. If not, He would withhold it. Either way, she trusted God's judgment over her own. She trusted His love over her logic.

CHAPTER 23

*W*hen Frank woke in the hospital, dazed and tired, it had taken him a minute to realise he wasn't at home or in the camper, but in a hospital room. Now, as he sat with Maggie, her fingers intertwined with his as he thought about the things he had to consider, he wished he could go back and relive the events of the past few days because they were all a blur. Last thing he remembered, he and Maggie were dining out for her birthday. Some birthday, ending up here.

"Aortal valve replacement is a serious surgery, and not always recommended for everyone," the doctor said as she held his gaze. "However, Mr. Goddard, you're generally in good health for your age, therefore, the procedure is what I would recommend. This problem won't improve on its own. It will only get worse, and in your case, it's already advanced. You're suffering from what's called aortic regurgitation. This is where the blood leaks back into the heart, which is why you were experiencing chest pain and shortness of breath."

Maggie reached for his hand and gripped it tightly.

Meeting her gaze, he gave the most reassuring smile he could muster. Truth be told, he was more concerned about her than himself. With God's strength, he'd survived the loss of Esther and Julian, and he had no doubt that God would get him through this. Maggie had suffered through challenges as well, but he'd much rather she didn't have to suffer again.

"You'll be in the hospital for about a week after the surgery," Dr. Greer continued. "The surgery will be done under general anaesthetic and will take several hours. I'll make an incision about 25 centimetres long along your breastbone," she said, indicating the place on a model. "As I mentioned to your wife earlier, you'll have a choice between a mechanical valve made of synthetic materials or one made from animal tissue, usually bovine."

"A cow?" Maggie questioned.

"Yes," Dr. Greer replied. "Cow tissue is closely related to human tissue physiology. Animal valves have a lower tendency to result in clots, therefore, you wouldn't need lifelong treatment with anticoagulants which a mechanical valve would require. The documents will explain the entire process and the options in greater detail. After the surgery, it will take a few months to get back to normal." Her gaze shifted between him and Maggie. "However, with the type of work your wife told me you do, I think you may want to reconsider the responsibilities you undertake. Your physiotherapist will advise you further. You'll need to see one to help with your recovery."

Frank balked internally but said nothing. She was probably right, but he didn't have to like it.

Dr. Greer continued. "I know this may seem frightening, but I've done this procedure many times with a high rate of success. There's nothing to worry about."

"What are the risks?" Maggie asked, leaning forward.

"I'd be lying if I said there weren't any. There's always the risk of complications, but the risk of not proceeding outweighs that."

"So, he could die?" Maggie glanced his way, concern etched on her face.

The doctor nodded. "Yes, but your husband's overall health is good, and I have confidence that he'll make a full recovery."

Listening to her, Frank felt she was a good choice and would do a commendable job. It was no small thing entrusting someone to operate on your heart. "I'm sure I'm in great hands," he said.

The doctor smiled. "Do either of you have any questions?"

Did he have questions? Too many, but most were things she couldn't help him with. He looked at the pamphlets she'd given him, information on the various types of valve replacements that were available, and all the risks and benefits of each. He still couldn't believe he was facing this. It didn't seem real. "No, Dr. Greer, I don't have any questions, but maybe later I might," he said. He glanced at Maggie. "Do you have any questions, love?"

She shook her head. "No." Her voice was solemn. Resigned.

"Very well. If you do, you know where to reach me. I advise you both to consider the options carefully, and once you've decided, inform the nurse, and we'll proceed from there."

Maggie stood and took Dr. Greer's hand. "Thank you, doctor. We'll think everything over carefully."

She walked the doctor out of the room and then turned to face him. She didn't say anything, but he could see the grave concern in her eyes. Forcing a smile, she returned to her seat. "So, we have a lot to think about."

He took her hand. "You're worried, my love."

"No, I'm not. Everything's going to be fine," she said, but her smile betrayed her. It didn't reach her eyes, and it wasn't as wide as usual.

"Maggie, don't pretend with me. I know you're worried. I can see it," he said gently. He reached for her cheek and caressed it. "Don't hold back with me."

She covered her hand with his and then kissed his palm. "I'm sorry, love. I won't do it again." Her eyes glistened.

He pulled her close and held her to his chest. "It's all right, Maggie," he whispered into her ear.

Her shoulders shook. "I'm sorry. I don't mean to cry."

"It's okay," he said, rubbing her back gently.

"I know everything's going to be alright, but I can't help how I feel," she continued, tearfully.

"This isn't how I expected our trip to turn out. I'm sorry."

She lifted her head. "There's nothing to apologise for, Frank. I'm glad that you're going to be okay and that we caught this in time." She smiled wistfully. "We can always travel later."

"That we can," Frank assured. "I promise you we will. No matter what, Maggie Goddard, we will finish this trip."

She smiled weakly, then leaned in and kissed his cheek. "Whenever you're ready to go, I am."

"How about now?" he joked. "I can fold up this bed and take it with me."

She laughed, and he felt better instantly. Seeing Maggie smile was like sunshine on a rainy day, and today it was pouring. "I love your smile."

"I love *you*," she replied.

"We're going to get through this, my love," he assured. "God never fails, and He promises to never leave us nor forsake us."

She closed her eyes. "Thank you, Lord."

The presence of God was tangible. It was such a peaceful, welcome feeling. Frank closed his eyes, too. "Father, I don't know what's going to happen, but You do. My heart's been burdened many times, but I've always tried to give it to You. Now, my heart isn't working right, and I'm giving it to You again. I ask for Your healing hand to be upon me and that You would guide the surgeons as they operate. I also ask You to watch over my family. This will be weighing heavily on them after everything we've been through, but I know that You will give us all strength as we wait on You."

"Yes, Lord," Maggie said softly.

Frank took a deep breath. "Father, may Your will be done in my life. For Thine is the kingdom, and the power, and the glory, for ever. Amen."

"Amen," Maggie whispered after him.

When Frank opened his eyes, she wore a small but genuine smile that reached all the way to his heart. He squeezed her hand. "Let's not worry about it anymore, Maggie. We've given it to God. He'll handle it from here."

"I know He will," she said, her smile growing.

He lifted her hand to his lips. "I love you, Maggie."

"I love you, Frank."

He was blessed. Gazing into her eyes, he knew he was. He had the right woman by his side. She trusted God as He did, and together their faith would get him and their family through. It had before, and it would again.

TWO DAYS LATER, Maggie was sitting in the waiting room as Frank underwent surgery. The family sat together praying as another hour went by. She didn't think time could crawl as slowly as it was now. Every time she looked at the clock on the wall, she expected it to be later than it was, and still, there was no word from the doctors.

"It feels like we've been sitting here forever," she said, turning to Joshua, who sat beside her. Stella was at the hotel checking in with Elizabeth and Sean. She'd be back later with food. The hospital cafeteria was nice to eat in, but the food wasn't great, so Stella had taken it upon herself to prepare simple meals for them all.

"I know. It feels like we've been here for days instead of hours," Joshua agreed. "It's been three hours already. How much longer will it take?"

"Dr. Greer said it would be five hours or more in total, depending on how many valves need to be replaced," Maggie explained.

Joshua nodded. "We just have to be patient."

Maggie held his hand. Before, there was so much distance between her and Joshua, but now, there was no distance at all. First, Julian's death, then Joshua's marriage, and now Frank's illness; they'd all helped to knock down the walls. "He'll be fine, Joshua. I know it."

"At least he won't have to do this again since he's getting the artificial valve," he replied.

Maggie nodded. "Yes. It was the best choice for us. A bovine replacement would have meant he'd have this surgery every ten years, and that wasn't acceptable to your father. To either of us. Each surgery would mean more time on his back, away from what he loves, and more stress on the family." *And more risk*, although she didn't say that. "He was thinking of all of you when we made the decision."

"Dad's always thinking of us," Joshua said with a sombre smile. "Even when he's about to undergo life-threatening surgery."

"He loves you."

"I know he does. That's something you never have to doubt with Dad."

"You understand why he didn't want to discuss this with the entire family, don't you? He knew it would be difficult, especially on your sister," Maggie said.

Joshua nodded slowly and ran a hand through his hair. "Yeah, Dad knows Liv too well. She would have been a mess hearing all the details, not to mention the research she'd feel compelled to do to ensure he was making the best decision possible. We'd still be waiting for her findings if he'd asked her opinion." There was a hint of mirth in his voice, and Maggie smiled. They needed some levity under the circumstances.

"Do you think she understands that?" she asked.

"I'm sure she does," Joshua said. "I think that as long as Dad gets through this, she'll be fine. She's worried, that's all, and with her tendency to take control, not being a part of every aspect is hard for her to take. She'll get over it."

Maggie glanced in Olivia's direction. Frank's daughter was huddled with her husband a few seats away. She'd been upset when her father told them he was undergoing surgery and she didn't get to have any input. Nate did his best to comfort her, but Olivia was still upset up until the time her father went into surgery. As if she knew they were talking about her, she lifted her gaze and looked in their direction, her head angling.

Maggie sighed. She patted her stepson's hand and got to her feet. "I'll be right back."

He glanced at Olivia and nodded. "Yeah. I'll be here."

Maggie walked slowly as she approached Nate and Olivia. Serena was at the hotel with Oliver, and Janella was asleep two chairs away. She'd had difficulty sleeping; Maggie blamed being back in a hospital again. Whatever the reason, Janella hadn't slept since they'd arrived in Perth and now, she was completely exhausted. She'd fallen asleep minutes after Frank went into surgery, and no one wanted to wake her.

"Olivia?" Maggie said softly.

She nodded. "Yes…"

"May I speak with you a moment?" Maggie glanced at Nate, hoping he'd understand she wanted a moment alone. He did. Kissing Olivia's cheek, he excused himself and vacated his seat.

Maggie lowered herself into the empty chair.

Olivia narrowed her eyes and straightened. "Did something happen to Dad?"

"No," Maggie said softly. "I wanted to speak to you about earlier."

Olivia's nostrils flared. "What about it?"

"I'm sorry we didn't involve you in the decision," Maggie said. "Your father wanted to make things easier on everyone. You understand, don't you?"

"We always make decisions as a family, even on small things, then Dad makes this choice on his own? It didn't seem fair." Olivia breathed heavily. "I only wanted to be part of it. To make sure he'd be okay."

"Your Dad knows that," Maggie assured.

"I'm scared," Olivia said, covering her face with her hands as tears spilled onto her lap.

Maggie rubbed her back. "I understand. I'm scared too."

Olivia's head shot up. "You are?"

"Yes," Maggie admitted. "I know God's taking care of your father, but it doesn't mean I don't feel fear, although faith trumps fear in the end. It's my flesh that's scared, but my heart believes. God sees the heart."

"I love my dad, Maggie. I love him a lot. After losing Mum and Julian, he's all that's left of my family. Yes, I have Nate and the children, and you and your family, but it isn't the same."

"I know. There was a time when it was the five of you. Now there's only three, and you're scared of it becoming two."

Olivia sniffled. "Is it ridiculous to be afraid of being an orphan at my age?"

Maggie wrapped her arms around Olivia's shoulders and felt the young woman melt against her. "There's no shame in it, Olivia. God knows your fears. He knows your heart. He'll keep you through this. He'll keep all of us."

She sat there, holding her stepdaughter as she wept and finally grew still, her breathing changing from the jagged breaths that tears elicited to the smooth, rhythmic rise and fall of sleep. It was the best thing. Hopefully, by the time she woke, Frank would be out of surgery, and there would be good news for her to hear.

Olivia shifted against her shoulder and Maggie glanced in Nate's direction. Catching her cue, he came over and took her place, resting Olivia's head against his chest. He nodded and thanked her.

Standing, Maggie shook her arms. She needed to do something—she'd go stir crazy just sitting. She headed towards the exit. A walk would do her good.

"Where are you going, Maggie?" Joshua asked as she passed.

"I need to stretch my legs. I'll be right back," she replied.

He gave a nod and smiled.

She passed by the maternity ward, her feet carrying her and her mind following. She stopped to look at the newborns. They were so small and fragile. She thought of Frank and the state he would be in once the surgery was over. It seemed the fragility of life was felt most at the beginning and the end.

"Maggie?"

She turned to find Janella behind her. "Janella, what are you doing here?"

"I came to look for you. I wanted to be sure you're alright. Josh told me you went for a walk."

Maggie smiled meekly. "I just needed to move. Sitting still wasn't doing me any good. I find that when I walk, I think better."

"I feel the same." Janella inhaled deeply. "Maggie, I want to talk to you."

Maggie frowned. "What about?"

"I'm not going to Darwin," she answered in a rush.

Maggie's jaw dropped, and she shook her head. "No, Janella, you have to go. You've been accepted. You've already told the children your plans. You can't change your mind now, not after you've come so far. Not when you can make such great strides for yourself and your children. They want you there with them."

Janella met her gaze. "I can't leave you and Frank like this, not when he's in such a shape. The family needs me, and I can't abandon them."

"You're not abandoning us," Maggie said, placing a gentle hand on her arm.

Janella's eyes glistened. "It's settled. I'm staying."

"I don't think that's the right choice for you," Maggie insisted.

"How can you say that? Look at everyone, they're a mess. We need to stick together to get through this," Janella said. "Frank would want us to stay together and be the family he wants us to be."

Under different circumstances, Maggie would agree, but not this time. Frank would never want Janella to stay at Goddard Downs because of him, not when she had such opportunities elsewhere.

"Janella, you're always willing to sacrifice your needs for others, but Frank would never accept you doing this for him. He wouldn't want you to give up on your hopes and dreams because he's ill."

Janella's gaze shifted away from her to the newborns behind the glass. "They're so sweet when they're small. The world is so innocent and simple for them. Their choices are easy. There are none. When you get older, there seems to be a never-ending stream of choices to make, and the options aren't easy." She turned back to Maggie. "But sometimes you have to choose what's best for others over yourself."

Maggie smiled. "Sometimes, you have to choose what's best for you."

Their gazes locked and Janella remained silent. Her eyes reflected her inner conflict, but applying pressure wouldn't help her make the right choice. "You should pray about this," Maggie said quietly.

"I already did."

"Yes, and the Lord answered you," Maggie reminded her. "Don't be eager to change your mind again once He's said yes. Seek Him first. Know what He's saying to you." Maggie paused and rubbed her arm. "We love you, Janella, and we love having you close, but don't use this as an excuse to run away from your dreams again."

Janella nodded but didn't speak. Maggie slipped her arm around her shoulders. "Come on, let's go back and see if they've finished the surgery. We can talk about this more when Frank's awake."

"Okay." Janella released a heavy breath and nodded.

Glancing at her friend as they walked, Maggie hoped she'd make the right choice, but she couldn't force Janella. Everyone had a path to take, and they each had to make their own decisions. She'd pray that Janella would make the right choice for her and her children, but right now, Frank was foremost in her mind, and she needed to get back to him.

CHAPTER 24

*S*ean smiled as he put the last filing cabinet in place. Frank and Olivia were going to get a surprise when they returned to the station to see how he'd reorganised the office in a way that made more sense. The older files were now further away since they weren't needed as regularly as the newer ones. He archived those older than seven years and placed them in storage bins in an older container behind the shed. He'd also moved the desk so that whoever was using it could better take advantage of the natural light.

"Looking good," Elizabeth said, poking her head into the room. Her dark hair was in two braids on either side of her head. She looked like a little girl, but she wasn't. Even with her hair in braids and a graphic tee on, she was beautiful, and Sean couldn't take his eyes off her.

"Thanks. I think it turned out well. Frank and Olivia should be very happy with this new setup when they get back, but I don't expect Uncle Frank will be back to work anytime soon."

Sean took a deep breath; the words were difficult to say. He couldn't imagine the station without his uncle. Though they'd called to say the surgery had been successful, his uncle still had a long way to go before he recovered fully. It had only been a few days, and his uncle still had a couple more to spend in the hospital before they were scheduled to come home, but it would take a while before they could get back to the station. Frank couldn't fly so soon after surgery, so they'd have to drive back in the rig.

Elizabeth walked into the room, leaned against the doorframe, and smiled. "See, I always knew you had it in you."

Sean laughed. "Did you?"

"Oh yes," Elizabeth replied, grinning. "I knew."

"How?"

"There's a lot more to you than you think, Sean Goddard. Right now, you're getting to see that. This place is running so smoothly. Your uncle would be proud."

He stepped towards her. The thought that his uncle would be proud was enough to make his heart beat harder. "You really think so?"

"I know it," she said confidently. She walked to the desk and picked up the schedule Sean had organised. She handed it to him and smiled.

Everything was in order. He had lists for every task that needed to be done, who was to do it, and when it was to be completed. It was the reason he always did the planning for his and Josh's trips. Despite what people thought, he was the more organised one. If only he could get his life as ordered as his schedules.

With no one to answer to, he felt strong. His family's

absence from the station allowed him to make decisions, and the results were evident. It felt good to see the choices he was making reaping rewards, even if there was no one to see it, other than Elizabeth. People had never given him a chance to shine. He guessed he always wanted that feeling, and now he was getting a taste of what it was to be someone of worth instead of the person looked down on. "Why do you believe in me?"

Elizabeth looked at him as if he'd asked something strange. "Why wouldn't I?"

"Apart from Uncle Frank and you, no one ever has," he answered softly.

"You don't give them a chance, but for some reason, you let me," she continued.

"How could I not? You don't give up," he said, laughing. There was a glint in her eyes as their gazes met across the room, and for a moment his heart felt as if it would burst through his chest.

"Hey, Sean, the guys are waiting," David said as he stepped around the corner. He stood in the doorway with his hands in his pockets, his gaze shifting between them.

Sean swallowed the lump in his throat. "We should get going, we don't want to be late since there's a lot to do," he said, tucking the clipboard under his arm and walking past Elizabeth. There he was, making eyes at her when there was work to be done. The station didn't run itself. That was his job.

He strode to the truck and jumped in. David did likewise. Sean started the engine and headed for the construction site. They started work at seven every morning, but on Mondays, he started meeting with the men to ensure they were all on the same page for the work that needed to be done that week. He felt empowered as he stood talking to the workers who listened and did what he asked.

When the meeting was over that morning, he and David shed their jackets, donned their gloves, and joined the men who were mixing the cement to secure the pylons.

"You're doing a great job, Sean, you know that?" David said as they shovelled constituents into the mixer.

"Elizabeth mentioned the same thing. I'm not sure I believe her any more than I do you," Sean replied.

"Why not?" David looked at him pointedly. "Why would we lie?"

It was a good question, and one Sean couldn't answer. Perhaps it was easier for him to believe they were messing with him than it being true. Good things never seemed to last for him, and if things were going well, he didn't want to mess it up like he always did. He smiled. "No, I guess you wouldn't."

"That's right. If I say you're doing a good job, then you're doing a good job," David reiterated. "Your family will see it, I'm sure."

"I don't know. Hoping for that might be a waste of time. I've done so many bad things that it's hard for people to believe anything different about me."

"That doesn't mean they can't," David replied, lifting a shovelful of gravel and tossing it into the mouth of the mixer.

Sean threw sand in behind it. "Doesn't mean they will, either."

"Have faith that your family will see past your mistakes and realise how well you're doing now and will continue to do into the future."

Sean shrugged. In the days since the construction started, he and David had spent a lot of time together. There were only three adults in the main house now, and that made conversation limited. However, it also meant Sean was talking a lot more because Elizabeth and David were two people who didn't allow him to wallow in his self-doubts and fears. They encouraged him to be bold and take chances and believe that he could contribute in a way that would make others take notice. Though their words were getting into his head, it had only been a few days, and he wasn't completely sold yet, but he doubted his family would ever truly see past his mistakes.

They continued shovelling in the aggregates until the mixer was full. After that, they moved onto helping the men who were digging trenches to clear the water from where the pylons would be erected. They needed to clear the water and allow the earth to dry out so they could pour in the cement. They'd already cleared the way for the first two, but six more needed to be done. By the time they returned to the house for lunch, they were both aching and tired.

"Sit there," Elizabeth said, pointing to a chair near the window.

"I was going to take it with me," Sean replied. He didn't usually sit to eat. He normally fixed himself a plate and headed back outside or sat at the desk and checked the schedules. He didn't give himself a chance to be lazy. He kept busy, and things worked well. It also meant he didn't have to spend too much alone time with Elizabeth. Spending time with her made him think too much, and sometimes he didn't want to do that.

"I said, sit." She held the back of the chair firmly and looked him squarely in the eye. Her tone left no room for argument. She was such a feisty woman and there was no denying her.

He complied.

"Good," she said, patting him on the shoulder. She grabbed her plate and sat across from him. "How's it going today?"

"Fine," he replied.

"Are you avoiding me?" she asked.

Her question came out of nowhere and took him by surprise. "Of course not."

She chuckled. "Yes, you are." She shook her head and continued to laugh. "You're a terrible liar."

"I am not," he retorted.

She took a bite of her chicken sandwich. "Oh yes, you are. I can see through you as clearly as I can see though that glass window I just cleaned."

He glanced in the direction she indicated. Was he that transparent? He didn't think so. But she had a knack of seeing him when others didn't.

"Don't lie to me. Okay?" The look in her eyes shot right through him.

He sighed heavily. "Alright. I won't."

"Good, because there's no point to it. I'll find out anyway." She chuckled.

"Fine, I'll remember that," he replied. She was like that, always challenging him. When he wanted to say no, she said yes. When he was saying yes, she'd say no, but it wasn't about being argumentative, more that she was trying to get him to do what he didn't want to do. There was a lot he didn't want to do, but she wouldn't let him get away with it. Strangely, he enjoyed this conundrum. She made his life interesting, but he couldn't let his feelings get in the way of something good. Trying to make more of what they had would lead to trouble. She was his friend, and though he'd never had a female friend before, he wasn't about to mess up the good relationship he had going with her.

"Auntie Elizabeth?" Issie called, wandering into the room with Sasha and William trailing behind.

Elizabeth turned and smiled. "Issie, I wondered when you were coming in. Did you have fun playing?" She pulled the child onto her lap, and Issie hugged her immediately.

"Yes. Are Mummy and Daddy home yet?"

"Not yet," Elizabeth replied sweetly. "As soon as they are, you'll be the first to know."

"Okay," Issie replied. "Will they be gone long with Grandpa Frank? Is he feeling better?"

Elizabeth glanced at Sean over the top of Issie's head.

"Of course, he is," Sean said quickly. "Your grandpa is one of the strongest men I know. He won't be sick for long." He sure hoped he was right.

Elizabeth smiled approvingly. "You heard what your cousin said. Your grandpa's doing better, and your mummy and daddy will be back soon. You don't have to worry, sweetheart. The doctors are taking good care of him for you."

Issie huffed. "They better. I love my grandpa, and if they don't take care of him, then I'm going to tell."

Sean laughed. "Who are you going to tell?"

"God," she said frankly. "Grandpa says that when you have a problem, you tell God, and He takes care of everything."

"That's right, Issie. You are such a smart girl," Elizabeth stated. She hugged Issie to her. "Come on, let's go outside. Who wants to eat indoors anyway? Do you want your sandwich now?"

"Yes, please!" Issie said excitedly, as if a sandwich was the world's best food.

Elizabeth packed up her plate and one for Issie and William and headed for the door. "Are you coming?" she said, looking back at Sean.

He smiled. "Sure."

He followed them outside but didn't get involved as Elizabeth played with the children, taking bites of her sandwich in between running around with them.

Finally, they stopped running and Elizabeth joined him at the outdoor table. "Did you hear from Josh today?" she asked as she flopped onto the chair.

"I did. He said Uncle Frank's doing much better, but he's in pain from the surgery. He's recovering slowly, and in three days or so, they'll let him leave and they can start back home as soon as he feels well enough."

"Is Josh flying back, or will he drive with Maggie?"

"He's driving with Maggie." Sean didn't expect his cousin to do anything less. He did the right thing whenever he could, and driving with Maggie was the right thing to do. She would need help caring for his uncle and driving at the same time. That was a lot for one person to handle.

"I'm glad he's going with her. Someone should," Elizabeth replied.

"I prayed for my uncle," Sean blurted.

"You did?" The sound of surprise and joy was mingled in the question. It made him smile.

"Yes, I did."

"Wonderful. I'm glad to hear that. I've been praying for him, too," Elizabeth replied. "I guess you aren't the complete heathen I thought you were. There's something salvageable in there," she continued, poking him lightly in the chest. Her touch made his breath falter.

"I'm not that bad," he laughed, but then he grew serious. "I never had any use for God before, that's all."

"Issie, bring William back here," Elizabeth called. The little boy was picking up pebbles and throwing them at a dry patch of grass. Once Issie had William by the hand and was guiding him back, Elizabeth returned her focus to Sean. "What do you mean? You don't *use* God. You love Him."

"He's never loved me," Sean said solemnly. If God loved him, then He wouldn't have let him get into the messes he'd gotten into. He would have kept him away from them. He would have made his life better.

"That isn't true," Elizabeth said, her brow raised. "God, in the form of Jesus, came to earth to die for you because He loves you and wants to save you from your sins."

"If that's true, then He'll make Uncle Frank well again. If God loves me so much, that's what He can do for me. I don't care about my life, but my uncle means the world to me. If He can do that, then I'll believe He loves me." He stood and sharply turned from the table to go back inside.

"Sean!" Elizabeth called after him.

He turned and faced her, not wanting to argue, but ready to.

She grinned. "He loves you. End of story."

CHAPTER 25

*A*fter being home more than a week, Frank still felt terrible. Propped up in bed, his fingers traced a path beside the incision that marked his chest bone. At least the worst was over. In the hospital, the pain from the incision and the tubes coming out of him from every angle, draining away blood and fluid, and wires to control the function of his heart, was awful. Pads on his chest tracked his blood pressure and flow, and the airflow to his lungs. He'd never felt weaker or older.

The first few days after he woke from the surgery, the doctors spent most of their time ensuring his heart was beating normally and that his appetite was returning. He had no desire for food to start with, but eventually, his appetite did come back, but it wasn't the same. Nothing was.

Even his voice sounded different as he called to his love. "Maggie?"

"Coming," she replied brightly, appearing in the doorway a

moment later, a smile on her face and long rubber gloves on her hands.

He smiled at the sight of her. "You're cleaning at this hour?"

She nodded. "I was hoping to get it done before you woke up."

"Sorry to spoil your plan." He grinned as he patted the bed beside him. "Spare me a moment?"

"Only a moment?" She chuckled lightly as she slipped off her gloves and set them on the dresser before sitting beside him on the bed. Laying her hand on his thigh, she kissed his cheek. "What can I do for you?"

His chest hurt, but it wasn't why he'd called her. He had all the pain medicine in the world on his bedside table. It was her presence he needed. "Nothing. I just wanted to see you."

Her cheeks turned a pale pink. He loved to see her blush. She leaned closer, resting her head gently on his shoulder as her arms wrapped gently around him. He missed her firm, strong hugs, but since the surgery, even she treated him with kid gloves. He couldn't wait for life to return to normal.

He sighed. "I hate this," he whispered against her hair.

"I know," she replied.

His jaw clenched. She could only understand so much. How could she truly understand how he felt as a man who'd been active his entire life but was now forced to stay in bed, weak and tired, day in and out, only leaving the house to go to Kununurra three days a week for physiotherapy to help him rehabilitate? "Sometimes, I wonder if I'm ever going to be whole again."

She looked up at him. "You will. I know you will."

"It doesn't feel that way. Every day it feels like nothing's changing. I can't do anything. I'm so tired all the time, and the exercises they take me through at therapy make me feel I'm older than I am."

"You wanted to get healthier," she said, grinning.

"But not like this." He let out a heavy sigh. "I wanted to be setting my own pace, not trying to keep up with someone else's. I thought I'd feel stronger doing exercises, not weaker. I feel like an old man, and Dr. Greer said it could take months to get back to normal, and my physiotherapist says I should stop some things entirely."

"They were just suggestions. Driving cattle and long rides, that's all. Avoiding the heavier tasks. You can still do everything else."

"That *is* everything," he complained. "If all I can do is sit at my desk and do paperwork all day long, what point is there? I've never been a man to sit still. I've always worked, ever since I was a child. All I can remember is running around this place, climbing on my horse and taking a ride, helping my father work on the machinery, tending the cattle. Even now, with the work on the bridge, I would have been out there helping to get it done. What use am I sitting here doing nothing?"

She straightened and looked him in the eye. "Don't say that, Frank. You've just had major heart surgery. You have to be realistic. It will take time to regain your health and strength." Her expression softened and she placed her hand gently on his cheek.

As he gazed into her eyes, he could see her love, her tenderness, and her care, but she couldn't see his pain. She felt for him, she wanted to understand, but she couldn't. Not really. She may have lived for a short period on a station when she was young, but it wasn't her life. Goddard Downs was his. Everything he wanted was here. Everything he *was*, was here. Not being able to take care of it, watch over it, as his father had before him, and how he expected to for the rest of his life, was inconceivable to him.

"Let's get you ready," she said, taking him by the arm to help him up from the bed. His mother was coming for a visit. After she'd heard about his surgery, she insisted on coming out. He'd rather she didn't. He didn't want her to see him like this, but there was no telling her not to come. No matter how old she got, his mother was determined and always got her way.

He took a deep breath as Maggie helped him swing his legs slowly off the bed. It hurt, but he was getting used to the pain. It was getting a little duller each day, but it was still there. Everything with time, Maggie kept telling him. Even God was saying it as he read from the Book of Ecclesiastes each day. There was a time and season for everything, and this was his season of recovery. If only knowing that made it easier to bear, but it didn't. He wanted to get back to normal *now*, not later, but he didn't have a choice.

Maggie helped him bathe and dress before she returned to her cleaning. She wanted to finish before his mother arrived. He ate breakfast while she worked, watching her closely as she moved from one area of the house to the other. If he was well, he would have helped, but he couldn't. He couldn't even drive for another five weeks. He was completely dependent on her, and it wasn't a feeling he relished.

A man took care of his family; that's what his father always told him. Now, he was the one having to be taken care of. His children stopped by almost daily to look in on him, especially Olivia. He'd never seen his daughter so worried. It broke his heart to be the cause of her anxiety. As her father, he'd always taken care of her, comforted her, and he'd been the one who made the pain better. Now, she was the one trying to do that for him, but whenever she looked at him, all he could see in her eyes was fear.

She was experiencing a personal crisis. He could understand that. God never promised a life without challenge, and sometimes it took time to figure things out and come to the place where you could say, *Your will, not mine, be done.* She was still figuring it out.

Thankfully, she didn't have the station to worry about since Sean had risen to the occasion in a way no one had imagined but that Frank had always hoped. His leadership was impressive, and Frank was glad he was there to help run things now that he wasn't in the position to do so, and Olivia was almost paralysed.

His mother arrived just after eleven with his brother, Steven, Sean's father. Frank was sitting on the deck watching the water when Maggie brought them out. "Frank, look who's here."

"Mum! Steven!" He tried to stand.

"Don't get up on our account," his mother said. "You have to get your rest." She hobbled towards him with the help of her walking stick.

"I rest enough, Mum," Frank answered.

She looked at him with clear eyes and a warm smile. "How are you, my boy?"

He didn't want her worrying, just as he didn't want Olivia

worrying. He wanted to assure them both that everything would be fine. His mother had other things to take care of, more important things to worry about, like her own health. She was getting old, and he wanted whatever time she had left filled with only good memories and experiences. "I'm good, Mum. Getting better each day. Before you know it, I'll be back in the helicopter helping the boys with the cattle."

Maggie narrowed her eyes as she stared at him but she didn't say anything. She knew what the physiotherapist had said, what Frank refused to accept.

Steven leaned forward and extended his hand. "Good to see you, brother."

Frank took his hand and shook it. "And you." When he'd heard it was Steven who'd be bringing his mother to see him, he'd been surprised. He'd expected his sister to bring her. He didn't even know Steven was in town.

"Yeah, I was in town visiting Mum. Thought I'd bring her out since I haven't seen you in a while."

"Yes, it has been a while," Frank said.

"So, who's taking care of the station while you're out of action?" Steven asked as he sat in the chair Maggie pulled out for him after she'd helped their mother into one.

Stifling a grin, Frank met his gaze. "Sean."

His brother scoffed. "Sean? You're letting Sean run things? That's not a good idea."

"And why not?" Frank countered.

Steven shook his head. "You know Sean. He brings trouble wherever he goes. You can't trust him. He's not responsible."

Frank's jaw clenched. "You should be happy to know that

Sean has done a great job managing everything on his own since my surgery. The entire place."

Steven folded his arms, a blank expression on his face. "I still say you should find someone else. This is a big place. Sean isn't capable of looking after it."

His brother's dismissal of his son was disheartening. Frank didn't know why he couldn't see past Sean's former mistakes. He was different now. Frank knew from the moment he'd returned to Goddard Downs that something inside his nephew was changing for the better. He only needed a chance. Why did Steven never see fit to give him one?

"Why don't you stop by the main house and see him?" Frank said. "How long has it been since you spoke? A year? Two? You might be surprised what you find when you talk to him."

Steven exhaled deeply. "Nothing I haven't seen in him before."

Maggie looked at him sadly. "You should talk to him and see for yourself. He's changed a lot."

Steven gave a half-smile and a nod, but Frank could see in his eyes that he had no intention of speaking to Sean. No matter what, Steven couldn't see his son as anything other than trouble. Frank had no idea what it would take to change his impression of Sean, or how long it might take, but he prayed that one day his brother would see his son as the man he'd wanted him to be and was now becoming, and not the loser he still saw him as.

Frank turned his focus to his mother. "Mum, how've you been?"

"I'm doing better than you. Heart surgery." She shook her head. "I don't know. As old as I am, I've never had that."

"I know, Mum."

"You need to take better care of yourself, my boy. Cut back on the fatty foods. That's what gives you heart trouble," she scolded gently. "I used to tell your father the same thing. He didn't listen, either."

Frank sat up. "You told Dad that?"

"Yes. After *his* father had a heart attack, I told him he needed to eat better, but he didn't listen. He did what he wanted. Always did."

"Mum, you're saying Dad and Grandpa both had heart problems? Did anyone else?"

Her brow creased, the deep lines more prevalent than he'd noticed before. "Most of the men in your father's family had heart trouble of some kind. Heart attacks and things like that. I can't remember all of them," she said. "But it was the food they ate that caused it."

Frank shook his head. "No, Mum. It wasn't just the food. From what you're saying, there's a history of heart problems in our family. It could be hereditary."

She frowned. "You're saying this could happen to any of you?"

"It's something we should look into." He turned to Steven. "You should too."

His brother chortled. "Be serious, Frank. I feel fine."

"So did I before this happened. I'm sure Dad and everyone before him thought the same as well." Frank's steady gaze didn't waver. "Take this seriously, Steven."

Their mother smacked Steven on the hand. "Listen to your

brother. I don't want anything to happen to you as well." She turned to Frank, her eyes glistening. "You gave me such a scare, son. When they told me you were in the hospital, I wanted to come, but everyone said it was too far for me to travel."

He leaned forward and took her hand. "It's fine, Mum. I'm glad you're here now."

She patted his knuckles. "I'm glad as well." She lifted her wrinkled hand to his cheek and patted it. "You were always such a good boy. You took this station over when your dad died, and you've done wonders with it. I don't know if I've ever told you how proud I am of you."

"Mum..."

"Frank," she cleared her throat, "I know this is going to be difficult for you. You've never been a man who stood still, not even when you were a boy, but things happen for a reason. You made it through that surgery, and you'll get better in no time, I'm sure. God gave you a second chance at this life. Others in this family didn't get that, but you did. I take it that God has something planned for you."

"Mum," Steven said.

"Hush," she countered, giving Steven the stern look she used to give them as children. It was a look that always silenced them. It still worked, and Steven sat back and crossed his arms.

Frank stifled a laugh. It was funny how even as grown men they could still feel like children in the presence of their mother.

"Frank, I want you to take it easy," she continued.

"I will."

"No son, I mean it. I know you. You'll say that you'll take it easy, but you won't. And then you'll try to convince Maggie that you're fine and you can do things as normal." She smiled at her daughter-in-law. "Not that she'll fall for it." His mother winked.

Maggie chuckled. "You're absolutely right, Mary."

Frank smiled. "Are the two of you ganging up on me?"

"No," Maggie replied, moving to sit beside him.

"Son, I want you to take time to review your life. It's been a good one. A very good one. But there comes a time when we have to take stock and look at things differently."

His brow furrowed. "What do you mean?"

"I mean, this is a new chapter in your life. Be open to turning the page."

He understood, but he didn't want to. He wasn't willing to accept it. Yes, he felt different, even before the surgery, but that didn't mean he was too old for this way of life. It didn't mean that he was getting bored or that there was something else for him. *Did it?* He was a cattleman. That's who he was, and who he'd always be. Still, something in the back of his mind kept pricking him. *For My thoughts are not your thoughts, neither are your ways My ways, declares the Lord. For as the heavens are higher than the earth, so are My ways higher than your ways and My thoughts than your thoughts.*

CHAPTER 26

anella was pensive as she drove to the cottage. Maggie needed help with Frank. Men were never good patients, and Frank could be the worst. Goddard men didn't take illness well, especially when it meant they couldn't do the things they loved. Frank loved the station and the responsibility of it, being a part of every aspect. Janella didn't expect him to take being in bed easily. Maggie had her hands full, and Janella was doing her best to help by bringing meals as often as possible. Today, she was bringing enough to last the next few days. It would take the load off Maggie, who was making three trips a week to and from Kununurra for Frank's therapy. Others had offered to take turns, but Maggie said they were needed on the station more than she was, and Frank was her husband. It was her place, and like a true Goddard woman, she was taking the reins and caring for her husband no matter what.

Janella glanced at the bundle of food on the passenger seat. She was glad they'd decided to keep Frank at the cottage instead of the main house, even though they'd had to set up a makeshift bedroom downstairs. He'd never keep still at the main house. He'd want to be involved in every aspect of the daily activities, and he didn't need that right now. What he needed was to rest and relax so he could get better quickly.

She stopped the Jeep outside the door of the cottage, carried the food to the door, and then called out. "Maggie?"

The door opened a minute later. "Janella! I thought you were coming by later. Come on in." She stepped aside, and Janella followed. "Let me take that," Maggie said, holding her hands out. She took the basket and carried it to the kitchen.

"Where's Frank?" Janella asked, following behind.

"He's taking a nap," Maggie answered. "He's very tired today."

Janella nodded. "It's expected. It'll get better. He just needs time."

"I know," Maggie replied. "It's just difficult for him to accept that he needs to slow down for a while."

Janella took a seat at the kitchen table while Maggie put the food away. She liked visiting with Maggie. Her friend needed the company, an opportunity to let her feelings out. It couldn't be easy to watch Frank in such a state and not be able to make it magically better for him.

"How are you feeling, Maggie?" she asked.

"I'm doing well."

Janella angled her head and studied her. Maggie might have uttered the right words, but her tone suggested she wasn't doing well at all. "Maggie."

Her friend stopped putting the food away, turned and flashed a meagre smile. "I'm a little tired."

"You should get some rest. Let me do that," Janella offered, getting to her feet.

"I can do it," Maggie insisted. "I have to keep the routine as normal as possible. Frank needs to feel that things are going well. If I start sleeping in the day and acting like something's wrong, then he'll worry. I don't want him doing that."

"I see," Janella replied. She took a deep breath. Maggie was doing her best, but it would eventually take its toll on her. She needed to rest as much as Frank, but Janella understood why she felt she had to keep going. She'd felt that way after Julian died and the children were grieving. She put all her energy into them, and though she was hurting, she did her best to keep life as normal as possible. She put a hand on Maggie's back to comfort her.

"Maggie?" Frank called from the makeshift bedroom. "Could you bring me some water, please?"

She turned to get a glass from the cupboard, but Janella stopped her. "Let me do this. Take it easy. Maybe you can close your eyes for a few minutes on the couch?"

There were slight bags under Maggie's eyes. With the distance between them, Janella hadn't noticed them before, but as she looked closely now, they were clear.

"Maybe a minute," she replied.

"Maybe twenty," Janella said with a smile. "Don't worry, I'll take care of Frank."

Maggie collapsed onto the couch and snuggled down with a cushion under her head. Her eyes were closed before Janella could pour the water. She loved Maggie and Frank, and she'd do anything to help them. Taking care of Frank for twenty minutes was the least she could do.

She wandered to the makeshift bedroom. She'd not been in there before because Frank insisted they visit him in the living room. He didn't want them seeing him bedridden. He was proud in the best possible way, not wanting people worrying about him, and going out of his way to make sure they didn't, even if that meant suffering discomfort.

"Janella?" he said when she walked into the room.

She smiled. "Maggie's getting some rest. I brought your water." She placed the glass on the bedside table and pulled up a chair from across the room. "How are you today?"

Frank raised an eyebrow as he took his pain pills. "Don't worry about me, Janella. How are *you* doing?"

"I'm fine." She smiled, but just like Maggie had done moments earlier, she hid her true feelings.

"Thanks for helping."

"You're welcome." She fiddled with her earring and felt his gaze on her. "I brought some meals over. Your favourites."

"I look forward to eating them," he said. "But since you're here, I have a question. Why are you still here, Janella? I thought you were going to school in Darwin."

She nodded, still unable to meet his gaze. "How can you ask that, Frank? You know I'm needed here."

She'd tried to put school out of her head, but it was impossible. Every day her thoughts drifted to what she'd put aside. It wasn't forever, only until they didn't need her as much around the station. But yet, she felt sad. Bitter, almost.

"Janella," Frank said, reaching for her hand.

She looked up, unsure if she could handle the look in his

eyes. She couldn't say what was on her heart, but she also couldn't turn away. "Yes?"

"You want more, Janella. I know you do. I know how excited you were when you accepted the spot at culinary school. You were excited about everything you would learn, the people you would meet, and of being closer to Caleb."

His words tugged on her heart. It was all true. She wanted to go. She still did. She'd be lying if she said that she hadn't thought about what life would be like in Darwin with her children. What it would be like for her to attend culinary school, get her certificates, and make Sasha, Caleb, and Julian proud. Her husband always wanted more for her, even more than she wanted for herself, and for that brief moment, she'd thought she might actually obtain it.

"Janella, you don't have to tell me. I can see it in your eyes, and when Sasha comes to see me, I see her disappointment. She was looking forward to living in Darwin. I'm sure Caleb was looking forward to having you there, too."

"They understand," she protested. "They know you need us here and that as a family, we have to support each other."

"You're right. We support each other." He patted her hand. "And we support you, Janella. You and the children. We want what's best for you. *I* want what's best for you."

She gave a half-smile. "I know."

"Then you know why I can't let you stay."

Her eyes shot open. "Frank, what are you saying?"

He squeezed her hand. "I want you to go, Janella. I want you to leave Goddard Downs and go after your dreams. I want you to see the world Julian desired for you."

She couldn't speak. Tears filled her eyes as she sucked in a ragged breath. She closed them and let the tears roll down her cheeks.

"You know, Janella," he continued, "sometimes I wonder what Julian would have done if there hadn't been the station to take care of."

She looked up through damp lashes. *What did he mean?*

For an instant, his expression reflected sadness and contemplation. "Julian was always ambitious. I always imagined that he'd stay in Darwin after he finished school, but when he came back, I knew it had more to do with you than the station."

She shook her head. "No, Frank. He came home because of the station. For the family."

"No, Janella. He came home for you. He loved you. He always did. From the first day he met you, you took precedence in his mind and actions. He knew you'd never leave the station, although he believed you could do whatever you put your mind to."

She was speechless. "Are you saying he would have left the station if I'd wanted to?"

"I don't doubt it. He and Olivia were a lot alike. They were both driven." He let out a heavy breath. "But their hearts were equally big. Love brought them both back to Goddard Downs. Olivia's love for me and the family after Esther died. For Julian, it was you."

"Why have you never said this before?"

"I didn't think it would make a difference, but I can see it's the right time for you to hear it now."

"Why?"

"Because you can't stay. I won't let love, even love for this family, make someone *I* love sacrifice more than they have to."

It didn't make sense. "What are you talking about?"

"I love my family and this station. Maybe I let that love and wanting to keep you all close blind me to the fact that life exists outside of the station. Just because moving away wasn't for me doesn't mean it couldn't have been for any of you. Julian certainly believed it."

"He loved this station. He wanted to make you proud. It wasn't because of me he stayed."

"He did, but if I'd told him he could leave and someone else would take over, and if you were willing, I believe he would have left a long time ago."

"But he wanted to maintain the family's legacy," she said, her eyes still blurry with tears.

"Yes, he did. But it wasn't his priority. You were. I want you to consider this, Janella. We all have to take a chance in life, a leap of faith, and sometimes that requires us to leave those we love behind and see what else is out there."

A knot twisted her stomach. She dipped her head and sighed deeply. The words were difficult to get out, but she had to try. "I've been trying not to think about Darwin, but it's so difficult."

"You could have been there already," he said. "Why shouldn't you go now?"

"Because you need me," she cried.

"Your children need you more, and they need each other. The three of you could use some time together. You still have some healing to do after Julian's death, and it's what he would have wanted for you." He took her hands. "He loved you so much. He wouldn't go anywhere without you."

"He always took care of me." Her heart warmed with the memories of her husband's love and protectiveness. "He never even let me go shopping on my own. He didn't like me driving alone."

Frank laughed. "That was my boy. He was a gentleman."

"He was wonderful." She sucked in a breath and met Frank's gaze.

"He was," Maggie said softly, her hands settling gently on Janella's shoulders. Janella hadn't even heard her come in.

She felt the weight, not of Maggie's hands, but of her desires and losses. She'd been living under that weight for so long, but she didn't want to live under it anymore. "I want something more," she blurted.

Frank's hands held hers as Maggie massaged her shoulders. "Father, King Eternal," Maggie prayed, "You are God and God alone. Into Your hands we place Janella's hopes and dreams. As she embarks on this new stage of life, we ask that You guide her along its path. Make her way straight, her steps ordered, and show her Your plan for her and the children."

"Yes, Lord," Janella agreed with a sniffle. She could almost feel the weight beginning to lift.

"We all have a place in Your kingdom, Lord," Frank said. "A place and a purpose we can hardly imagine, but You don't reveal the entire plan at once. You give us only what we can handle, enough to keep us going so we don't run away, and not too much that we run towards the end too quickly and miss all You have in store for us on the journey. Lord, let Janella enjoy the journey You're about to take her on. May she let go of what was, and embrace what can be. Father, lead her and my grand-children, and help them to find their unique places in this world. Let Your will be done, on earth as it is in heaven. Amen."

"Amen." Janella opened her eyes and met Frank's smiling face. She looked at Maggie, who was also smiling, and swallowed the lump in her throat. "I guess I have to tell the children I've changed my mind."

Frank and Maggie laughed together. "I think you do," he said. "But I'm sure they'll be okay with this change."

"I hope so, because I won't change my mind again," she assured, dabbing her eyes with a tissue. "I'm going to do it."

Maggie lowered herself onto the bed beside her and Frank. "Yes, and we'll help you. Whatever you need, we're there for you."

Janella nodded gratefully. It was such a comfort knowing she had such support. She would do this for herself, her children, and Julian. She would brave the unknown and overcome her fears and reservations. She would prove to herself that she could make it, just as Julian, Frank, and everyone else believed she could. She was more than the confines of the station. With God's help, she would venture into the world.

She took a deep breath. She hadn't come for this, but now that she had a plan, she needed to get back home. There was still work to do and a lot to organise before leaving for Darwin. Plus, she didn't want to become more emotional. "I should get going. I've got to start on lunch. A lot of hungry mouths to feed." She stood and wiped her nose with the tissue. "I wish Elizabeth could've stayed. She was a big help for the couple of days she was here."

She faced Maggie. Her friend looked brighter, even though the bags remained under her eyes. She pulled Janella into a warm hug. "We love you, Janella."

Janella squeezed her back. "I love you, too. Thank you for everything."

CHAPTER 27

*M*aggie escorted Janella to the door, her heart lighter, even if the fatigue still lingered. She felt good as she walked back to the bedroom and found Frank sitting up in bed with a grin on his face. She climbed in beside him. Snuggling close, he wrapped his arm around her shoulders as she rested her head against this chest.

"That's a good thing you did, Frank," she said softly.

"Janella needed to hear it," he replied. "She needs to start over."

"We all do." Maggie looked up, blinking rapidly. The words she wanted to speak were on the tip of her tongue. Not wanting to utter them, she had to.

Frank pulled her closer.

"You know what you said to Janella about there being seasons?" she started.

Her husband's voice was low as he replied. "Yes."

"You know the words were for you as well, don't you?"

Silence.

She looked up at him. His gaze was fixed straight ahead, and he was barely blinking. His breathing was slow, his chest rising and falling rhythmically against her body. Finally, he whispered a response. "I know."

"I know you want everything to be as it was. I want that too, but what your mother said and what you just told Janella might also be something for you to consider."

He looked down at her but didn't speak, although his Adam's apple moved up and down as he swallowed.

"Maybe God has other plans for you, Frank."

"Maggie…"

"Hear me out," she interrupted. "When we were on the road, just the two of us, I didn't hear you mention the station once. Not once, other than when they called about the bridge. You were having too much fun to even consider it. We were enjoying the plan God had for us, the one that we didn't even plan for ourselves. It was beyond what we'd hoped."

"That's true," he said reluctantly.

"So why can't it be that God has some other plan for you than you thought? You've dedicated your entire life to one pursuit, but perhaps the season to focus solely on the station is over. Maybe it's time for you to stretch your wings, so to speak, and embrace what's out there for yourself."

"Am I old, Maggie? Over the hill? Is that what you're saying? That I can't live this life anymore?"

"No," she said quickly. "Of course not."

"I feel old. Sitting here every day, pain in my chest, not able to do what I love. It makes me feel old," he said, his voice cracking.

"You aren't old, Frank, and you could never be in my eyes. No matter what's happened to your body, it doesn't mean you've suddenly aged and become an elderly man. Age is a number and feeling old is in your head. Don't let what's happened get to you. Don't allow it to make you feel any different than you want to feel. You'd already determined you wanted to get healthier, and now we both have even more reason to do so."

"I'm not a teenager anymore, Maggie."

"Neither am I, but that doesn't mean we have to act as if we're two-hundred years old. We need to rethink the direction our lives are going in. Perhaps the Lord is trying to lead us somewhere else. We can't pretend that things haven't changed, but it doesn't mean we have to throw our hands in the air and give up everything. We need to see what God has in mind for us. What His plan is, just like we were thinking after we met Mable and Ned."

Frank exhaled a jagged breath, his bottom lip trembling. "I don't know what else I can do," he said, his voice cracking more. "Being on this station is all I've done my entire life. I can't imagine doing anything else. I wouldn't know what to do."

"Frank, my love." She caressed his cheek with her hand.

"I'm a cattleman, Maggie. Born and raised. My father was the same before me, and his father before him. It's not just what we do, it's who we are."

Maggie shook her head. "That isn't true. You're more than a cattleman, Frank."

"Am I? I'd planned my whole life around this station. It never occurred to me that it could take any other path."

She took his hand, caressing his knuckles with her thumb. "Your life can go anywhere. You can do anything. What does the Word tell us? *We can do all things through Him who gives us strength. Through Christ.* Just because you did something all along doesn't mean you're limited to it. God can use you for anything. All you have to do is avail yourself to His will."

FEW THINGS in life frightened him, but the prospect of change, this kind of change, was one Frank thought would never give him a moment's pause, but it was. He was almost sick at the prospect of losing the life he loved, of everything he knew and cared about. Who was he if not Frank Goddard, owner of Goddard Downs? Cattleman. Businessman. Father. Grandfather. He could think of all the titles he'd held in his life. There didn't seem to be a time when he didn't have a label, and now he was facing losing the one he'd held the longest and worked hardest at.

He tried to hold back the tears by sniffling and blinking, but nothing worked. He wasn't someone who cried often, but now, he felt as if his world was falling apart, and he didn't know what to do. He'd never been so out of control in his life, so helpless and unsure. It was terrifying. Thank God Maggie was beside him. "I'm scared, Maggie," he whispered.

She wrapped her arms around his middle, her touch warm and comforting. "You don't have to be scared. I'm right here with you. Whatever God has planned, it's for both of us. You and I are one for the rest of our lives. I'm not going anywhere. I'll be with you no matter what."

Her words provided comfort. "I'm not going anywhere either," he assured, holding her close. He stroked her hair. "Do you know what I couldn't stop thinking about in the hospital?"

"What?" she asked.

"I kept wondering what would happen if I didn't make it and you were left alone. I was afraid I might not see your face again in this life. When they wheeled me into surgery, it was all I could think of. You were the last person on my mind as I went under. I asked God to protect you, and to make sure you were taken care of if anything happened to me."

"Frank, please. I don't even want to think about that," she said, her voice heavy with anguish.

"But you have to hear it. I need you to. I faced death, Maggie, something I didn't anticipate having to deal with for many years to come. I faced it, and I made it. I made it because of the Lord and because you were there to hold my hand through it. Even now, you're holding my hand, holding me up, praying for me. My life wouldn't be the same if it wasn't for you. God sent you because He knew I'd need you. He knew this day would come."

"And that together we're stronger than we are alone."

He nodded. "One can chance a thousand, and two can put ten thousand to flight."

Maggie smiled. "Something like that."

"Will you hold me up if I can't stand?" he asked solemnly.

"I'd hold you up if you couldn't move," she answered. They both laughed.

As he looked into her eyes, love shone brightly back at him. He traced her hairline with his finger. "I love you so much, Maggie. I know you're right and that God has everything in

267

His hand and that whatever He wants is what's best, but I need you to keep me grounded through this."

"I'll be here, Frank. No matter what, I'll be here."

"Thank you," he said, kissing the top of her head and breathing in the sweet scent of her hair.

MAGGIE SQUEEZED her eyes closed as she listened to her husband. It was difficult to see him so afraid, but it was also calming. It was good to know that there were no secrets between them, not even the difficult process of a man admitting his fear. Fear wasn't of God, and though he felt it, and so did she, they had to keep the faith. They needed to trust God.

"Don't tell the children what I said," Frank said softly.

Maggie smiled. "I wouldn't tell a fly, Frank."

"I have an image to uphold. I'm the strong silent type." There was laughter in his voice, and it brought a smile to her lips.

She snuggled closer. He slowly lowered himself further down the bed until they were both flat against the pillows. She slid her leg over his. "Frank."

"Yes?" She could hear the fatigue in his voice.

"You don't have to worry, not about the station, us, or the family. God will take care of us. *Even to your old age and gray hairs, I am He, I am He who will sustain you. I have made you and I will carry you; I will sustain you and I will rescue you.*"

Beside her, she could feel Frank relaxing, his breath slowing to an even pace. She didn't move but allowed herself to relax as well, her breath eventually echoing his. She closed her eyes. Whatever God wanted, she wanted. He'd spared her husband and promised to take care of them. God's Word was always true. He'd never failed them before, and He wouldn't fail them now.

God, I thank You for today, for yesterday, and tomorrow. I thank You that whatever You have planned for us is already accomplished and that Your desire is for us to prosper and be in good health. Christ died that we might live. Help us to live the way You want us to. Help us to walk the path You've designed for us. Help us to trust without reservation. Help Frank overcome his concerns and embrace Your will. In Jesus' precious name. Amen.

CHAPTER 28

*L*ife had returned to normal now the family was back at Goddard Downs. Olivia had swept in with a whirlwind of plans and expectations and displeasure about the changes Sean had made to the office, and he returned to his place as a no one. It was alright. He'd known it couldn't last forever. Being someone important at Goddard Downs was a pipe dream. No one but his uncle and Josh would ever see him as anything more than the good-for-nothing cousin.

He sat with his arms folded, slumped in his chair, and wishing he were out at the site working on the bridge. The family was gathered for a meeting, the first since everyone had come home. Even Uncle Frank was present, although no one was comfortable with him being there. The family still worried about him, afraid that the stress of the station would send him back to the hospital, or worse. Sean thought otherwise. He was sure his uncle could handle it, and if God was real, as Elizabeth said He was, and if He loved him, then Uncle Frank would be just fine. He needed to be, because Olivia wasn't up to running the station alone.

Since his cousin's return, she'd fumbled over the mucky stuff. When it came to numbers, facts, and figures, she was brilliant, but when it came to the dirty business of the station, counting cattle, marking, cleaning, maintenance, she was completely lost. Sean tried to help, but she wouldn't listen. She kept acting as if she knew it all, but she didn't, and what was more, she was distracted by her father. His illness made her uneasy, and Sean understood why. Who wouldn't be afraid and worried when their father had almost died? That was why he was keeping quiet. She didn't need to hear the mistakes she was making. Instead, he made sure the messes were cleaned up without her knowing. The family was clueless. Everyone but David, that was. They were becoming quite close since everything happened. Sean no longer considered him simply as Serena's husband, but as a friend.

"Thank you for being here," Uncle Frank said calmly. He smiled at each of them. Sean looked up long enough to meet his gaze, but he didn't plan on paying much attention to the discussion since nothing would involve him.

"I don't think you should be here," Olivia said.

You could almost hear a pin drop. Everyone stared at her and then at Uncle Frank, who simply smiled. "Thank you for stating your feelings, Olivia. I think it best that we pray now."

Sean marvelled at how calm his uncle was amidst Olivia's outburst. Everyone knew she meant well, but her anxiety was making her more abrupt than normal. "Sorry," she said solemnly.

Uncle Frank nodded and bowed his head. "Father, we thank You for allowing us to be here today. We know that You, and no one else, are the author and finisher of our faith. We commit this meeting, and this station, into Your hands. May Your will always be accomplished, and may Your purpose be revealed in us now and forever. In Jesus' name. Amen."

Amens chorused around the table. Even Sean repeated the word.

"First, let me commend all of you on a job well done in taking care of this place during my illness and recovery. I'm not back to normal yet, but I'm getting there."

"It's only been a couple of weeks, Frank. No one expects you to be back to normal so quickly. I'm sure it won't be long, though," Nate said.

Frank smiled. "Thank you, Nate."

Nate nodded silently. He was a good guy; Olivia was lucky to have him. He was the kind of steady, loving, and dependable man she needed in moments like this when she was scared. Everyone had someone. Everyone but Sean.

"The first thing I want to mention is the office," Uncle Frank continued.

Sean sat up immediately. What would he say about it? Olivia had already voiced her disapproval. The day she came back she complained she couldn't find anything, and she didn't like the new location of the desk. It was disheartening to hear, but Sean had kept his mouth shut.

"You did a great job, Sean."

The corners of Olivia's mouth turned down. Sean was speechless.

"I'm glad you took the initiative. It was about time someone sorted that space out. I know Olivia was surprised, but how you've arranged it makes more sense and it's more functional now. Isn't that right, Olivia?"

She nodded her head reluctantly and glanced at Sean. "Yes. You did a good job, Sean. Everything's more streamlined, and the files are easier to find. I'm impressed." He could tell it irked her to utter those words, but they made him grin.

"We all are," Nate agreed.

Sean looked around the table and met approving smiles and nods from the rest of the family. His grin widened. He'd never had such approval before. He almost didn't know what to do. "Thank you."

Frank looked at him, a smile still on his face. "I believe the office isn't the only thing we need to commend you on, Sean. I believe you've got an update for us on the state of the bridge. You've taken the lead on this project when we were all otherwise occupied. Why don't you tell us how things are coming along?"

The lump in his throat threatened to choke him, but Sean refused to be intimidated by it. Elizabeth's words to him as she left the station echoed in his mind. *Be who you are. Don't hide your accomplishments. Claim them.*

He cleared his throat. "The project's coming along ahead of schedule. We've had some good days. The pylons have been set in place, and we've already started working on the main structure. At this rate, we should be finished a week early, maybe a bit more."

David smiled. He knew as well as Sean that being able to finish the bridge earlier than planned, plus the repairs that had been completed around the station, would put Sean in good stead. He hadn't done it for that reason, but he was pleased that the work he'd done hadn't gone unnoticed.

"The place is looking good with the repairs," David commented suddenly.

Sean shot him a look. Why was he bringing that subject up? He didn't need more spotlight.

"That's also true." Uncle Frank met his gaze. "Seems we should have let you do more around here long ago. I'm glad you were here to help when it was needed."

"I wanted to," Sean replied. "I was happy to."

"We're all grateful for what you've done," his uncle continued.

Sean was silent. What more could he say? He was two seconds from drowning under the attention. He coughed as his cheeks warmed.

"Before I continue with other business, does anyone have anything they wish to share?"

Olivia straightened. Her expression was sheepish as she tucked a strand of hair behind her ear. "There's something important we need to discuss. With recent events, the question of the future of Goddard Downs has become an issue."

Sean sucked in a breath. He'd known this was something that would eventually be raised, but he didn't think it would be so soon. He supposed it was on the minds of everyone. Uncle Frank had run the station for most of his life, but when he became ill there was no clear indication of who should be in charge. Sean had stepped up because everyone else had been needed elsewhere.

Uncle Frank tapped his fingers on the table and nodded slowly. "I'm glad you brought this up, Olivia. I understand this isn't an easy thing to discuss, but being who you are, you had to speak up."

She nodded. "Yes."

"Then I think it's time I made my announcement."

Sean's head snapped in his uncle's direction. Uncle Frank's words sounded close to ominous. Sean held his breath. He held it even tighter when Maggie's hand slid across the table to hold his uncle's. Sean swallowed his anxiety.

"Announcement, Dad?" Olivia looked confused. Joshua looked equally perplexed and glanced at Stella beside him, but he kept quiet and waited for his father to speak.

"Yes, Liv. I have something important to share with you." He paused and took a breath. "As you know, following my surgery, I've had to make some changes, and I've had to think more about what the future holds for Goddard Downs, Indigo, and this family. Maggie and I have discussed it, and I've decided that it's time for me to step down from running this station."

Gasps rippled around the table. Sean sat forward. He couldn't believe what he was hearing. His uncle was stepping down from running Goddard Downs?

Joshua spoke first. "Dad, are you serious? You're stepping down? Who's going to take your place?"

Uncle Frank smiled. "I'm very serious, Joshua. It's for the best. I've dedicated my entire life to this station and the people here, but it's time for me to do something else. I think God's calling me to something different. It's a little frightening. I'd be lying if I said it wasn't, but I know it's the right thing, and this is the right time."

"But who's going to take over?" Olivia asked.

Sean expected his uncle to announce that Joshua would take control of both stations. Who better for the job? It had always been assumed it would be Julian, but with him gone, Joshua was the obvious choice. He had his life figured out, and he was the man everyone would look up to. He had everything going for him.

"Sean."

He snapped out of his thoughts at hearing his name. "Yes, Uncle Frank?"

"What do you say?" His uncle's head was angled.

Sean's brow wrinkled. "Say to what?"

"What do you say to becoming the manager here? You and Olivia. She can deal with the numbers, everything she already does, but I think you have what it takes to manage the rest of the station. You've been working here for years. You know this place as well as any of my children, and you've proven that you have what it takes to hold the reins of responsibility."

Sean stared at him. Was he hearing right? Was Uncle Frank out of his mind? His heart beat harder. *You can do it,* Elizabeth had told him. *You can do anything, with Christ.*

The room was silent, waiting for his answer. It was what he wanted, what he'd always wanted. A place where he could belong. Where he could be somebody. His gaze shifted around to the faces of his family, and for the first time, he wasn't looking at disapproving faces.

Olivia looked him in the eye. "Before you say anything, Sean, I want to tell you something. I haven't always liked you. I'll admit it. I thought you were trouble and no good for my brother, but you've changed. I've seen it. I think we all have. I know I wasn't happy at first about the office. I was stressed out about Dad and everything that had happened, and I'm sorry if I wasn't immediately appreciative of what you did, but I'm grateful."

"We all are." Joshua leaned forward and smiled.

"You've done a great job," Stella added.

One after the other, his family complimented him. Sean's lip trembled as his emotions began to overwhelm him. Before he knew what was happening, he was blubbering, and his uncle was at his side, holding him. He tried to push him away gently, to hide his face and control himself, but he wouldn't move. Sean stood, but Uncle Frank kept hold of him. "It's all right, son. You're with family here, and we love you."

Those words meant more to him than he could ever describe. Hearing his uncle call him son, to hold him as a father. All he'd ever wanted while growing up was for his father to hold him and approve of him. "Do you mean it?" he cried.

"Of course, I mean it. I can't think of anyone better suited for the job, and I want you to take it. Forget the past. Forget your problems. You belong here with us. Make this station your home, the place where you can make a difference. The place where you can be the man I know you want to be and can be."

How did his uncle know? It was like talking to Elizabeth. She always knew what he was thinking and feeling, even when he hadn't said a word. He took a deep breath, wiped his face with the back of his hand, then extended his hand to his uncle. "I would be honoured, Uncle Frank."

His uncle smiled and took his hand, shaking it firmly. "I know you'll do me proud, son."

AFTER THE MEETING, Sean retreated to his room. He was still trying to process what had happened. How, in a matter of minutes, his uncle had stepped down from managing Goddard Downs to appointing him and Olivia in his place. He felt like his head would explode. It was so much to take in. He needed to talk, alleviate the pressure, and then maybe it would feel more real. There was only one person he could talk to. He picked up the phone and dialled Elizabeth. Her voice was the one he wanted to hear. When she picked up, it was almost a relief. "Liz?"

"Sean. What's up? How are you doing?"

"I don't know," he admitted.

"What's wrong?"

He swallowed the lump in his throat. "Today, my uncle made Olivia and me managers of the station."

"That's wonderful!" The joy in her voice made him smile before he sobered.

"Is it? I don't know. I'm kind of nervous, to tell the truth."

"Don't be. Your uncle knows what he's about. He thinks you're right for the job, and you are."

"How can you say that?"

"Because it's true. Don't you see, Sean? God loves you, and He's making a way for you. He brought your uncle home safe and sound and then opened a door for you to get what you've always wanted—a place to belong. A place to call home. What did you tell your uncle?"

"I accepted." He swallowed hard. He could barely believe he had. *Had he made a mistake?*

"Don't shy away from this, Sean. Don't say yes today and no tomorrow. Your family cares about you. You need to keep pressing forward. You need to keep taking one step at a time. Don't look back. No matter what, don't look back. Put the past behind you and keep moving forward."

Her words even sounded like his uncle. "Why do you care so much?"

She giggled. "Because God cares."

"That's all?"

Silence.

"When are you coming out here again?" He suddenly wanted to see her more than anything.

"God has a plan for you, Sean, and it's at Goddard Downs. It's always been there. I'm glad you're finally seeing that."

"When are you coming?"

"I don't know," she answered, her voice dropping.

Her reply was disappointing, but he understood. She had a life. She couldn't leave it simply because he wanted to see her. "That's okay. I hope I can get to see you again soon. I like our squabbles."

"So, do I," she replied in a more upbeat tone. He could hear the smile in her voice even though he couldn't see it. It would have to be enough. "Bye, Liz."

"Bye, Sean."

CHAPTER 29

*J*anella stood at the foot of her bed and took a deep breath. The sheets were stripped, the pillows had no cases, and the pictures were no longer on the bedside tables or walls. She looked at the box that sat at the end of the bed and then closed the lid. It was the last box, the last of their life at Goddard Downs. She couldn't decide what to leave, so she was taking everything. Every item held significance, and she couldn't leave anything behind, even if it was only for two years.

"Mum, have you seen my bag?" Sasha asked, poking her head through the open door. "I thought I left it on my bed, but I don't see it."

"I put it next to mine behind the door," Janella replied, smiling at her daughter. "Are you sure you have everything else? Once we leave, there's no coming back anytime soon."

Sasha nodded as she grabbed her bag off the hook behind

the door and slipped it over her shoulder. "I'm sure. I triple-checked everything, just as you asked."

Calling her over, Janella wrapped her arms around her daughter and hugged her. Her little girl was turning into a young lady before her eyes. She pressed her lips to her forehead. "That's my girl. Now, go meet your uncle outside. We're just about ready to go."

Sasha stepped back and nodded.

"Take this with you," Janella said, picking up the box from the bed. Sasha took it and left the room, leaving Janella alone with her thoughts—her memories.

Love came in many forms. The room she was in was filled with love of every kind. She inhaled deeply as memories rose to the surface. The first time Julian brought her into this room. The first time they slept in the same bed as man and wife. The first time Caleb crawled into bed with them. And then when Sasha joined them. The first night she slept alone after Julian died.

She sighed deeply. There were so many memories.

Walking to the door, she glanced back before stepping into the hallway and closing the door behind her.

The whole family was waiting outside when she arrived. Joshua was driving them to Darwin in his truck. It was the only vehicle with enough space to transport all of their things and them to their new home. They'd arranged for her car to be transported separately, and it was already there waiting for her.

Her throat felt thick as she walked out the front door for the last time.

"Good luck, Janella," Serena called from where she stood on the verandah with Oliver and David.

Maggie and Frank stood near the truck and were smiling proudly. She walked over to them and took a deep breath. "Here we are."

"Yes, here we are," Frank said, gazing into her eyes. "Are you ready?"

She looked over her shoulder to where Sasha was talking animatedly with Joshua. Her daughter was so excited about their move. Caleb could hardly wait for them to get there as well. He'd been calling all morning to make sure they were still coming.

"Yes, I'm ready," she replied.

"Then you should go," Frank said.

She stepped forward to hug him. "Thank you, Frank. For everything you've done for me and my children. I'll never forget it, but don't worry, we'll be back before you know it."

He hugged her tightly. "Be open to God's leading, Janella."

She stepped back and smiled before turning to embrace Maggie.

Her friend squeezed her tightly. "I'm so proud of you for taking this leap. God's arms are open to you, Janella. He won't let you fall."

She nodded. "I know He won't."

Maggie patted her arm. "Go say goodbye and get on the road before it gets too late. I'm sure Caleb will be in stitches waiting for you."

The thought of seeing her son made Janella's steps lighter, and quicker. She walked over to Sean and hugged him. He wished her all the best.

"You do a great job here, Sean. Don't forget you can call me whenever you want to talk."

He smiled. "I'll remember that. Good luck, Janella."

Stella hugged her and wished her the best, whispering a short prayer for her before she moved over to speak to Olivia and Nate and the children. She bent down and hugged her niece and nephew.

"Have a good trip, Auntie Janella," Issie said. "Mummy says that when you get settled, we can come visit you, Sasha and Caleb. I miss Caleb. He's been gone a long time."

Janella chuckled. "I miss him, too, but we'll both get to see him soon. As your mummy said, once we're settled, you can come visit." She looked at Olivia. "I expect it."

"We'll be there," her sister-in-law replied, pulling her into a big hug. "I love you, Nella. Be amazing out there."

"Yeah, Janella. Show everyone in Darwin how incredible you are," Nate agreed.

She felt her cheeks warm. "I'll sure do my best, Nate. No promises, though."

"What are you talking about, Janella? Of course, you will. You can't do anything but be incredible. It's your nature," Olivia protested, her eyes glistening. "I'm going to miss you, sis."

"I'll miss you, too. Don't be a stranger. Call me often," Janella urged.

"I will."

Finally, she stood beside the truck and faced Joshua. Sasha was in the cab, having said her goodbyes first. "Ready?" Joshua lifted a brow.

She took a deep breath. "Yes."

They climbed into the cab. Frank pushed the door shut behind her while Joshua started the engine. She stuck her head out the window and waved until the station and her family disappeared in a cloud of dust.

She was on her way.

Sasha put music on and settled back in her seat between Janella and Joshua. Although it wasn't the music Janella would have chosen, she smiled as her daughter bopped along happily.

"I never thought I'd see this day," Joshua commented as they turned onto the road leading to Darwin, "but I'm glad it's happening."

Janella inhaled deeply. "Me too. I think Julian would be happy."

"I know he would. He wanted you to stretch yourself, step out of your comfort zone. And now you're doing that." Joshua glanced at her and smiled. "Yes, my brother would be happy. Very happy."

She leaned her head on her hand as she gazed out the window. "I wish he could've seen this, Josh," she said softly. "I would love to see the expression on his face at realising we're taking this trip."

"He'd be proud. He'd be the one driving you to Darwin." Joshua let out a small chuckle.

"I don't know what's going to happen once we get there," she confessed. "I mean, I know what we have planned, but I have no idea what God has in store."

"Anything can happen. Just be open to it. Take chances. Try new things. Meet new people. Don't limit yourself."

She listened to him but didn't respond. Although there was a lingering sadness over leaving Goddard Downs, Darwin was a whole new world waiting to be explored, and she was growing more excited every moment. She'd even written a list of things she wanted to do. Things Julian had written to her about when he was in school. Experiencing them would be like doing them with him.

THEY ARRIVED in Darwin the following day after spending the night at a motel along the way, and collected Caleb from boarding school before heading to their new home, an apartment on Woods Street. Once there, Joshua helped them unpack. It was a three-bedroom, two-bathroom near the water. With the money Julian had left, she'd been able to afford a place with a swimming pool and security. She wanted to ensure her children would be safe in the city.

Joshua pulled one of the big boxes from the back of the truck. "Where to?"

"Eighth floor," she replied. "The lift is right through there."

Joshua took off in the direction she was pointing while she passed some lighter boxes to Caleb and Sasha before picking one up herself.

"Let me."

Turning, she found a familiar smile greeting her. Her eyes widened. "Mr. Johnson!"

"Wade," he said, grinning. "You're moving in?"

She looked around for Caleb or Sasha, but they were already on the way to the lift. "Yes. What are you doing here?"

"I live on the seventh floor." He stepped forward and took the box from her.

This was unexpected. "We're on the eighth."

He gave a nod. "You lead, I'll follow you."

She locked the truck and walked towards the apartment building, Wade following close behind. "Who would've guessed we'd meet here," he commented.

She glanced at him as they stepped into the lift, a small smile lifting her lips. "Yes. Who would have guessed?"

FRANK'S DAYS were more peaceful now that he no longer faced the responsibility of the station. He still cared, of course, but he no longer woke with a laundry list of what needed doing on his mind. He slept later and woke lighter. Maggie did too. They were enjoying their late mornings together. However, this morning he was going for a drive with Sean.

"Uncle Frank, I'm glad you're coming out here today. I've wanted to show you the bridge ever since you came back, but I wanted you to have something more to see than just a simple frame."

Frank smiled. "I'm glad I get to see it today. I have to admit that I've wanted to come out for quite a while, but I knew I'd have to wait." He chuckled. "Although it wasn't easy."

"I understand." When Sean looked at him, Frank sensed that he actually did.

"I know I keep saying this, but I'm proud of you, Sean. I've been watching you take on your new responsibilities with gusto, and I have to say it's been heartwarming."

"I didn't want you to regret your decision," he answered.

"Why would I? I picked the right person for the job."

"I know you gave me this chance, but you have to know

that I'd rather not have it. I'd rather have you back to normal, doing things yourself."

Sean was a good man, and Frank knew this wasn't what he wanted. He wasn't someone who grasped for this kind of attention. In the past, he'd lived for the limelight of the rodeo circuit, but that was different. Out there he hid his true self behind the attention. Here, he hid from the attention so he wouldn't have to suffer the disappointment that came after getting his hopes dashed. Disappointment and rejection from strangers were easier to bear than from those you cared about.

If he hadn't needed the surgery, Sean would never have stepped up, never have taken the chance to shine and show the family what he was capable of. God had a plan. Frank raised his hand to his chest and felt his scar. It wasn't the way he would have chosen, but God's ways were far above his, and what the Lord knew and planned, he could never imagine. It was time for things to change at Goddard Downs, and the Lord knew it better than him.

Frank shifted his body in the seat and faced Sean. "How much longer are you going to wait?"

Sean frowned. "Wait? For what?" He glanced at him curiously.

"To give your life to God."

Sean was silent at first, his hands rigid on the steering wheel as he drove towards the bridge. "I've been thinking about it," he said quietly.

His response made Frank smile. "So, what's stopping you?"

"I told God that I'd believe He loved me if He brought you home safely and you were able to return to life as normal. It didn't exactly work out that way, did it?"

Frank chuckled. "I think God had it right. You can't or shouldn't bargain with God. If He'd given you exactly what you wanted, then you wouldn't be where you are now. I think you needed this more than I did."

Sean shrugged. "Maybe, but I'm not sure I'm ready to jump on the 'God bandwagon' just yet. I'm just believing in Him more."

"You're already halfway there, son, you just don't know it yet." Frank smiled and patted his shoulder.

Sean let out a heavy sigh. "You might be right, but I don't know if I'm ready for it."

"There's no 'ready for it'," Frank replied. "You either want it or you don't. If you do, then go for it. If you don't, then don't. Don't play with God, Sean. Don't put your hand to the plough and turn back. If you want God, then go after Him with all of your heart."

"I'm not you, Uncle Frank. I don't know how to live the way you do." There was a glazed look in his eye. "I don't know how to live the way any of you guys live."

"I didn't start where I am." Frank settled back in his seat and looked straight ahead. "There was a time when I struggled with God, but He eventually won. He always does." He swung his gaze back to Sean. "Love is bigger than fear. Bigger than doubt. I want you to know that I'm here, Sean. I'm here to help whenever you want it."

"I know. If there's one person who's always there for me, it's you." Sean turned his head and looked at him for a moment.

"No, Sean. The Person who's always been there for you is God. You just didn't know it. You couldn't see Him working because you didn't want to know Him, but He knows you. He planned for you and made a way for you. He's still making a way for you, and He'll do even more if you let Him. All you have to do is accept Him, let Him into your heart. He'll do the rest." As Frank uttered the words, he prayed they would find a place in his nephew's heart. That Sean would let God have a place in his life.

Father, it's time. Sean's wandered long enough in the valley of indecision. Let him experience Your grace and love. Let Him know You for himself. In Jesus' name. Amen.

EPILOGUE

"This bridge was built two years ago. At first, we thought it was just something we needed to make the station more accessible during the rainy season, but soon after it was finished, we realised its deeper significance."

The small hand of an eight-year-old girl shot into the air. "What was that, Pastor?"

Frank smiled. "We realised that it was the bridge between our past and our future. This right here, where we're standing, is the present, but there is always something behind and even more ahead."

"That's right," Serena said. "We should never forget the past, but don't let the past keep you from the gift of the present, or the hope for the future." She smiled at the growing group of children that were part of her programme. When it started it was half the size it was now, and each month they received new applications for participation.

Frank stooped so he could be on eye level with the child.

She had dark skin and hair, and her eyes were a warm, deep chocolate. "God says that when we sin and make mistakes, He's willing to forgive us and put those mistakes into the sea of forgetfulness."

"What's that?" the child asked, curiosity sparkling in her eyes. Frank loved to see it. It made his new vocation all the richer.

"It's the place where God puts forgiven sin, so He doesn't remember it anymore."

"So, He pretends it didn't happen?"

Frank smiled. "He doesn't pretend. It's as if you've been given a clean slate. He won't bring it back up and remind you of what you did once you've asked Him to forgive you. Once it's forgiven, it's over with, unless you do it again."

The child nodded. "Then you have to ask for forgiveness again."

"Yes, but you should only repent if you're sincere. Don't say sorry if you don't mean it, especially to God," he said, patting her head lightly and standing to his full height. "All right, children. I know you've had a fun day taking a tour of this part of the station, but it's time to head back for lunch. Everyone to the Jeep they came in. We'll be driving back shortly."

The sound of children's laughter and the murmur of conversation punctuated his words as Serena moved closer. "Great work, Frank, as always."

"I'm always glad to help."

"Having you be a part of this programme has been such a blessing. You've helped make it an even richer experience for the children, sharing your family's history, and weaving in nuggets of faith and God's love. I couldn't have done it."

Frank disagreed. "That's not true. I think you would've done just fine without me."

"I would have tried, but I don't know nearly as much as you do," she replied. "The children benefit from you and your experience."

"Just because you don't know doesn't mean that God can't use you powerfully, Serena. He already has. None of this would exist if not for you. You're the one who made all of this happen." He wrapped an arm around her shoulders. "Come on, your mum and Elizabeth are expecting us."

Serena walked beside him, her arm around his waist. She leaned against his shoulder. "I love this work," she sighed.

Frank smiled. "So do I."

When they returned home, Maggie, Elizabeth and Jonah were setting out lunch. The more people they had at the station, the more hands were needed to feed them, and there were a lot more people than before. Sean's management skills were turning the station into an even more thriving place to live and work in. They'd increased their herd at Goddard Downs, and he'd hired more people to help out. It made the work easier and the benefits greater. Frank didn't worry about it, because Sean and Olivia had everything under control.

"My love," he said, kissing Maggie on the cheek as he walked up behind her and slipped his arms around her waist.

"Frank," she chuckled. "There you go sneaking up on me."

"It's easy to do when you're so focused on what you're doing." He laughed as he peeked at the spread they'd laid out for lunch. "Looks delicious."

"Jonah did a great job. I'm glad he decided to come back and help. He's been such a blessing," Maggie replied with a smile. She turned around to where Olivia was sitting with the children. Little Oliver was running around now and was quite the handful.

"Come here, little guy." Frank picked him up and kissed him on the forehead.

"He's been having a great day," Olivia commented. "You should've seen him. He got into the cabbage patch and tried to eat the leaves right from the bed." She laughed softly, her eyes bright and her belly big.

"And how's this little guy?" Frank asked, touching her stomach gently.

"He's good. Kicking all the time." Olivia laughed. "He's going to be a football player, I think."

"Whatever he does, I know he'll be great at it," Frank stated confidently. He'd been praying for his new grandchild every day since Olivia told them she was expecting. The family at the station was growing, and with it, so was the love and laughter.

"How will you handle the drive to Darwin?" Maggie asked. Janella's restaurant was opening in two weeks, and they were all going to Darwin to support her.

Olivia smiled and tucked some loose hair behind her ear. "I'll have to take a few breaks to stretch my legs along the way. Nate won't mind, since he's used to it. Thankfully, I'm not getting sick anymore. I still can't believe Janella took such a step. It's incredible." She faced Frank. "You always said she could be a chef, and now she owns her own restaurant."

Julian's Dream. The name made Frank smile. Janella's decision to name her restaurant after his late son meant a lot. It was as if Julian's dreams for her were finally realised.

"I can't wait to see Sasha and Caleb again," Maggie said. "I know we saw them at Christmas, but it seems so long ago now."

Frank remained silent. How he missed Janella and his grandchildren, but their lives were in Darwin now. They were doing well there, and he was happy about that, although Goddard Downs wasn't the same without them. But loving people sometimes meant you had to let them go, it didn't, however, mean they had to be strangers.

"WHAT DO YOU THINK, Sasha? Does this shade of pink suit me?" Janella held up the dress in front of her as she shifted her weight from one leg to the other.

"Pink always looks good on you, Mum," her daughter replied. She was considering a dress for herself, a blue one with green flowers. "This store has great clothes."

"That's why we always shop here," Janella said with a smile. At first, life in Darwin had been strange and she felt out of place, but now, after two years, it was home and she loved it. Her children loved it, too.

"Mum, do I have to be here?" Caleb asked. His voice cracked as he spoke. He sported several whiskers on his chin, an extra five inches of height, and a voice that couldn't quite decide whether it wanted to be baritone or alto.

"Go find yourself something to wear. No one said you had to stay with us," she replied with a grin. Looking at Caleb she saw more and more of Julian. Her handsome son was doing well in school, playing on his school's basketball team, and was topping his class.

He smiled. It was Julian's smile, and it made her momentarily melancholy. "Great," he said. "I'll be back."

"I'll find you when we're ready to go," she replied. Caleb left seconds later, his long strides taking him to the men's department while she returned to her dress shopping. She wrinkled her nose at her reflection. "I'm still not sure about this dress, Sasha."

"Am I interrupting?"

Janella's heart thudded louder in her chest as she turned around. Wade was standing behind her. "Wade! What are you doing here?"

He shrugged. "I was passing by and thought I saw you. I decided to see if I was right," he replied with a grin. "I guess I was."

Janella felt her cheeks flame. It was one thing to have her son with her while dress shopping, but quite another to have a man watch her, even though Wade had become a good friend, but another opinion couldn't hurt, could it? "I'm dress hunting," she said, holding the dress up. "What do you think?"

He angled his head. "I think it will look lovely on you." His gaze travelled over the dress until it lifted to her eyes.

Her stomach did a flip. It did that whenever he looked at her with those kind eyes. She quickly averted her gaze and turned around before he saw her blush. "I'm…I'm not sure it's the look I want to go for."

"Especially on this occasion," Sasha said. She looked at Wade and smiled. "Hi, Wade."

"Hi, Sasha."

Janella could hear the smile in his voice. She glanced at the mirror and saw his reflection. He *was* smiling while looking right at her.

She laughed nervously, wondering if the dress suited her body. She'd lost weight since coming to Darwin, but she still had her curves. It didn't always make shopping easy, but she'd learned what flattered her and what didn't.

He walked over to one of the racks, pushing aside some of the garments until he finally stopped at one and pulled out another dress. It was also pink, but featured a halter top, high waist and flowing skirt. "What about this one?"

She took the dress and held it against her body. Although it wasn't her typical style, it looked nice held against her. "I might try it on."

He smiled. "I think you should."

She took the hanger from him, their fingers touching for a moment as it passed between them. Her stomach clenched, but she ignored it. She had to. Walking to the changing room, she thought about the feelings she'd been experiencing lately. Feelings for Wade. They were unexpected, but not entirely unpleasant. But first and foremost, he was a friend and a neighbour, the first true friend she'd made when she moved to Darwin, plus he worked at the children's school. Was it inappropriate to be having these thoughts?

She slipped into the dress, which fit like a dream. She considered her appearance in the mirror and laughed at what she saw. Where had Janella Goddard gone? The woman looking back at her wasn't the woman who'd come to Darwin. The frumpy clothes were gone, her hair was cut and styled professionally, and she now wore makeup. Not a lot, just a little to freshen her appearance. If Frank or the rest of the family saw her now, they'd hardly recognise her. She stepped out of the dressing room to find Sasha and Wade.

"Wow." The look on his face was worth trying on the dress. She couldn't remember the last time anyone gazed at her the way he was.

"Thank you," she replied, smiling.

"You look amazing, Mum. You have to get that dress," Sasha commented with a grin. "Good choice, Wade."

"Thank you, but your mum makes the dress," he replied, his gaze fixed on Janella's.

Invite him to the opening. The thought jumped into her head from nowhere. She didn't want him getting the wrong idea. They were just friends. Yes, they'd hung out with the children many times together. He'd made himself their personal tour guide when they moved to town, ensuring they could find their way around until they got familiar with the city. After that, it had become normal for him to drop by, and she would test her recipes on him, but it was nothing more than that, just friendly interactions. "I better change out of this."

"We'll be right here," he replied. He turned to talk with Sasha, who was eagerly sharing her dress choices with him. Janella turned for the changing rooms but stopped when she heard him ask Sasha, "All this shopping. What's the occasion?"

"Mum's restaurant is opening in a couple of days. She wanted us to look special for it," Sasha replied.

"Of course. How could I have forgotten?"

Janella swallowed the lump in her throat as something prompted her again to invite him. "Wade?"

"Yes?" he answered, turning to look at her.

"If you're not busy, would you like to come to my restaurant opening on Saturday evening? It's at seven." She didn't know why, but her heart raced as she asked the question. It shouldn't matter if he said no, but for some reason it did. *He's a nice guy. Your friend. Of course it matters.*

"I'd love to." He smiled broadly, revealing his white teeth.

She felt like a breathless girl of eighteen. "Great. It'll be wonderful to have you there."

"Wade…" Caleb's voice cracked as he approached and smiled at the older man. "Nice to see you. I need a male perspective. Can you come and help?"

Janella feigned insult. "And what does that mean?"

"It means I need someone to help me pick the right outfit for the opening," her son replied. He grinned as he glanced at Wade. "Ashley's coming."

"I see," Wade replied. "Well, that does make a difference. I can help if your mum's okay with it."

"Of course. Help him find something nice for…Ashley," she teased. "I'll get Sasha squared away here and then we can go."

"Meet you by the register?" Wade asked, lifting a brow.

"Sure." She nodded as she placed a hand on her daughter's shoulder, her heart swelling with something she'd thought she might never feel again. As he walked away with Caleb, she faced Sasha. "Have you made up your mind yet?"

Wade and Caleb met them at the register fifteen minutes later. Janella paid for the clothes, and they left the store. Wade walked with them. He was headed to the camping store nearby, he told her. He loved the outdoors, and every few weeks he took the weekend off to camp. Caleb had joined him a few times, but despite her son's insistence that she should come too, she'd refused. She may have gone if she hadn't been worried about what it might look like.

"I think I need to say my goodbye here," Wade said as they neared the store. "I'll see you guys later."

"Bye, Wade," Caleb and Sasha chorused.

He turned to leave but spun to face them a second later. "Janella, I know this is out of the blue, but would you like to have dinner with me tomorrow night?"

Her breath caught. She felt a soft nudge. "Go on, Mum. We can look after ourselves," Caleb said with a grin.

Wade looked about to burst waiting for her answer. "Don't pressure your mum, Caleb. She can speak for herself," he said, his gaze still on her.

She started to refuse. The words were on the tip of her tongue, then she stopped as a still, small voice spoke. *Go. Live. It's a new season.*

She looked at her children, at their smiling faces and approving looks. It was time. She'd opened herself to every possibility but one—loving again. Perhaps she was ready to try. She couldn't be sure what would happen, but she would never know if she didn't take the chance. She met Wade's gaze and smiled. "I'd love to."

The look of relief on his face made her laugh. "I'll come by at seven?" he said.

She gave a nod. "I'll be ready."

He backed away with a wide grin on his face as he held her gaze. Finally, he whirled around and strutted into the camping store, whistling.

Sasha and Caleb laughed. "Mum, you're going on a date!"

The words were sobering. "I am. How do you feel about that?"

"We like Wade. He's nice," Sasha replied.

"Dad would like him," Caleb added.

Those words struck home. Janella pulled her son close and hugged him. "Do you really think so?"

"I know so," he replied. "But stop hugging me, we're in public."

Teenagers! Janella let go and they continued on their way. There was still a lot to do for the opening, and now she wouldn't have tomorrow night. She needed to make some adjustments to her schedule to ensure everything was ready.

THE ENTIRE GODDARD clan was there to celebrate the opening of Janella's restaurant. Frank stood beside Caleb; his young grandson was growing into quite the young man. "I still can't believe how tall you've become."

Caleb grinned. "Mum tells me that all the time. I'm way above her now."

"Where is your mum?" Maggie asked.

Caleb glanced around the room and pointed to where she stood on the other side. A man was with her, and she was smiling. It was a smile Frank hadn't seen in a long time. Sean and Elizabeth were standing not far from them, engrossed in conversation, but that wasn't anything new. When you saw one you saw the other. Frank hoped the two would finally make things official, but as of yet, there was no news on that front.

He wasn't sure what Sean was waiting for, but Elizabeth was a good woman, the kind he needed in his life.

"Do you see them?" Maggie whispered.

"Who? Sean and Elizabeth, or Janella?"

"The first two," Maggie replied, smiling.

"I do."

"When do you think they'll finally admit they're in love?" She intertwined her fingers with his.

"When they're ready. Elizabeth is a patient person. She's waited this long. I think she can wait a bit more."

"You think he'll make her wait much longer?"

"I hope not," Frank replied. "I wouldn't mind having another wedding at Goddard Downs."

Maggie grinned at him. "And this time you can officiate."

Frank's smile broadened. He liked the idea of marrying Sean and Elizabeth. It would be a blessing to be able to play such a role in their lives, but only God knew when or if that would happen. In the meantime, there was someone else he needed to consider.

"I'll go get Mum," Caleb offered before crossing the room to where his mother stood. Janella turned and waved at them before speaking to the man beside her. They both started towards them a moment later.

"Frank! Maggie!" she exclaimed, throwing her arms around Maggie's neck and then his own. "I'm so happy you all could make it."

"How could we miss this?" Maggie said, laughing.

"You've done an amazing job here, Janella," Frank agreed as he glanced around the room, nodding at the tasteful décor, the dark woods, and the vibrant colours that spoke to her heritage, and the muted lighting that set a relaxed, but elegant ambiance.

"Thank you, Frank. I think it turned out well," she said, still smiling. She turned to the man beside her. "Frank, I'd like you to meet my friend, Wade Johnson."

The name rang a bell. She'd mentioned him before. The man who'd befriended them when they first arrived. Frank smiled and extended his hand. "Nice to meet you, Wade."

"You too," he replied. "I've been looking forward to meeting you. Janella's told me a lot about you."

Frank looked at his daughter-in-law. "I look forward to getting to know you better," he replied, giving her a reassuring smile. It wasn't easy for her to take this step. He'd suspected that she was starting to open her heart again, but he wasn't sure she was completely ready to step into it. Now, perhaps she was, and he wanted her to know that he approved. She couldn't grieve Julian's loss forever. She had to move on eventually, and Frank felt that there was no better time than now. Everything was going well for her; it was the time to try new things, to even try love again. He squeezed Maggie's hand gently. She looked at him and he smiled. She was his second chance, so why couldn't Wade be Janella's?

She looked at her watch. Waiters and waitresses were coming out with glasses of champagne and distributing them to the guests. "Is it that time already?"

Wade winked at her. "You're on."

Frank took the glass offered to him and waited silently as Janella spoke to the room full of people.

"Good evening, everyone. Thank you for coming out tonight to the opening of *Julian's Dream*."

Everyone applauded and Janella continued. "As most of you know, this endeavour was a dream I thought about many years ago but told myself I could never do. I was wrong. At the time, I was married to a wonderful man whom I loved dearly, but circumstances took him from me far too soon. However, it didn't mean the dream was gone. I only started living it after he was gone. I took a bold leap of faith, and I haven't looked back since. This restaurant is named in honour of him, and it honours the confidence he had in me when I didn't have it myself." She met Frank's gaze. "It's for the love he gave me and the support he always had for me. It's for my family, the Goddards, who are the best bunch of people you could know. They're always there for each other, and their love is sincere and without limit. I raise a toast to you, my family, Frank, Maggie, Josh, Stella, Olivia, Nate, Sean, Caleb, and Sasha. Also, my friends, Elizabeth, Jonah, Serena, David... Wade. I toast you and thank you for caring for me, loving me, and helping me to come to this place. I thank God for you all." Tears dampened her cheeks. She sniffled and wiped them away. "Enjoy your evening, everyone!" she said in closing, raising her glass and taking a long sip of her champagne. Everyone joined her.

Frank held Maggie's hand and his heart was full. The circle of his family had grown so much, and the people who'd entered it were now all so much a part of him it was as if they'd always been there. God had shown Himself to be powerful, merciful, and loving. Through the trials and the tests, He'd brought them to this place of peace and appreciation for one another. They'd lost loved ones, but they'd gained new ones. God never stopped. He always moved forward. He always had a plan, even when they couldn't see it or understand it. And it was all for their good and for the extension of His Kingdom.

Thank You, Lord. Thank You for what You've done in our lives. If it weren't for You, where would we be? I don't dare think of it. I know that what You've done is more than I could have ever imagined. More than I could have asked for. You've filled my family with more love than I could think possible, and You're not done yet. There's tomorrow, and the next day, and the day after that. We're going to keep loving each other, and we'll extend that love to those You bring into our lives. It's been a long trek, Lord, but we're finally here, in this place of peace, but our journey isn't over. Whatever You see fit to bring our way, we will trust You. The Goddard family believes in You, no matter what. Your love never fails. Your mercies are new every morning. Great is Your faithfulness, oh Lord. Thank You for building the bridge between our past and our future. I praise You with all my heart. Amen.

NOTE FROM THE AUTHOR

I hope you enjoyed this fifth book in the *A Sunburned Land Series*! Frank and Maggie's story continues in book six, *Christmas at Goddard Downs* - you'll find the first chapter below.

Enjoyed "Slow Trek to Triumph"? You can make a big difference. Help other people find this book by writing a review and telling them why you liked it. Honest reviews of my books help bring them to the attention of other readers just like yourself, and I'd be thrilled if you could spare just five minutes to leave a review (it can be as short as you like).

Keep reading for your bonus chapter of "Christmas at Goddard Downs".

Until next time, take care and God bless.

Juliette

CHRISTMAS AT GODDARD DOWNS - CHAPTER ONE

Kununurra, far north Western Australia

On a steamy December afternoon, Elizabeth Martin parked her red Subaru XV outside the well-maintained weatherboard home where Mary Goddard, the matriarch of the Goddard family, had lived with her daughter and son-in-law for fifteen years.

A fall the week before had damaged the paper-thin skin on the ninety-nine-year-old's left arm and leg. Dr. Thomson had wanted to admit her to the hospital for fear of infection, but stubborn as always, Mrs. Mary, as everyone knew her, insisted she'd be fine.

Elizabeth agreed with the doctor but knew better than to argue with Mary Goddard, who still possessed all her faculties, including her clever mind, sharp tongue, and quick wit.

As Elizabeth opened her car door and climbed out, a wall of intense heat, heavy with the scent of jasmine, engulfed her, but she was used to it, having lived in the far north of Australia most of her life. She grabbed her medical bag and headed towards the white timber gate as Frank Goddard, Mary's eldest son, exited the front door and strolled along the flagstone path.

Although Kununurra was a three-hour drive from Goddard Downs, Frank had started visiting his mother regularly. She was in good health, but last month, she'd lost two of her closest friends, both younger by several years. Frank had officiated at their funerals and seemed to realise his mother could go at any time.

Still, he whistled as he walked. But that was Frank.

"Hey, Liz." He jogged a few steps closer and gave a wave. "Mum said you were coming this afternoon. Good to see you."

"And you. How is she today?" Elizabeth hoisted her bag strap over her shoulder and tightened her ponytail.

"Much the same. Still insisting she'll be fine to come for Christmas. You know how she is." His crystal-blue eyes sparkled in his sun-weathered face.

Yep. Elizabeth knew. She also understood his mother's desire to spend Christmas with her family at Goddard Downs where she and her late husband, William, had lived and worked and raised their four children. The cattle station held many memories for her, and perhaps she sensed it might be her last opportunity to spend Christmas there.

"All being well, I'll bring her out tomorrow." Planning to spend Christmas at Goddard Downs as well, Elizabeth had already offered to take Mrs. Mary. Now she wasn't so sure she wanted to spend Christmas with the Goddard family. She loved them. Of course, she did. They were like family to her.

That was the problem. If she went to Goddard Downs, everyone would expect her and Sean to announce their engagement, but things had cooled between them, leaving her wondering if he'd ever propose. She'd even considered popping the question herself, then begun questioning if they were suited. *And* if she could give up her job to live at the cattle station he co-managed with his cousin Olivia.

Did she want to live at Goddard Downs?

And what about Bree's offer to travel the world with her and nurse wherever they found themselves? Elizabeth never cared to travel, but her spirit felt restless. She needed a change, and the idea appealed.

But could she walk away from Sean?

He annoyed her, but she also loved him.

Or at least, she thought she did.

If only God would make it clear what she should do.

Frank opened the car door and rested his hand on the frame, hot air shimmering from the open door. "Great. If there's any problem, call me. I know what my mother can be like."

"She'll be fine."

"You're a legend, Liz." He slid into the driver's seat, then popped back out. "Oh, I almost forgot. I hope you're hungry. Sarah's been baking."

"I wondered what the smell was. I thought it was the boabs."

His gaze turned to the flowering bottle-shaped trees lining the wide street. "Could be a bit of both. The flowers are glorious this year."

Elizabeth nodded. "They certainly are."

He climbed into the vehicle and started the engine, tipping his wide-brimmed hat before driving off.

Elizabeth let out a breath. Time to attend to Mrs. Mary. She headed along the grevillea-lined stone pathway to the front steps.

Before she climbed them, the door opened, and Sarah, Frank's older sister, stepped onto the verandah. "Hi, Liz. I thought I heard someone chatting with Frank. Come in out of the heat."

"Thanks. Looks like a storm's brewing." Elizabeth gestured to the menacing cloudbank approaching from the east.

Standing aside for Elizabeth to pass, Sarah followed her gaze. "They said it could be a doozy."

Great. Just what they needed. Being the wet season, storms were common, but short-lived. This one looked different. "I hope Frank stays ahead of it."

"I doubt he will, but he'll be fine. My brother's used to driving in these conditions."

Elizabeth could only pray Sarah was right. The roads grew dangerous quickly. How many road accident victims had she helped treat over the years? They were mainly tourists unfamiliar with the roads, but even as skilled and experienced as Frank was, one tourist driving too fast on a slippery road could wipe him out.

Sarah followed her down the hallway. Christmas music played on the radio, and silver tinsel framed the kitchen doorway.

"Would you like a drink and some Christmas nibbles before you start?"

"Sounds lovely. Perhaps afterwards?" Elizabeth needed to attend to Mrs. Mary.

"No problem. Mum's expecting you. Let me know if you need anything. I'm boxing up treats to hand out at the carols tonight."

Elizabeth entered the living room while Sarah continued to the kitchen. A neatly decorated Christmas tree dominated one corner, its twinkling lights splashing colour on the wall.

Frail in an oversized upholstered armchair, Mrs. Mary smiled, crinkling up her wrinkled face.

"How are you doing, Mary?" Elizabeth set her bag on the carpeted floor and began inspecting the bloodstained bandages, which had only been changed the day before.

"I'm fine. I'm not sure why everybody's fussing."

Hmm. Mary's voice had weakened since her fall. Was she putting on a brave face? Hiding how she felt?

Probably.

Elizabeth tsked, wagging a finger at her most stubborn—and vulnerable—patient. "You know why. In this heat, the risk of infection is high."

"It's cool in here."

It *was* a lot cooler inside than out. But still.

"And Sarah keeps a clean house."

Elizabeth shook her head and clucked her tongue as she removed the last bandage. "That's not in dispute."

"Good. So, there's no problem."

And that was that. Elizabeth would never win an argument with Mrs. Mary. Instead, she inspected the wound on her arm. "But we still need to be cautious."

"I've had worse wounds than these in my lifetime."

"I'm sure you have. But you weren't ninety-nine then."

"Ninety-nine..." Mrs. Mary sighed. "I keep forgetting my age. Go ahead and do what you must." She turned her head and stared out the window, golden sunlight gleaming on dust motes floating in the air.

Elizabeth removed the gauze. Phew. The wound wasn't nasty. "It's not looking too bad."

"See. I told you." As Mrs. Mary craned to peek, her eyes twinkled.

"You did. We'll give it some air before we redress it. Now, let me look at your other wounds."

"They'll be the same."

"Perhaps, but I still need to check."

Air puffed from Mrs. Mary's thin lips so fast the gentle lady barely contained a raspberry. Then, as Elizabeth sank to the beige carpet to unwrap a leg bandage, Mrs. Mary's cold fingers grasped her shoulder, stilling her administrations. "Now, tell me what's going on between you and my grandson."

Beneath the weight of that frail hand, Elizabeth's shoulders fell. She removed the dressing on Mrs. Mary's leg. "Not much, I'm afraid."

"That's what I heard. I thought you'd be married by now."

Elizabeth's shoulders fell further. So had she. "He hasn't even proposed."

"Silly boy." Mrs. Mary tutted. "I'll have words with him tomorrow. You'll have a ring on your finger by Christmas, mark my words."

Right. He probably hadn't even bought one.

Mrs. Mary squeezed her shoulder. "He does love you. He's just unsure of himself. That's all."

Little surprise there with the way Sean's father, Stephen, belittled him. Elizabeth winced, thinking of how Stephen responded when his older brother appointed Sean manager at Goddard Downs after stepping down. "Why can't Stephen see Sean's changed? Offer encouragement—*just once.*"

"Both men are stubborn ones—all us Goddards are. That makes it hard admitting we're wrong."

"True that." Elizabeth swallowed hard, but she couldn't force down the ache in her chest. Couldn't Stephen see what that would mean to his son? No longer the reckless drunkard who only thought about the next rodeo, Sean changed when he surrendered his life to the Lord. But his father's refusal to believe the change was permanent left him questioning his ability to stay true to his new-found faith.

"By God's grace, one day Stephen's opinion will change, and he'll say so. But until then, Mrs. Mary, you're right. Sean's battle with insecurity is real." Tipping her face up towards the Goddard matriarch, Elizabeth slid her hand atop Mrs. Mary's, pressing her fingers against her shoulder. "I don't know. I'm not sure he's ready for marriage."

"Nobody's ever ready for marriage, but so long as a couple love each other and put God first and they're committed to working through whatever comes their way, they'll succeed." Mrs. Mary angled her head, fixing watery but alert blue eyes onto Elizabeth's. "The question is, do you love him?"

Good question. One Elizabeth had been asking herself for days. How did she know? She'd never been in love before, but when she and Sean were together, her heart swelled, and the world looked different. Better. Brighter. They sparred, but they also laughed and shared things they never shared with anyone else.

Was that love?

She drew a long breath as she redressed Mrs. Mary's wounds. "I think so."

A faraway look slackened the elderly lady's face, smoothing out her wrinkles as if carrying her back in time. "Love's a strange thing, but if you're unsure, ask yourself how you'd feel if you never saw him again."

A weight pressed on Elizabeth's chest. She couldn't imagine it. "I'd feel lost."

Mrs. Mary faced her. "I think you have your answer."

Maybe. But if he wasn't ready, she couldn't force Sean to marry her, could she? Perhaps she *should* go travelling with Bree. Give him space to figure out what he wanted.

But what if he decided it wasn't her?

Could she risk it?

She secured the last bandage and pushed to her feet. "There you go. All done."

"Thank you, dear. Now, Sarah's got some Christmas treats ready for us before you go."

Elizabeth smiled and bent to hug the elderly woman's bony shoulders. "I'll let her know we're ready."

Sarah bustled into the room carrying a tray loaded with Christmas goodies and a pot of tea. She placed the tray on the polished timber coffee table, poured three cups of tea, and insisted Elizabeth fill her plate with the home-baked treats.

"You must think I never eat." Elizabeth laughed as she bit into the Christmas cake, groaning with pleasure when the rich flavours burst in her mouth.

Sarah eased into an armchair and sipped her tea. "I know how hard you nurses work and how little time you have for baking."

That *was* true. When Elizabeth arrived home after a twelve-hour shift, the last thing she felt like doing was cooking. Plus, baking wasn't her forte.

After a pleasant hour, she took her leave and said she'd collect Mrs. Mary the following day to drive her to Goddard Downs for Christmas.

She didn't have the heart to tell her she might not stay.

I hope you enjoyed this first chapter of 'Christmas at Goddard Downs'. Order your copy to continue reading.

OTHER BOOKS BY JULIETTE DUNCAN

Find all of Juliette Duncan's books on her websites:

www.julietteduncan.com/library

www.julietteduncanbookstore.com

Beneath the Southern Cross: The Dawn of a Sunburned Land Series

Love's Unwavering Hope

Love's Rebellious Spirit

Love's Distant Dream

Love's Precious Moments

Love's Faithful Journey (Coming 2026)

A Sunburned Land Series

Slow Road to Love

Slow Path to Peace

Slow Ride Home

Slow Dance at Dusk

Slow Trek to Triumph

Christmas at Goddard Downs

True Love Series

Tender Love

Tested Love

Tormented Love

Triumphant Love

Transformed by Love Christian Romance Series

Because We Loved

Because We Forgave

Because We Dreamed

Because We Believed

Because We Cared

Billionaires with Heart Series

Her Kind-Hearted Billionaire

Her Generous Billionaire

Her Disgraced Billionaire

Her Compassionate Billionaire

The Potter's House Books...

The Homecoming

Unchained

Blessings of Love

The Hope We Share

The Love Abounds

Love's Healing Touch

Melody of Love

Whispers of Hope

Promise of Peace

Heroes Of Eastbrooke Christian Romance Suspense Series

Safe in His Arms

Under His Watch

Within His Sight

Freed by His Love

<u>Stand Alone Books</u>

No Going Back

The Preacher's Son

Promises of Love

Tumbling into Tomorrow

<u>The Madeleine Richards Series</u> (Pre-Teen/Middle-Grade Series)

Rebellion in Riversleigh

Trouble in Town

Problems in Paradise

ABOUT THE AUTHOR

Juliette Duncan is passionate about writing true to life Christian romances that will touch her readers' hearts and make a difference in their lives. Drawing on her own often challenging real-life experiences, Juliette writes deeply emotional stories that highlight God's amazing love and faithfulness, for which she's eternally grateful. Juliette lives on the beautiful Sunshine Coast of Queensland, Australia, and she and her husband have five adult children and eleven grandchildren. When not writing, Juliette and her husband love exploring the great outdoors.

Connect with Juliette:

Email: author@julietteduncan.com

Website: www.julietteduncan.com

Juliette's bookstore: www.julietteduncanbookstore.com

Facebook: www.facebook.com/JulietteDuncanAuthor

BookBub: www.bookbub.com/authors/juliette-duncan